WITCHFIRE

Witchfire
An Airship 27 Production
www.airship27.com airship27hangar.com

"Witchfire" © 2007 Ardath Mayhar and Ron Fortier
Cover by Rob Davis, "Witchfire" logo by Anthony Schiavino
Cover and interior illustrations © copyright 2007 Rob Davis
Production and design by Rob Davis

ISBN-13: 978-0615691770
ISBN-10: 0615691773

Third Edition

Printed in the United States of America

10 9 8 7 6 5 4 3 2 1

AIRSHIP 27 PRODUCTIONS PRESENTS

"WITCHFIRE"

a fantasy novel by

Ardath Mayhar & Ron Fortier

with illustrations by Rob Davis

"He hoped she would be young and pretty..."

Prologue

-1-

When she was very young, she had sat as a novice at the feet of Mother Kalavela, learning the ancient arts.

"There are three elements, giving us all life," Kalavela had said. "Fire. Air. Water. You must learn to master all three, it is true, but never forget that it is fire that is the giver and the destroyer. It is fire that warms the universe.It is fire that nullifies the cold powers of darkness.Witchfire."

The old woman sat hunched in her unlikely tweed suit, her face tracked with light and shadow, as well as with wrinkles provided by long living and deep thought. Morgan remembered drawing a deep breath, as if inhaling the truth that had been given to her. Yet she had shivered, nevertheless.

-2-

Ralph Zimmer prided himself on his knack of reading character from slight clues. At a glance, he could judge people.The walk, the expression, the general carriage might tell almost anyone what he wanted to know, but Ralph's talent lay deeper than that. He intuited, immediately and accurately, what sort of a person was approaching even from a good distance.

Now he stood in a clump of pines, hidden from any chance glint of light from the nearby street lamp. He was tense with waiting. Patience, although a necessary quality in his missions, was never something he enjoyed. Rather he endured. All his talents would come into use soon enough. This warm July night was his element: it was too early for the theater crowds, yet too late for strollers or lovers. The hour was his ally, for now only solitary people were apt to cross his path.

His hands were a bit damp. The plastic handle of the butcher knife was pleasant within his grasp, though he felt his muscles beginning to tighten just a bit. That had been triggered by the footsteps approaching along the cement walk.

They were light, fast, and crisp. Pumps, he guessed. The click-click was distinctly feminine. He licked his lips and leaned forward to peer through the concealing foliage. He hoped she would be young and pretty. The pretty ones were always more satisfying than the plain Janes. The pretty ones had so much more to live for. As she came into view, moving quickly along a branch path, he was elated.

She was tall, her long legs carrying her along energetically. High heels, full plaid skirt, spotless white blouse whose short sleeves revealed her tanned arms… she was damn near perfect in all respects. He continued to stare. The long black hair was black as a gypsy's and rode on her shoulders and back like a lion's mane. Regal.

She was beautiful like the models that graced the covers of Vogue. Classic, but not cute. A dark complexion, almost Mediterranean, with a wide forehead, arching brows and a slender nose over full, sensual lips. Her haughtiness derived from distinct cheekbones and piercing green eyes that seemed to dart about like fireflies. Gypsy. The word fit her perfectly.

She walked with the sure, rapid gait of a city woman, clutching her small brown purse to her side. She moved through the quiet little park as though it was her own living room. Totally at ease in her surroundings. That sureness told him she was a businesswoman. Law or corporate finance, maybe. There was no trace of the indefinable hesitancy that surrounded women who looked to men for protection.

She was much different from his last two targets. More difficult, perhaps, but variety was the spice that seasoned his strange hobby. It gave an extra pleasure to the death that he dealt.

She was coming quickly, almost parallel with his position. He tensed for a spring into the path. With the first... the waitress... he had been clumsy and had almost lost her. The second had gone much better. Practice made perfect as the old saying went. Now he knew exactly what to do and his muscles responded smoothly, the habit becoming established.

Yet he somehow wasn't fast enough. The woman stopped in her tracks and turned toward the shadow in which he had just begun his motion. He froze. Could she see him? Impossible! There had been no sound, no motion of a leaf or branch. She stood calmly, looking into the darkness with such directness and assurance that he felt breathless. Caught!

Bitch! He thought. I'll carve you like a chicken!

Her voice fell between them so softly that he wondered if he was actually hearing it all. Had his mind wigged out? But the words were there, as if rising from inside himself.

"Come out of the trees. Come now!"

Zimmer felt a spasm of terror grip his heart. The woman brought her hands up chest-high. They were empty, and he found the time to wonder what had become of her purse. Then they moved purposefully, and he forgot such unimportant matters. The woman was moving her hands, describing patterns in the mottled light and shadow of the lamp and leaves.

"Come out! I command you in the sacred name of Adonay!"

Something seized Zimmer in an irresistible grip. The web patterns caught him, moving his feet as he tried frantically to resist. With heart-wrenching shock, he realized that he was moving into the open area of grass, before the spot where she stood. Panic fought with mutinous limbs, but they kept on walking forward, as if the connection between brain and legs had been broken... or short-circuited. He had never been so scared in all his life.

As he came near to the woman, she made a different sort of gesture. Suddenly, he found his fingers losing their grip on his knife. The blade seemed to weigh a ton as his lifeless fingers relinquished the hilt. The knife, instrument of passion and vengeance, fell to the grass.

His feet stopped short, too near to his tormentor. Now he looked into eyes so green that even the streetlight's glare could not leach their color. They blazed with emotion. Hatred?

Anger? He never was able to identify or understand what it was he saw there.

The voice whispered, "Agent of the Dark, the Destroyer, the force of anti-life, you have taken lives for your pleasure. You have desecrated bodies and sent souls, unready, into that which is beyond. Now you must atone for your crimes."

Despite his overwhelming fear, Zimmer was no coward. He steadied his voice, as well as he could manage, and croaked, "Look, Lady, I don't know what you're talking about. Honest! Let me go! Please?"

Her bewitching hands flickered. Another pattern formed, and Zimmer's world dissolved into a sea of pain. He caught his head between his hands and screamed. As he crumbled to the grass, his body twisted, convulsing with agony.

Still he heard the voice, strained through the nets of torture. "Only when you confess your crimes, not once but as many times as need be, will you be released from this punishment."

He screamed, his throat aching with the effort. His brain seemed to flame, his skull to shatter with the surges of agony. His cries echoed across the park. He couldn't bring himself to worry that they would bring policemen hurrying to see what was happening. Even when heavy footsteps pounded across the turf beyond the next band of trees, he could not control his voice.

The woman looked down at him, the green eyes glowing strangely in the lamp light. Then she turned and was gone into the trees behind which he had hidden.

Guns drawn, two officers panted into the clearing. Zimmer was still screaming. One of the cops dropped to his knees and felt the suffering man over for injuries.

"Okay, Buddy, I can't find a thing wrong with you. Shut up and tell us what's the matter?"

Zimmer kept on screaming, louder and louder.

"Paul, get an ambulance out here. Maybe this guy's bleeding inside or something. I can't see anything wrong on the outside of him."

"Right, Frank. Won't take ten minutes to get one here."

"I did it," Zimmer keened before the one name Paul could move. "I killed those two girls!"

The patrolmen exchanged glances. Frank knelt again beside Zimmer and touched his shoulder. "What the hell are you saying? You killed somebody?"

Zimmer knew he was betraying himself. That he would suffer for that as much as he was hurting now, but it didn't matter. The pain, which had been devouring him, began to fade the instant he made his confession. His only thought was to fight free of that all consuming pain, no matter what the consequences might be.

"I killed the two girls in the park, last week. I did it! You got to believe me! My knife is in the grass over there. To your right!"

The standing cop moved to the spot Zimmer indicated.

"Son of a bitch! Frank, he's not kidding. There's a knife here, all right. Big enough to carve a steer."

Zimmer laughed, light-headed with relief. He stretched, moving his head cautiously. He laughed again... nothing mattered now. The pain was gone. Just like that.

Frank, his gaze fixed on the laughing man, pushed back his cap and whistled. "I'll be damned. We got us the Park Butcher, it looks like. But he's crazy as a bedbug."

Zimmer, reveling in his freedom from pain, didn't care. He didn't know that every time he tried to renege on his confession he would find himself in self-same agony again.

He never knew that only in one way had he assessed his intended victim correctly. She with the glowing green eyes was indeed a businesswoman.

Her business was witchcraft.

Chapter 1

Thomas Axel thumped his fist on the polished teak of his desktop. His square face was red with annoyance.

"Dammit, Darryl! What's taking so long? When I employ people, I expect results!"

Darryl Waitman turned off his ears for a long moment. Let the old man run himself down. As he waited, he looked about the room, feeling with all his acquisitive senses the power emanating from it. Its very furnishings breathed the elegance that only world-controlling affluence can attain. The wine-red rugs, ankle-deep: the elaborate teak wood desk that was hooked through a computer network to all parts of the globe, the fine paintings on the walls all breathed effortless control.

He looked unobtrusively at the chair in which the president of C.C.I. was sitting. It was almost a throne. The man who ran Construction Consortium International held strings in his pudgy hands that could halt materials needed by projects in Moscow or Beirut or San Francisco.

He would sit in that chair, Waitman knew, if he only had the wit and the patience to manage that brand of power. He was only thirty-eight, the youngest Managing Vice-President in C.C.I.'s history. Tom Axel might be the tenant of the throne, now, but he was old. He couldn't last for much longer.

Yet the old fool had an iron core to him. Waitman had learned that, watching the old man wheel and deal, manipulating unwitting dupes, eliminating dangers to himself and his empire with malicious relish. As one cutthroat to another, he respected the man as much as he could find it in himself to respect anyone. And he admired him unstintingly for his genius in covering his tracks. Between inspired accountants, which he had been a master at hiring, and six feet of good, rich earth, which the old man was not averse to using to cover up delicate matters, he had kept his reputation and that of C.C.I. impeccable for almost half a century.

Darryl knew where a couple of those graves were located, as well as who was inside them. That information might, one day, give him an edge he needed. In the meantime, he found that his name, Waitman, was all too appropriate. Even poetic, if one was fanciful.

There was a pause in the babble from the chair. Darryl looked into the older man's eyes with the honest assurance he had cultivated so carefully.

"Rest assured, Mr. Axel, Lucien Wicker has the reputation for efficiency that you require of such people.

"As well, he can perform his... ah, services... in ways that never suggest foul play. The ordinary specialist in the field invariably does leave certain identifiable traces. Wicker's jobs, on the other hand, pose puzzles that the police cannot solve and wouldn't believe even if they could."

Axel stubbed out a cigar in the loaded ashtray. "I hope, for your sake, that you're right about that. If this Appleton thing isn't handled fast, he might get his information to someone who could and would use it against us. We cannot have that. Damn sloppy work on the part of Accounting. Inexcusably sloppy."

I warned you, Waitman thought. But he said, "The matter has been corrected, Sir. We dismissed several people. Others have disappeared completely. You can be sure that the affair is being handled effectively. I also believe you will find Mr. Wicker to be a most useful ally."

"Employee!"

"Not quite, Mr. Axel. Wicker is a unique man. A very dangerous man with unequalled talents. He does not place himself in a subservient position for anyone. Not even C.C.I. He is no minor contractor of services. He is powerful. Very powerful, if you understand my gist. But he is also one hundred percent dependable. I have been given complete assurances of that."

Axel fumbled another cigar from an inner pocket. Waitman whipped out his platinum lighter.

The president squinted through a cloud of odorous smoke. "You've used this Wicker chap before?"

Thanking his stars for the air conditioning, Waitman coughed softly. Then he nodded. "Twice. Most successfully." But he was thinking, If the old bastard keeps this up, I probably won't have to kill him after all. He'll do himself in with those awful cigars.

Axel was speaking again. "This one had better be successful. All our tails are in the crack, this time. Appleton could blow the whistle on the entire worldwide operation. A trillion dollars a year, right down the bloody hatch and all of us off to prison. Or worse. We've done a bit of housekeeping, along the way. If the law began looking into all our operations, they just might locate some of the dust we've swept under the rug. If you take my gist?"

Waitman nodded. "I think, when all is said and done, you will agree that Mr. Wicker is just the answer we've been looking for."

As if on cue, the intercom buzzed. Axel cocked his chair bolt upright and barked, "Yes, Lilith?"

"An outside call, Sir. Lucien Wicker."

"Put him on."

Click-pause... Waitman could hear it from where he sat.

Then, "Is this Thomas Axel?" The voice, even at such distance, was cool, assured, and somehow disturbing.

"Yes, dammit. Speaking."

"The Appleton account has been successfully terminated."

"Excellent. Most excellent. There will be a bonus in this for you, Wicker."

"Money is, of course useful. I may also ask a favor, sometime in the future. If, naturally, my services are suitably appreciated."

"Waitman will be in touch with you. Everything will continue to be done through him."

"As you wish. Good day, Sir." The line fell silent.

Tom Axel blew a cloud of foul smoke into the air and beamed. He was very content. Whereas Darryl Waitman leaned back in his leather chair and watched, eyes slitted.

Soon, he mused. Sooner than you think, old man. You're starting to lose your grip. I can see it happening. And when you lose, I'll win.

CHAPTER 1

Morgan Rein bolted her door, hit the light-switch, and threw her purse onto the sky-blue sofa. Her white Angora cat, sleeping there, opened one eye, saw it was she and closed it again.

Morgan moved to the window, where she paused before drawing the draperies, staring down onto the display of lights below her high-rise apartment. The city looked like a field of sparkling jewels fanning out to the dark horizon beyond. The stars above competed with their own natural brilliance. It was a beautiful night.

The cat stretched, washed one paw reflectively, then drew himself into a dignified position, paws together, tail curled neatly around them. He sneered delicately at the purse that had waked him.

"Good evening, Scratch," she greeted. The cat winked at her deliberately, curled up and put his furry head on a cream-colored pillow.

Morgan smiled and glanced at her watch. Almost midnight. It had taken her longer to go across town than she had thought. She unbuttoned her blouse, hurrying toward the bathroom. She dropped her clothing into a hamper and turned on the shower. Beneath the warm spray, she turned, scrubbed, and washed her long, silk-smooth hair. She must be clean for the ritual.

She walked naked to the closet and drew out the long robe of white linen. Freshly laundered, it smelled of soap and starch, and she pulled it over her head. Her skin warmed to its familiar touch. A green ribbon from the drawer confined her still-damp hair snugly. That touch, too, was familiar, reminding her of long-ago matters.

She glanced into the full-length mirror and was satisfied. She was ready.

In the living room, Morgan went to one of the long bookshelves that lined its walls. A weathered volume slid into her hand, its leather worn and fragile, now. She crossed the room to slip between the draperies without opening them. She went through a glass door onto the balcony. The breeze was cool on her skin, and subtle scents of her green and blooming plants filled the small rectangular space.

Her bare feet were chilly as she moved to the end of the balcony, where a small wrought-iron table held two candles in silver holders and a silver dish filled with sweet incense.

Morgan opened the book: the pages fell apart at the center, where two newspaper clippings had been placed. She lighted the candles, laid the book between them, and sat to read once again the bits of newsprint. The tiny puddles of light from the candles revealed again the stories of the two women. Dead women, now.

They had names, jobs, lives, and personalities that the cold print had not addressed. Betty Phillips, cocktail waitress, the clipping said. But Morgan glimpsed, inside herself, a round, merry face, with round eyes. Something else... a child. A most beloved child. But the news account made no mention of that either.

Paula Eaton. Morgan closed her eyes to see a slight figure dancing, entranced by the music and its own motion. Someone else... parents? Audiences? Someone in the background, beaming approval for her dance.

She closed the book and held the clippings in her right hand. Her eyes closed, she prayed to the dual faiths that she professed. Then she touched the paper to the candle flames. She held them, even when the small fires reached her fingertips, and as she felt the pain she sent toward those spirits, removed untimely from the world, all the peace she could find in her own spirit.

The moon floated serenely above her. Lights were going out below. After a time, Morgan rose and went back into her apartment, carrying the book carefully. She restored it to its place on the shelf. She was weary to the bone. The powers upon which she called drew much of their potency from her own flesh.

Again she showered, toweled, and climbed between the cool, smooth bed linens. She sighed with a calm, inner relief. Her profession was a difficult one, trying at times, and distressing at others. She closed her eyes, her dark lashes curling on her cheeks in the dim light coming through the blinds.

A face swam into view, behind her eyes. Lucien! Morgan sat upright, her hands against her heart. She had seen his face clearly. It had been dark with anger.

But why think of Lucien? Why now? It had been so many years! And now she was armed against him, as she had not been as a child. Mother Kalavela had alleviated the hell he had made of her childhood, over the years. She had been taught how to cope with such practitioners of the Dark.

Still there had been no word of her brother, no trace of his existence upon the inner chart of her mind for so very long... surely...

She drew a deliberate breath, held it, and expelled it just as deliberately. Her taut nerves relaxed. The panic reaction that had almost overwhelmed her in that vulnerable span between sleep and waking had eased.

If Lucien still lived, still worked his ugly craft, she could do nothing about it tonight.

Tomorrow, rested, she might investigate this odd apparition.

CHAPTER 3

A bedraggled young man wheeled his motorcycle into the basement garage of the apartment complex and leaned it against a post. Locking the ignition, he absentmindedly brushed back a sopping wet strand of chestnut brown hair. The stream of water from his jacket collar poured down his cheek and he cursed quietly. The Harley was cheap to run, no doubt of that, but if foul weather was going to set in and rain much, he'd better think about getting a car.

It was no day to be outside, even on a sensible assignment. Whereas this was all utter nonsense! He rummaged in his saddle pouches, producing a small tape recorder and a Polaroid camera. Thankfully they were both still dry, he noted with relief.

The security in the lobby looked at him suspiciously when he introduced himself. He knew he looked pretty unimpressive. More like a drowned rat than a bona fide member of the scientific community. He raised his chin and managed to say with some assurance, "Doctor McCoy to see a Miss.. Mrs.?… Morgan Rein."

The guard, a big bruiser with a walrus mustache, hit the call button for apartment 751.

"What is it, Biff?" asked a musical voice.

"Fellow wants to see you, Miss Rein. Says his name is Dr. McCoy." His tone was doubtful, his glare still holding the man under tight scrutiny.

"Yes, of course. Send him up, Biff. Thank you."

"You're welcome, Ma'am." He motioned toward the elevator doors to his immediate left. "Seventh floor, to your left as you come off the elevator."

Biff continued to look suspicious and McCoy felt that he would be quite willing to come charging to the rescue of Miss Morgan Rein, if she should need it. Interesting?

He half turned toward the lift…then he looked back at the stoic guard. "I'd like to ask you a question. If you don't mind?"

"What?"

"Miss Rein. What is she like?"

Biff's face crunched like a bulldog about to take a bite.

"I've never met her," McCoy hurriedly finished.

The guard relaxed. Then, obviously caught up in his mental imagery, he actually smiled. "A real lady, Doc. Polite. Friendly. Goes to bat for the help, when we need it. She's good people, Miss Rein. Take my word for it."

The elevator door slid open and McCoy stepped into its empty box. "Thanks," he called as he tapped the number seven button.

Small puddles formed about his feet and he felt his wet socks squish inside his shoes, as he was borne upward.

"A scientist shouldn't have to make his living like this," he said aloud.

He should be safe and snug in the lab, with the test tubes twinkling all around and Alice's Bunsen burner perking black coffee. Sergei should have sent Alice on this assignment, anyway. A woman was better equipped for this sort of thing. What did he know about witches and herbal medicines?

The problem had begun when Sergei had insisted on having an entire research lab staff attend a seminar on ancient drugs and their uses in modern medicines. Sergei had a forceful way of insuring that his subordinates went along with his wishes, though he was never overtly pushy. The entire team had, predictably, gone.

Then the unexpected had happened. A stunning woman had given an even more stunning lecture on healing herbs, their origins and uses through the ages. Her suggestions for modern-day applications had been logical and usable. It had seemed incredible to him that someone so young (not to mention attractive) had lived long enough to amass such a wide volume of knowledge on the subject.

After the lecture, they had all gone forward to meet the lecturer. That had been wonderful. McCoy had been all set to ask her for a date, when she dropped the bomb on them.

Sergei had voiced the question that had nagged him and the others as well. How had she managed to acquire such a wealth of knowledge. Morgan Rein, quite calmly, had replied that, being a seventh-generation practicing white witch, she had access to centuries of accumulated lore on many such subjects.

Sergei, affirming McCoy's long-held belief in his questionable sanity, had been instantly captivated at the notion. "My dear, you must give us some of your time," he all but gushed, like some fawning high school student. "This is most intriguing. It might, also, be useful to our work. Would you consent to a full taped interview with one of my staff? We need to catalogue all this marvelous material properly."

To McCoy's disdain, she had agreed. Somehow, he had known that he'd be the one picked for the job. And here he was, soaked to the bone, waiting to interview a witch. He sneezed and the elevator stopped at the seventh floor.

As he sloshed along the carpeted hallway, he wondered why he hadn't protested more vigorously. Surely he could have squirmed out of the task, if he'd really put his mind to it. Sergei wasn't a complete ogre and would have relented had he mustered an argument against the assignment. And there it was. The truth. A tiny part of him had wanted to do this. Had wanted, in fact, to meet Morgan Rein again. She was gorgeous. He was a man. All the degrees in the world couldn't eradicate the feeling he'd had when she took his hand in their too brief introduction. Those green eyes… he wanted to look into them again.

The doorbell chimed. He had no idea what to expect as he shook himself, trying to throw off his strange mood, as well as the worst of the damp. Green eyes or not, he was a thorough going professional. He'd do a good job of this, like it or not.

The door opened to reveal a vision in Nikes, denim jeans, and a black T-shirt with MAGIC emblazoned across the front in letters three inches high. Her long hair was tied back in a bun that should have looked severely practical. It didn't.

"Dr. McCoy… how nice to see you again. Do come in."

She ushered him into a large room that was filled with light, even with the overcast of the gray day outside. White walls held small, intricate paintings that glowed with stained-glass hues. A blue couch centered the creamy rug and a white cat sat upon it. The haughty animal looked at him appraisingly, as if to pass judgement. Books lined the walls… thousands of them, their muted colors showing gaily against the white paint.

McCoy turned to her. "Beautiful."

He was not speaking solely of the room and the twinkle in her eyes told him she was aware of that.

"Thank you," she said graciously, comfortable with the awkward compliment. "Here, let me take your coat. You're drenched."

He handed over his jacket, which had proved not to be as water repellent as advertised. Morgan hung it in the closet by the front door and said, "What a nasty day. Would you like some tea? I'm sure it will make you feel more human, after such a soaking."

"A special brew?" he squinted his eyebrows together.

She laughed and he loved the sound. "Nothing mysterious, I'm afraid. Just some chamomile tea with a touch of cinnamon and honey."

"Sounds delicious." He hated tea.

She led him into the small but well-appointed kitchen. He looked about at copper pans shining on the walls, the herb and spice racks beneath the cupboards on the wall.

"You really do have a beautiful place here."

"Thank you." She reached across the counter-top for a kettle, which she filled and put on a burner. "I was lucky to get it. Especially so near the center of town."

The fluffy cat joined them, leaping easily onto the counter between them. He regarded McCoy coolly with round pink eyes. His claws worked in and out against the Formica.

Morgan smiled down at it. "Scratch, this is Dr. McCoy. He is a friend and you are to treat him like one." She rubbed an ear and a rolling purr came from Scratch's throat. McCoy extended a cautious hand. The feline arched its back beneath his palm and continuing purring. He knew the animal had accepted him and for some strange reason that pleased him immensely.

"Hi, Scratch."

The kettle whistled and filled two mugs with boiling water. Then she spooned fine powder into them from a large canister beneath one of the herb racks. The warm scent of cinnamon and the flowery smell of honey joined the subtle aroma of the chamomile. They stood in the kitchen to take their first sips from the mugs. The beat of the rain against the windows seemed to make the brew even more comforting.

Morgan led the way to her small round table and they sank into padded chairs. He tasted the tea again.

"This is really good, Miss Rein." To his own surprise, he was being truthful. "It takes the chill right off."

"I'm glad you like it. But please, call me Morgan. I hate formality."

"Then you must call me…"

"Dancer?" her eyes laughed at him over the rim of her mug.

"What?" he was startled. "Now how did you know that?"

"Dr. Sergei called to make the appointment and said that you would be the one coming. I decided to do a little bit of research on you. That's all. No witchcraft needed for such a simple task. In most cases, the obvious ways are the best and the most efficient. Witchcraft takes too much out of you ever to be used lightly."

McCoy winced at the word. He hated thinking that this lovely, vital young woman was subject to such superstitious delusions. Still he managed to smile. Part of him was flattered she had bothered to learn who he was.

"Research, heh? What else did you find out about me?"

Morgan chuckled. It was if she'd followed every twist of his thinking. "Dancer McCoy, borne in Bangor, Maine, the oldest son of Paul and Martha McCoy. Named Dancer because your mother was a frustrated dancer and hoped you would follow in the steps of her movie idol, Gene Kelly. Naturally, you went into the sciences instead of entertainment. Sons are always a contrary lot."

The editorial aside made him cringe jokingly. He hoped she wasn't some kind of secret man-hater. That would truly crush him.

"Graduated from MIT and did post-graduate work in physics at the University of California at Berkeley. Presently twenty-eight years old and a research fellow at the Andrews Institute of Science in this city.

"How's that?"

"You forgot my doctorate."

"Oops, sorry." The smile flashed again. She was enjoying this. "Doctorate from MIT a year ago. Of course I also found a few other things that I'm keeping to myself for the time being."

"Really?" He looked at her with newfound respect. She hadn't found all that at the library. "Accurate. But why go to so much trouble?"

Her emerald eyes were aglow with some inner merriment. "Why, Dancer, we witches have always been a cautious lot."

"I see."

"I don't think you do. Not yet. Many of us still believe that giving our true names to others gives them a kind of handle on us. There is true magic in a person's name. That being the case, I like to know about the people who come to learn about me.

And besides..."

She paused as if weighing what she was about to say next.

"Besides what?" he prompted.

"Well, as a scientist, you deal with concrete fact. You desire to know everything that you can about any given phenomenon before you begin investigating it for yourself. Right?"

"Right. Science is based on corroborative data."As a practicing witch and consultant, I deal in people. I have, by the way, a degree in behavioral psychology as well as one in applied psychology, from William and Mary. I like to know about the people I deal with. I particularly wanted to know about you."

"Why?"

She flushed faintly. "Because when I met you at the lecture, I liked you. More than a little. I hoped you'd like me, too."

McCoy swallowed a scalding gulp of tea and started choking. Morgan jumped up and thumped him solidly on the back.

"Okay," he gasped. "I'm all right now."

"I'm sorry. Did I embarrass you just now?" The eyes were dancing again.

An irrepressible grin dawned on his face. "Yeah, I guess you did. Feel free to do it again."

Morgan's smile was radiant. They began the interview and the hours raced by like a freight train riding the rails of burgeoning friendship.

Just like that the tapes were filled and the photos taken. They were talking quietly when Morgan suddenly stood up and her face went pale. Scratch, at the very same instant, wailed eerily and leaped onto the table between them. Dancer, caught off guard by both of them, could only stare in bewilderment.

The cat was staring into Morgan's eyes. She looked for a long moment and then nodded decisively.

"Hurry," she said. "Something's happening downstairs."

She bolted across the apartment and out the door without waiting to see if he followed. Dancer had to run to catch up.

"What's going on?

The elevator arrived and they jammed into the small box. Morgan punched the lobby button hard. There was a wild, frantic look about her.

"Tell me! What is it? What's wrong?" Dancer demanded. He couldn't believe the abrupt change in her expression and demeanor. Now she looked as cold and sharp as a razor. Something had struck a nerve. He realized he was seeing a side of Morgan that few could have seen before this.

She made a hand gesture and the cat, which had somehow followed them, jumped into her arms. He mewed into her neck as she smoothed his fur with both hands. The elevator lights flashed the passing floors. She looked at McCoy apologetically.

"I'm sorry. Scratch isn't exactly a pet. He's a familiar. I would have told you, but I could see it made you uncomfortable."

Dancer swiped a hand over his unruly hair. "I don't understand. What is happening here?"

"Scratch sensed something happening in the lobby. Something... wicked. I felt it too, but less strongly than he."

"You mean you can communicate with him telepathically?"

"Not exactly. It's more an empathic than a telepathic connection. We sense each other's moods and feelings. Nothing clear, in words, just feelings when they are strong enough. And Scratch, like any cat, has senses we don't have."

McCoy was doing his best not to laugh. He didn't believe a word of this. He couldn't think for a moment that she was taking it seriously. Yet here they were speeding down to the lobby for no sane reason that he could fathom. Remembering the moment of warmth in her apartment, he said nothing more. But he watched her closely.

My God! He thought, She's really worried! What does she expect to find down there?

Morgan's knuckles were white as she gripped the side rail with one hand. She bit her lip with impatience as the slow machine descended. Her eyes were focused on the descending numbers as if her will alone could make the damn thing go faster.

Two minutes later, Dancer had his answer. The door slid opened to pandemonium. They saw Biff leaning over a small figure in a gray suit. It was a middle aged man with thin, wispy gray hair and dark ash colored glasses, now askew on his round, horror-masked visage.

Scratch leaped up and landed squarely on the top of the guard's now abandoned desk. Better to survey the chaos from a raised perspective. And chaos it truly was.

"Mr. Appleton! Mr. Appleton!" the guard was shouting, trying to lift the little man. As he raised the man's body, a gush of water spurted from his mouth.

Biff looked up, his expression stunned. Water continued to flow from the man in his arms. It spilled out over his lips and onto his suit in a continuous flow. McCoy couldn't believe the volume of liquid pouring from the distorted mouth.

There was a gurgling sound and McCoy turned to see it was coming from a water cooler set along the back wall. Through the glass he could see the level dropping but nothing was coming out of the spigot. That was impossible!

"Hold him, Biff!" Morgan cried. "I'll try to help."

McCoy felt both foolish and helpless as he watched the girl close her eyes and go stiff where she stood. His skin prickled, as if some electrical force were being generated nearby, but there was no visible source. The pulse of water slowed to a trickle. There was a gasp from the man in Biff's arms. The pale eyes, behind wire-rimmed glasses, focused for on instant on McCoy.

"Shee…" came the bubbling whisper…"Shee-shee-aye."

A gush came in an irresistible flood. McCoy turned to see the water cooler chug again at the same time. As water spewed out of the man, the tank's level continued to fall. There was some kind of connection between it and the poor guy on the floor, but his mind refused to accept what he was seeing. The body arched and struggled against Biff's strong arms. Then the body went limp, just as Morgan fell, full-length, at McCoy's feet.

Scratch yowled.

CHAPTER 4

Lucien Wicker laid the phone gently in its cradle. His thin face, with its knife-cut creases, was completely composed. His mind, however, was racing. The possibilities he was considering brought him as near to excitement as he allowed himself to come, in these days of his maturity.

Construction Consortium International... power unlimited, unquestioned, cloaked beneath the mantle of progress and development and many indebted nations. He had maneuvered a long time to work into a position from which he might obtain a hold upon C.C.I. Now a lever had been delivered into his hands, almost without effort.

He smiled, the sharp creases from nose to chin deepening. His eyes, dark and secretive, didn't change expression, however, as he took from a file cabinet a thick dossier.

Fate was working with him. Tom Axel was too old a hand, too shrewd an operator to have hired him with no questions asked. That tough old buzzard was in his present position and had reached his advanced age by being more cautious and more ruthless than anyone else in the game.

Now his vice-president was another matter entirely.

Darryl Waitman. Wicker flipped open the dossier and his smile widened. Too young. Too soft. Whatever he might think of himself, Waitman had slipped into the seat of power by a far easier route than old Tom Axel. His sinews, mental and physical, had not been forged in the fires of battle.

It was obvious the young executive was waiting for his boss to die or become incapacitated to the point at which he would be forced to retire. Lucien had found it easy to locate Waitman's underworld contacts. Specialists who made it their business to eliminate unwanted people in unsuspicious ways. The implantation of suggestion had been childishly easy for Wicker. Now all he had to do was sit back and wait.

His first two assignments had been dull. Small fry, on both occasions, had learned by accident something potentially damaging to the directors of C.C.I. The poor idiots hadn't even known what it was they knew... if that made any kind of sense. Or why they died. He had pinched their hearts a bit and they had gone quite naturally. He didn't even raise a sweat.

Waitman had been inordinately pleased and Wicker had known that eventually something of real importance would be put into his hands. Assassinations were things that C.C.I. shunned, whenever possible, after those first years in which Axel was securing his own top spot.

When the call came about the troublesome accountant, Appleton, Wicker had picked up his ears. He tried to seem avid for the offered money, knowing that any other motive would have been suspect to the avaricious Waitman. He had known, too, that for this occasion he must produce something spectacular. Baffling. Leading nowhere. Yet still exotic. Axel would be watching closely this time. He must be convinced that Lucien Wicker was a man too valuable to allow to remain outside the C.C.I. ranks.

Wicker shuffled the contents of the dossier and put it back into his files. It was a certainty that Appleton had known something very dangerous to C.C.I... or to Axel, which amounted to the same thing. The demand for immediate action told him that the pencil pusher must have intended passing on what he knew to someone able to use the information. So it was there, in his consciousness, at the moment he died.

That death had been one of his more original ploys. He had toyed with the notion of that method for some time. He had grown tired of creating spontaneous human combustions. He got a wry chuckle from the press reports of the random cases that had been his practice, performed upon people he considered useless. Yet that had palled, in time, and had looked about for something different. Something unique.

He could have pinched Appleton's heart, but Axel would never have been quite certain that his death wasn't a natural one. He could have shut off his air supply... but there was a psychic bond between killer and victim. At the moment of death, the sensations of the dying person were transmitted strongly to his or her killer. Wicker knew himself to be entirely too claustrophobic to endure that sort of death. Even second hand.

Fire and air being eliminated, that left water. The teleportation of sufficient quantities from the nearest water supply directly into the lungs of the victim had struck him as something completely out of the ordinary, and inexplicable to the authorities. It had worked beautifully, though he had not taken the time to try it out in practice. The news stories, afterward, made him laugh for the first time in years.

Now he had spun the first strand of his web. Waitman had called to arrange for the rest of the payment and Wicker had taken advantage of that opportunity.

"I understand that you are next in line for presidency of C.C.I.," he had said casually as they talked. "It must be wearisome, waiting for time to take its natural course. Don't forget that I am a specialist at shortening waiting-time for the... deserving."

There had been a slightly suspicious silence at the other end of the line. Then Waitman's voice carefully said, "I must admit that I do grow impatient, at times. Perhaps we might discuss this... philosophical question over dinner one night."

Wicker knew at that moment that he had him. The fool had snapped at the bait like trout after a wiggling worm. The price for his services would not be money this time. He would seek a written guarantee that he would be given the vice-president's chair when Waitman ascended to the presidency. Once he was there, it would be a simple matter of waiting for a decent interval to elapse before removing the last obstacle between himself and control of C.C.I. A really beautiful plan, he thought. Simple and beautiful.

Only one thing marred his total satisfaction. Why had he seen, at the moment of Appleton's death, the face of Morgan Rein? The vision had shaken him to such a point that his control had faltered for a second. He frowned and rose, moving toward his bedroom. Wicker didn't like surprises. They were not part of the plan.

If his outer rooms were standard well-to-do young man on his way up the corporate ladder, as conceived by an expensive interior decorator, his bedroom was not. No human being had ever entered it and emerged in any condition to describe it. It was the only area in his home where he felt really comfortable.

Crimson draperies covered the walls, the doorways, and the glass wall. The black carpet was springy beneath his feet, and the candelabra on the wrought-iron stands, once lighted, cast an unsteady light upon his bed and the … desk. He always used that term when he thought of the altar, no matter how inaccurate it might be. Others than he saw through the mantle of flesh and bone. He took no smallest chance of being discovered. Not until he was ready.

He dropped his clothes on the floor of the big closet. He washed carefully, then slipped a midnight blue robe over his head and down his tall, lean body. He cinched its waist with a black silk cord and arranged the hood to cover his entire head. Then, barefoot, he walked to the altar.

Outside his window-wall, it was dark. The glass mirrored the candle flames, the crimson shell of the room and the black figure on the black rug. Amid the muted brightness of crimson, the black-on-black seemed to open a space in space. He smiled and brought from a drawer a dish of herbs. That went into the middle of the altar. Another candle burst into flame and he used that to kindle the dried leaves. A strong, unpleasant odor filled the room, the stench of death and decay.

Wicker threw back the hood. His black hair straggled about his face, disarranged by the garment. Quickly, with practiced economy of motion, he traced the pentacle in chalk about the altar and himself. A pinch of herb and a candle went into each point. When he had finished, he knelt beside the altar and extended his arms widely.

The invocation to Lucifuge went smoothly, but he felt no responsive tingle in his body. Only when he spoke the words of Power did something move inside him that told him he would achieve his goal. "Aglon—tetragram-vaycheon—stimulamaton esphares…" his voice sounded in his own ears. Demanding and somehow dreadful.

A stillness enwrapped the room, shutting out the remote sounds of traffic twenty stories below. The flames froze above the candles, unflickering. Chill grew about the pentacle on the black rug. Wicker remained motionless, on his knees as the cold reached its ultimate intensity.

"I would look into the mind of one dead. Recently dead, Lucifuge, I require this of you!"

His voice was lost in the muffling crimson. There was no answer, but he had expected none. Other sorcerers were answered by their demons, but he had never known that to happen during his conjurations.

He closed his eyes and sank back onto his heels. Erect of spine, shuttered of countenance, he sent his spirit forth into the dimension of death. Dark mists closed behind it.

When he reopened his eyes, the chill was gone. The frozen stillness had vanished and the candles had burned halfway down their black lengths. Supple as if he had not knelt for half the night with his legs folded beneath his weight, Lucien rose.

"So, Mr. Appleton. You did, indeed, know something of great importance. With this knowledge, I could bring down that great business empire into ruin. But what good to me would be a ruined empire? It is a lever. It may be a weapon. I will cherish it, never fear. You have not died in vain, little man. With this in my hands, I have more than one road before me."

He pinched the candle to darkness. Then he moved unerringly across the room

"I have no weaknesses!"

to fall upon the great round bed. Exhaustion wrapped him, seeming to hollow out his bones.

Yet even as his eyelids closed, he saw the face of Morgan again. He groaned unconsciously. Why? Why Morgan? What had she to do with any of this?

He had destroyed her powers through all those long years of their childhood. He had almost killed her, until they sent her away with the old woman who had been their dead mother's infant nurse. There was no way in which his sister could threaten him now. Still, he had recognized very early that her powers could have been the equal of his own.

He had been cautious for years after their father's death, which severed the last remaining bond between them. He had made subtle inquiries through all the dark covens he knew. Not one contained a woman of her years. No whisper of the name Morgan Rein came to his attention, for all his careful questioning.

If she remembered him at all, it was as Lucien Rein. The name Wicker was his own wry joke.

Why Morgan? The question was an annoying insect that would not fly away. Why Morgan? Why Morgan?

He dropped into sleep with it whirling around in his mind.

CHAPTER 5

Morgan inhaled raggedly, exhaled in a little moan. McCoy rose from the blue chair that matched the couch and bent over her. She was pale... her tan looked odd, as if it had been painted over dead-white skin. Her eyes had sunk into dark circles and there were lines from nose to chin that he hadn't noticed before. She looked drained.

When her eyes opened, their vivid green was at once aware and filled with hurt. "He died!" she remembered, her voice coming out faint.

"Yes. I think he was all but dead when we got there. I've never seen or heard of anything like that before in all my life.

"What is it you were trying to do?"

She closed her eyes for a moment. A tiny wrinkle formed between her brows. "I think that I succeeded for a instant. That other... will... was too strong for me. I wasn't prepared for anything so strong. I had no time to think it through. But I tried to stop the transfer of water ..."

"The water cooler!" McCoy interrupted.

"What?" Morgan opened her eyes.

"There was a water cooler not twenty feet away from him... and the water just seemed to ...I don't know? Go out of it?"

"And into him," Morgan finished. "That's how it was done. But I managed to block it for a second. Didn't I?"

"I think so. That's when the poor bastard try to say something."

She sat up, alert and sharp. "What? What did he say?"

"I'm not sure."

Morgan grabbed his arms. "I have to know!"

"The police asked me that, too, you know. But it still didn't make any sense. I thought he was saying something about a woman. He started to say, 'She'. Then he stopped and began again and it sounded like she-she-aye. He was still too full of liquid for it to come out plainly."

The emerald orbs were filled with fire. "He was trying to talk through all that water. It would naturally distort anything he said. But Dancer, I looked into his eyes. They knew, were very much alert to whatever was happening to him. He was trying to tell us what... or who... was killing him."

"Who?" McCoy's face registered puzzlement. "Morgan, I don't presume to understand how it is possible for a man to drown in a hotel lobby miles away from any body of water. But that is what I saw. Okay. So it's a mystery. But that's all it is. A scientific oddity. That's all."

"No, it isn't. It was craftwork, the darkest kind. Someone with great arcane powers murdered that poor little man."

"That's crazy!" He started pacing about in front of her. The nervous habit of combing his hair with his fingers returned. Scratch, comfy on the opposite chair, watched him with cat curiosity.

Morgan sat up gingerly, taking another deep breath. She shook her head. "No, it is the craft and Scratch and I sensed it from the beginning. I realize that is hard for you grasp, but if we are to deal with this challenge, then you must put aside your doubts and trust me."

McCoy stopped his marching. "You're talking about murder, here. Right."

"Nothing less."

He threw his hands up in the air. "Okay. Just for the sake of argument, and my own sanity, say it is this magic mumbo jumbo. Why should we get involved? Isn't it a job for the police?"

"They would be in over their heads. I'm sure you are well aware of the adage, it takes a thief to catch a thief."

"So?"

"In this case it will take a witch to…"

"…catch another witch." McCoy fell back in his own chair and Scratch went over to join him. Leaping up into his lap, it made itself comfortable there and McCoy stared at it more confused than ever. Morgan smiled. It was Scratch's way of making the man at ease in a world he had never imagined. A world which was now opening to him with evil designs.

"All right," he said to the cat and then her," I'm in, but we still don't have much to go on. Just his garbled last words."

"Yes. She-she-aye."

"She!" Dancer snapped his fingers. "Maybe he meant SEA! After all he was filling up with water and that had to be the topmost thing on his mind."

Morgan negated the idea. "No. As you personally identified, it was fresh water from the cooler drowning him. I sensed it as well while trying to interrupt the transfer. Besides, even if you drown in it, the sea isn't malicious. There is nothing personal in it, even if it capsizes you."

"Thanks, I'll remember that the next time I go sailing and take a dunk."

Morgan ignored his attempt at humor. "What else sounds like that? She. Sea. What if it is simply the letter C itself?"

She whirled up from the couch and whisked a thick book from one of the shelves. "Here, let's look in the City Directory. It has all the industries, organizations, and corporations in the country who are based here. Let's run down everything that begins with a C."

"C.C." he added. His face lit up. "Aye… I! C.C.I.! Damn it, you may be on to something after all."

In twenty minutes they had a list of seven names with the Cannell Corporation, Inc. and ending with Czerny Canning International. McCoy, now sitting beside her at the kitchen bar, scanned the sheet of paper with renewed interest.

"There's a lot of power stored up among all those big guns. How in the blazes would anyone be able to find out what one of them might have against a poor little mite like this Appleton fellow?"

"Easily," Morgan replied. She reached for the telephone on the counter and dialed a number.

McCoy heard a faint buzz, then a click.

"Charlotte? Morgan Rein. Could you run a quick check for me? Yes, I can hold." There was a second long pause. "No, my command number is still the same. Right. The name is Appleton, Ronald Xavier. Apartment 348, my address. Yes, that's still the same, too. Fine. Terrific and thanks."

She hung up and smiled at McCoy. Her color was returning.

"This will only take a few minutes. This friend of mine is a computer hacker. She has access to everything and anything out on the web."

"You don't have a computer?"

"I don't trust them."

"But you get help from hacker."

"Compromise is a necessary part of life. Beside it's much faster than out-of-body seeking when I work for a client. Saves on the energy like you wouldn't believe."

The phone rang before McCoy could think of anything to say that wouldn't sound as dumbfounded as he felt. Out-of-body seeking indeed!

When Morgan replaced the receiver in its cradle, she was smiling, her eyes shooting green sparks that he felt should have scorched the creamy rug. "And there we have it. Mr. Ronald X. Appleton is… or was… employed as an accountant for Construction Consortium International.

"And who, pray tell, is in a better position to discover misdeeds among the higher-ups than a confidential accountant?"

"A discovery so big it would require murder to cover it up."

"Exactly." She sounded like a grown up version of Nancy Drew, whereas he most definitely was not one of the Hardy boys.

"What is it?" She sensed his hesitancy.

"C.C.I. is one mighty big outfit to accuse of wrong doing, Morgan. Especially murder. They handle the raw materials of the entire world. Like Caesar's wife, they've got to be above reproach.

"They also, for your information, fund a lot of the very work we do at the Institute. I can't just go up and start yelling that C.C.I. went and murdered their accountant. Particularly when nobody can say for certain what was done to kill the poor bastard in the first place. Witchcraft aside, for a minute.

"I'd be out on my ear in a flash and nobody would be any better off."

For all his logical arguments, she seemed unworried. "I don't' want you to, Dancer. You go about your life and work as if nothing had happened. If something is sinister at C.C.I., it's going to take methods you don't want to know about, and wouldn't believe if you did, to unearth it."

McCoy felt himself growing flushed. Though he had known this woman for less than two days… about three hours on a personal level… he found that her opinion of him mattered more to him than he'd have thought possible.

"Listen," he said, "I'm not backing down here. I want to understand what happened down there in the lobby as much as you do. You asked me to trust you and I will. You can count on me for anything you'll need. Hell, I've been out of job before and I can always find another one if I have to. Just promise me that you'll be careful in this thing." He reached over and took her hand in his. "I don't really believe in hunches, but if I did, I'd say I have a hunch this affair is nothing to get messed up in. It feels totally creepy… and dangerous."

Morgan tightened her grip on his hand. Her fingers were cool to the touch. "I may need your help, Dancer. But I wonder if you can accept some of the things I must do. The ways I must do them are strange and I know how you feel about my profession. Your skepticism radiates from you almost tangibly. Still... I do believe in hunches. I will need, I suspect, a dependable ally in this, and you, sir, all but reek of dependability."

They both laughed, the tension broken between them. She went to the table and gathered up his forgotten recorder and camera. "Now you'd better go, before the police come up here asking more questions. They'll get around to me, I'm sure, once Biff tells them I was there."

McCoy agreed, taking his gear. "Right. I didn't know exactly what you'd want to tell them, so I just told them that you took one look and just fainted dead away. Biff was too busy to take in what was happening with us. I hope you don't mind... they shouldn't even ask you questions at all. Unless you want to tell them that you knew something was about to happen.."

"Huh, huh," she shook her head. "No, way. You did the right thing. I just hope they don't use my name in the news stories."

"Don't see why they should. I got you out of there and up in the elevator before they arrived. Then I went back down and gave them my story. All I said was that we happened to be coming down together and when the door opened, we saw what was happening. The officer in charge didn't even ask for your name. They just took mine."

With his equipment in hand, he turned for the door. "When do you think you'll have any further information?"

Morgan opened the front door for him. "Come to dinner tomorrow night. I should have something to go on by then."

"Okay, and I won't ask how." One last gaze. Her eyes were lost in some secret domain and there was mischief there. He knew that she would do what had to be done, regardless of the risk involved. "Please, be careful, Morgan."

Then he was gone and she closed the door behind him.

CHAPTER 6

Next the police came and went. Their questions were routine and the detective in charge looked bored and anxious to be done with the whole mess. They stayed all of fifteen minutes. Long enough for Morgan to corroborate Dr. McCoy's account. It was a lie and she detested lying. But then again, it was a little one and offered up for the greater cause she had dedicated herself to.

Morgan listened with relief to their steps diminish down the long corridor as she straightened her disarranged couch cushions and drew the draperies against the approach of another night. Scratch got up from his couch perch and lazily jogged to his red food bowl. There was a good chunk of tuna fish there and he began nibbling at it with relish while his mistress tidied up.

Morgan was frantically anxious to delve into the Appleton mystery, but she knew she must wait until it was certain nobody would be requiring her presence. Her appearance, when she was out of the body, would have caused anyone who discovered her so to rush her either to the hospital or worse yet, the morgue.

Now she had both the time and opportunity. She moved into the kitchen, prepared herself a light meal and ate it standing at the counter. Scratch continued with his own meal, mewing every now and then to show his contentment. When at last she moved toward her bedroom, the Angora scampered ahead of her. He was waiting on the bed, tail quivering with excitement, when she entered.

With deliberate slowness, the young witch undressed, bathed and donned her white robe. Pulling back the gold and cream-colored bedspread, she arranged herself precisely between the sheets, as if for sleep. She folded her hands across her ribs, fingertips to fingertips.

Her heart beat warmly beneath, echoing in her pulse. She concentrated deeply, and the beat became slower and slower.

Now she projected her will into that other self that existed outside her body. She felt consciousness slipping upward, as if she were sliding out of herself from heels to head. After a while, she could look downward into her own face, which was now serene and pale in the wan light reflected from the windows.

Then she was out. Morgan floated for a moment above her body, making sure that all was well with it. The bright filament connecting her to it hung weightless on the air behind her like the gaudy tail of a kite, as she collected her knowledge and power. She paused, hovering like a constellation of stars in the still room. Then she shot through the wall, the dark sky of night, flying toward her goal.

As her ethereal self floated across the city skyscrapers, Morgan reviewed her collected intelligence. She had gleaned much from the friend's computer scans. She now knew the C.C.I. building, among other things, as well as she knew her own apartment. It would be all but empty now, tenanted only by the cleaning staff and security personnel. They wouldn't have the opportunity to see her. The distance to her target flashed past with almost the speed of thought. Having no real substance, she slipped through the wall of the steel and concrete high-rise as if it were mist. Bulls-eye, she thought with satisfaction.

She found herself, as intended, in the Chief Accountant's office. It was a large one, with walls lined with filing cabinets, filled, she suspected, with data that had not yet been entered into the company's computer systems. She ignored the terminal on the desk. The information about Appleton would not, she was positive, be located there. If the diminutive accountant had left any clue to his murder, it would be in some spot that was easy to overlook. She prayed such a clue still existed.

She concentrated, allowing the energies around her to tell their own stories. She received no unusual sensations from the bulk of the tan colored cabinets. None came from the desk or any of its drawers. But something was tugging at her. It was faint and Morgan refocused her mind not to lose the tenuous thread. Carefully, like a swimmer moving against a gentle current, she followed it through a closed door into the adjoining space, which held six desks.

Appleton! She felt a remnant of his personality in this room. This is where he had worked. And there... that had been his desk. She drifted to the metal piece and stopped beside it.

She sensed there was nothing in the drawers. Yet there was something? Of that she was convinced. Her feelings were strong on that count. She had to find whatever it was. She rotated slowly. The files behind the desk held no spark of interest. But there was something about the desk that drew her. Beneath a drawer?

Yes! Morgan extended her vision effortlessly. Requiring no real eyes, it went where she sent it and it needed no light for seeing. There was a sheet of paper taped to the bottom of the middle drawer.

Names and figures went into the secure storage of her memory. The brief note at the bottom was also committed to memory. Then she set herself to do the most difficult of all things... the manipulation of matter while in her astral state.

It was an arduous task requiring effort and patience. The paper lifted, with terrible deliberateness, free of its tape. Then she maneuvered it through a fine crack of the drawer onto the floor. There it rolled into a tight curl. She didn't attempt to struggle with the tape or any other kind of binding. Her mind was her best tool. Deftly she set her will about it and pulled it along with her as she rose up through the ventilation system in the ceiling. The small paper tube rolled along as if animated with a life of its own. It would have been easier to leave the way she had come, but that precious bit of evidence had to go with her. She dared not leave it behind for later retrieval. It was only by the purest luck, she had been able to find it. She had no doubts that others would do likewise were she to leave it behind.

Thus it popped out of outer wall shaft vent a half-hour later and was instantly taken up by a gust of wind. Delicately, Morgan pulled it through the air.

Dawn saw the glittering strand shorten, as Morgan's ghost-like self rejoined her body. As if she were a hand sliding into a glove, she moved into her waiting flesh. It moved uneasily to receive her.

The roll of paper fell silently to the sea-green carpet of the bedroom and rolled, just a bit, until it came to rest against the fringe of the bedspread.

Morgan gave an exhausted sigh, stretched luxuriously and fell into a deep, restful slumber.

She dreamed of days long past.

CHAPTER 7

She was seven years old again, standing in a damp cemetery in Paris beside her father and her brother. Death was a thing that she had just met and she had no comprehension of its finality. The steel-blue coffin had no connection, in her mind, with the warmth that was her mother. Yet she knew that Maman lay inside that box, which was sliding into the slot in the masonry tomb.

Only the anguish in her father's face told her that something had changed, terribly and forever, and for the worse. Armand Rein was a strong man. She had never seen him weep and hadn't known that he could. Yet now the tears were streaming down his olive cheeks, as his hand gripped hers so tightly that it was painful. Something too terrible to recognize was happening to her family. She peeped around her Papa's legs at Lucien, wondering if he knew the secret of this strange occurrence.

He stood on father's right, his thin face expressionless. That was normal, she knew. The pale face with the pointed chin seldom showed any sign of human emotion, whether of joy or anger or sorrow. He might have been watching a boat race or a passing plane or a dead cat, as their mother's coffin sank from view.

Although she had not known it then, that day marked the end of Morgan Rein's childhood. As the only daughter of a diplomat, she had known only abundance and ease. As the child of her mother, she had known the most sheltering and nurturing of loves. Now, though Armand was a sensitive man, he was unable to cope with his own woes. In his pain at the loss of his beloved wife, he didn't realize the depth of that loss to his daughter.

When her father shut himself away in his study, away from the world that had hurt him so deeply, to bury himself in his work and his library, it left Morgan adrift in an alien world. A new routine established itself in the house on Rue Chevalier. Like any other child, she unsuspectingly adapted herself to it, spending her scant free time in her room or her favorite spot in the garden behind the huge house.

There she practiced the secret arts that her beautiful mother had taught her. She made rocks float from the ground to circle like rough shaped butterflies until she let them drop again to rest. Sometimes she would force a flower into premature blossom, though she always felt guilty at shortening its already brief lifespan.

Best of all, was the waking time at night. She lay in bed, watching moonbeams move across the Persian carpet. Then she shifted dust motes into dim-lit ballets. Or she wafted her Teddy bear into comical dances in mid-air. At such times she felt Maman so near that she almost believed that a word might bring forth an answer, though she never quite dared to try.

School was another world entirely. She didn't realize that her schoolmates had no private play times as she did. She assumed that they could all do the things that she could, when they were alone. It had been her mother's single most imperative rule: You only practiced such talents in private. Never when anyone else might see.

Morgan had thus assumed that privacy was necessary. Perhaps the techniques wouldn't work at all, if someone else were present. She had never heard the word witchcraft. She only knew that she was never lonely and that Maman seemed the nearest when she practiced the things she had taught to her daughter.

She realized long later that Lucien had not been so ignorant. The darkness coloring his strange spirit lent him a precocity beyond his years. He had understood early the uniqueness of his talents. He comprehended very soon, so Mother Kalavela had told her, that their mother was a special order of being and that he, as her offspring, had inherited her special abilities.

They had gone back, years later, to trace his development. Kalavela had intuited that the boy had been quick to capitalize upon his skills. When older boys, bullying, had tried to make his life miserable, Lucien had no qualms about interfering with their physical processes. A mental tweak at stomach or chest and the resultant doublings-up with cries of pain had given him much gratification. He soon acquired a reputation as one who was best left alone. With his gifts, he was stronger than all the bullies put together.

Lucien had gained a group of toadying followers in that way and that had boosted his adolescent ego. He enjoyed their uncritical adoration. He ran the alleyways with them, enjoying to the full their unquestioning obedience to his malicious whims. Yet he had been intelligent enough to see, at last, the true nature of their discipleship. They were inquisitive about his powers. They wanted those for their own. Of course he had never entertained any intention of sharing that private treasure with anyone. Thus did he terminate his fraternization with his hangers-on.

At that point in his personal history, Kalavela was sure, he had decided that his road must be traveled alone. And then, to his dismay, he learned that his sister held gifts at least the equal of his own! Astonished and appalled by that discovery, he had cast about for a way in which to protect his own uniqueness.

He had run the savage streets long enough to observe the jungle of primitive survival. His instinct told him to kill Morgan.

Kalavela had told her more than once that her brother's true nature had never experienced or understood love. Their parents, she suspected, had been his immediate means of survival and ease. His sister, on the other hand, was not necessary to his comfort. To him she was simply a rival and an obstacle. He had absolutely no reservations about what he must do.

He secretly began following her about her daily routine, when she was not at school. Once he knew the rhythms of her days, he set about destroying her.

The first attack had been devastating and almost fatal. Morgan remembered it, with the intensity of her dream, entirely too well. She had a pattern or rocks floating in the garden, like a wall suspended in mid-air in the mellow afternoon sunlight. Without warning, one of the jagged bits veered from its position in her pattern to fly through the air directly toward her. It struck her full in the face. Before she could think or move, another assaulted her. She cried out in pain and terror as the rocks, like a nest of angry hornets, took flight against her. Desperately she had fled for her life. Only the timely appearance of the housekeeper had saved her life, for death had waited for her then and there.

She had not fathomed, then, what caused the bizarre event to happen. It had not occurred to her that her brother had ever noticed her, much less that he could feel hostility toward her. Morgan kept her mouth closed when her father questioned her about the cuts and bruises on her chubby, pink face. Armand had decided that it must have been some squabble with other children that had caused the injuries. An unfortunate thing, but nothing that would be repeated, he promised her and himself.

The second incident had been, in a way, more painful. She had been in bed watching her Teddy bear at his aerobatic dancing. The moon was bright on the golden-brown plump and furry bear. It almost seemed alive as it floated around her room. Suddenly the stuffed animal violently came apart in front of her.

The arms were torn away by some invisible force. The cotton stuffing sifted through the cold light from the suspended body. The head started twisting around and around, the button eyes gleaming in the light as they turned. Then it had fallen to the floor amid a rain of padding. While Morgan had watched, frozen with terror, her bed had then begun to rock. Gently at first, it had picked up momentum until she had to cling to the headboard to keep from being flung off.

Finally it ceased and fell to the hardwood floor with a bang. Shaking with fear, she had pulled the covers over her head and lain in silence wondering what new fears would come next.

"Maman," she cried. But there had been no answer.

Only the night… and the horror.

CHAPTER 8

Dancer McCoy sat in the blue chair with Scratch purring in his lap. He had just eaten the best lasagna that he had ever tasted. He was aglow with a delicate rose wine. Life didn't get much better than this. Then his lovely hostess handed him a slip of paper and spoiled everything.

"In your hand is a death list," Morgan said before going into the kitchen to clear away the dirty dishes. She'd insisted on finishing the meal before talking business and McCoy had no idea what discoveries she had made since they had parted company the day before. There was a keen brightness to Morgan's eyes and a hard edge to her voice. It spoke volumes without so many words.

He felt totally out of his element. "How do you know that?" he asked, looking down at the curled sheet of paper. "And where exactly did you get this?"

"That will make you terribly uncomfortable," she warned, returning to the living room as she dried her hands on a paper towel.

"Okay. I don't expect your computer friend hands out death lists," he offered. "I promise not to look skeptical… at least not any more than I can help. Just tell me how you got your hand on this?"

She dropped onto the couch and grinned impishly. "I went out-of-body," she confessed.

"Please, Morgan! No jokes. How did you get hold of this paper?"

"Truly. How else could I have gotten into the C.C.I. building, past the guards, into the chief accountant's office and from there into the actual account-ing department? In the middle of the night no less."

McCoy stopped scratching Scratch. His reaction was pretty much what she had envisioned. Still she pressed on.

"Come on, Dancer, there are some things that are just not humanly possible. Things that have to be done. Ergo, they have to be done by non-human means. I found that piece of paper taped to he underside of Appleton's desk drawer."

"Appleton's….? But how did you know which desk was…?"

She sighed impatiently. "Every spirit has its own signature. Something akin to fingerprints, you might say. The things a person handles, works with, plays with, and wears. All these hold an imprint of that person. Appleton's desk reeked of Appleton. It was easy to find."

Morgan leaned forward, her elbows on her knees. "Look, I know that you can't accept this intellectually, yet. Your analytical mind won't allow for it. But you really have to believe me here or we won't be able to work together at all."

McCoy did his best to look sincere. "Okay, I'll accept that as well as I can. But all I see here are a bunch of names, numbers and short note on the bottom. How do you know it's a death list? Your hacker friend again?"

"Exactly. I called her this morning. Every name on that list is that of a former C.C.I. employee. All of have died within the past six months. Every one connected in some way, directly or indirectly, with the finance and accounting departments as they relate to the new computer system management installed last year."

McCoy whistled. "So that means, counting Appleton, that outfit has managed to bump off six people in the past six months without making a ripple as far as the law is concerned. That isn't easy to do. Six people are dead, and to C.C.I. it's just business as usual. I really don't like this, Morgan. We are dealing with some pretty frightening people."

She nodded. She was looking at the paper still in his hand.

McCoy's intuition kicked in. "Then the figures beside each name could refer to the fee for the hit?"

"That's my guess," she agreed. The wine carafe was on the coffee table between them and Morgan poured herself another glass. The pink of the sunset struck the glass of the balcony windows, making the wine's color warmer. She sipped it, waiting for McCoy to proceed.

"What about this note at the end. 'If anything happens to me, notify C. Hines.'"

"I checked on that, too. Constance Hines is a corporate lawyer. She lives across town and has her office downtown. She was Appleton's cousin and they were very close, from what I've been able to gather. They were the last of the family left out here on the East Coast."

"You think he confided in her?"

"It's probable, but we must find out for sure. I tried calling her office, but she was out all day... probably making funeral arrangements for Appleton." Morgan's face took the stony expression that McCoy was beginning to recognize.

"And you think she might be in danger."

"Well, somebody did kill Appleton. Most likely because he discovered some kind of wrongdoing at C.C.I. Five other company people have died in entirely too short a time for it to be natural. If they were murdered, and every instinct I have says they were, then we're dealing with totally ruthless people. Monsters who wouldn't leave any loose ends. If they found out Ms. Hines exists... and that she is a lawyer, then they will see her as a threat." She left the rest unspoken.

McCoy swallowed the last of his drink and cradling Scratch in his arms, sprang to his feet. "What are we waiting for? We've got to find her and warn her!"

Morgan didn't move.

"Well? What?"

She wrinkled her nose. "Don't laugh. I've never ridden on a motorcycle before. I'm terrified of them."

He guffawed. "I don't believe it! You are too much. Here we are about to go chasing off after a gang of murderers and you're worried about riding on my bike!"

She groaned, reluctantly getting to her feet and marching into the bedroom. "There are things that even a witch cannot control and a bike is one of them."

She re-emerged having thrown a turtleneck sweater over her dark slacks and long-sleeved blouse. "She lives on the East Side. Her address is on the memo pad next to the wine."

McCoy gave the lazy cat a final rub about the ears and then laid him on the chair he had just vacated. He handed Morgan the death-list and picked up the yellow memo sheet. He glanced at the scribbled address and put it in his jeans pocket.

"I know the area well. We can be there in ten minutes."

They were at the door when the phone rang. Morgan pushed back her heavy hair and put the receiver to her ear.

"Morgan Rein," she said and listened. By her expression, McCoy surmised the caller was someone familiar.

"Yes," she continued. "But does it have to be right now? I was just on my way out on a matter of grave importance." There was another pause. "Of course, Claire, I understand. Very well, I'll be right there."

McCoy still had his hand on the doorknob. "What's up?

"That was Claire Maxwell. She's a dear friend and…"

"And?"

"A professional colleague."

"You mean another witch." He was enjoying himself way too much at her expense.

"Claire is more than that. She's my Coven Mother."

McCoy arched an eyebrow but was smart enough to keep his mouth shut this time.

"She wants to see me immediately on a matter of great importance."

"Hmm, you think it might have anything to do with… all this?"

"Possible. Claire is gifted. Nothing of metaphysical origin could happen within a fifty-mile radius of her without her knowing. She wouldn't elaborate over the phone."

"Okay, then. We'll split up. You go find out what she wants and I go find our Ms. Hines the lawyer."

"Good and you can drop me off. Claire's shop is on the way. But do hurry to find Hines as fast as you can, Dancer. All my craft instincts tell me we're surrounded by danger in this and we don't have much time to act."

"You're calling the shots. You just point me the right direction." His words were meant to reassure and his handsome smile did just that. There was more than craft magic at work here.

Morgan looked into his rich brown eyes. Dancer felt a bit giddy. Then she reached up to kiss him full on the mouth. Her lips were soft, moist and wonderful. There was a taste he could not describe. It was thrilling, and electricity tingled between them. McCoy was totally unaware, reacting to the oldest of all the magics, that she was placing a protective spell over him. Morgan, in her concern, had provided that his normal perceptions and reactions and reflexes would be sharpened to incredible heights, if there arose a need for that.

It was all she could do for him and the fluttering in her own heart.

* * * *

Claire Rowena Maxwell had been a name to conjure with, in fashion circles of thirty years before. At twenty, she had been a luminous beauty: the most famous model in the world. Now her face and figure had lost little of their breathtaking quality. In addition, she had gained a maturity that lent a distinctive style to her beauty. Though her short hair was frosted with silver, her eyes still generated a vibrancy that belied any idea that the spirit behind them had aged.

She now operated a chic boutique. Few knew that the poised owner of the thriving downtown enterprise, was the senior witch in the city's only coven of practitioners of Wicca. Those few were all in her inner circle, for she refused to publicize her secret life. Although nowadays many people espoused the Old Religion, Claire had grown up in a more conservative and less permissive era. She remembered the fears and apprehensions that circumstances had etched into the spirits of those who taught her the Way, back in her Massachusetts home. Let her peers walk openly, if they would and reveal their persuasions. She, on the other hand, kept them to herself. The humanitarian duties she performed were done in the strictest secrecy. She never sought thanks or praise and from such wisdom she learned the true reward of humility, inner peace and contentment.

When her doorbell chimed as the shop door opened, Claire rose from her desk and welcomed Morgan into her office. She smiled and hugged the girl, kissing her lightly on one cheek. The two shared a binding affection for one another. If Kalavela had been Morgan's surrogate grandmother, then Claire was a favorite aunt.

"Come sit down, dear," she invited, signaling to one of her clerks to attend to closing the shop. She shut the office door behind her.

The office was small but touched with the inspired hand of one who loved comfort. Claire poured coffee from a glass pot that was always full and ready to go. Then she lit a cigarette from an open pack on her desktop.

Morgan frowned. "When are you going to give up that filthy habit?" she prodded for the thousandth time.

"When I grow wings, my dear. Now don't go getting picky on me. You know very well that I relish my vices. I have so few that the ones I've managed to hang on to provide me with a great deal of comfort."

"Bullfeathers! You're incorrigible."

"And you, my child, are mixed up in something both frightening and deadly."

It was just like Claire. She got to the heart of any matter with one uncluttered thrust. No beating around some frivolous topic to waste all kinds of precious time. Time was too valuable a commodity to be treated so carelessly. Morgan took a sip of coffee then set her cup down.

"Yes," she admitted. "A man was murdered in my apartment building yesterday. He was drowned by psychic transference of water from a cooler twenty yards away into his lungs. Only a great talent could have accomplished it. I tried to intervene, but it was too late. He was almost gone… and the force behind the attack was much stronger than I suspected it might be."

"I see." Ashes fell from Claire's cigarette to the tidy floor, but she didn't notice. "Then I was correct. I felt the power at work. I had a sighting."

"Of the murderer?"

"Not clearly, I'm afraid. What I sensed was a terrible evil at work. You understand all too well how any practice of the black art permeates the atmosphere. This was particularly strong. Were you able to sense the source while you were struggling against it?"

Morgan hesitated for a long moment. She was uncomfortable with the question and fidgeted. Enough to spark her friend's ire.

"Morgan, don't be foolish. I depend on you for an answer. When I had the sighting, I held it tightly, trying to penetrate to its source and to probe its meaning. Your image came into my mind as I did so. Yours and then another's, this one fogged and obscure. Yet I saw your face beside that other and know there is a connection there.

"So, tell me, what does it have to do with you?"

Morgan sighed. "Two nights ago I trapped that killer in the park."

"Ah," Claire nodded. "I suspected as much. The newspaper accounts weren't too clear, so I knew it had to be one of us. Go on."

"Afterward, I returned home and offered the proper prayers. Then I went to bed. Before I could drop off I, too, had a sending. I saw the face of someone I haven't seen in many years. Someone I thought was dead."

Claire's eyes widened. "Who was it?"

"My brother, Lucien."

"Lucien..?" Claire's voice trailed off as she stared at her protégé. Her blue eyes mirrored genuine concern as her memories made all the right connections. "The brother who tried to kill you when you were a child... and nearly succeeded. The one Kalavela traced backward through time but couldn't follow into any future she could see."

"My tormentor and personal demon," Morgan finished. She took a last hasty sip from the cooling coffee. "Mother Kalavela always believed one of Lucien's wicked conjurations must have gone wrong and killed him. Nobody had ever succeeded in hiding from her, no matter how powerful his or her craft cunning might be. She was so sure that he was dead."

"But it was never confirmed, was it?" Claire blew out one last puff of smoke and crushed the butt in an ivory ashtray.

"No. When our father was killed, Lucien wasn't to be found. Nobody knew where he had gone the night before the accident. When Mother Kalavela couldn't trace him, I put him out of my life and out of my mind. I tried never to think of him again."

She laughed wryly. "That might have been a mistake on my part. A very big mistake."

"And the other night?"

"I had absolutely no reason to remember him at that time. I hadn't thought of him in years. The face I saw was that of a man, not a thirteen-year-old boy, as he was when I saw him last. This was a man in his forties. A very unpleasant man."

Claire opened her mouth to speak, but Morgan forestalled her. "After the murder, I made the connection. My vision had to be a forewarning. I believe that my brother must have been involved in the death of Mr. Appleton, though I cannot imagine in what way. Or why?"

The older woman lit a fresh cigarette. She exhaled, allowing the swirling smoke about her head to momentarily blur her comely features. Claire was not one to speak without thinking first. Morgan trusted her implicitly.

"You are assuming that Lucien has not only retained all his abilities, but has reinforced them with training of ..the wrong sort?"

"I am certain of it. Even when he was a child, he was terribly aware of the potential of his gift. Mother Kalavela found that in him at once. He was more cognizant, she said, than many of the adult witches she had counseled.

"He left the imprint of his talent upon everything he touched. That is highly unusual even for an adult, and terribly so for a child. He was working even then to learn all that he could. To attain any advantage he could find.

"Now, with all the years of such learning behind him, I am frightened to think how he must have increased his powers. The force I faced over the body of Mr. Appleton was one of tremendous unyielding strength."

Claire sighed. "I was afraid of that. Morgan, I am unable to advise you much in this. It is a personal challenge for you. No outsider could fathom it accurately. Including yours truly. The two of you are linked by the most elemental of bonds. Your common blood ties you into his affairs in a way that nobody else can approach or interfere with.

"He is a serious threat to our group, I am certain. I'm astonished that he hasn't sensed our existence and moved against us already. The art he embraces cannot tolerate ours. It is opposite and inimical."

Claire put her half smoked fag in the ashtray and rubbed her eyes with her fingers. The worry on her face was obvious but so was the resolve when she once again opened her eyes.

"Morgan, I have to tell you this. Lucien will destroy us, every one, if he can. We cannot see him or even sense him with any degree of accuracy, as you can see from my own feeble sighting. If you are willing to open your spirit to him, you can keep track of him. I believe this can be done without his realizing it."

She took another nicotine hit and went on. "Whatever plot he is engaged in is a dangerous thing. To us and the peace of the world at large. I can sense that strongly. That is the nature of the dark side of the power we serve. Are you strong enough to meet such a challenge?"

Morgan stared at Claire. She had never felt weaker, never more of a coward than she did now. Yet she knew that the witch was entirely correct. It was Morgan Rein's responsibility. It was her own battle to fight. She, of all the group, had the best chance of learning the truth and of seeing it to its end. And of surviving? That was another question altogether.

"I hope to be strong enough," she answered with a steady voice. "Have you disbanded the group, just as a precaution?"

"I did that this afternoon. It isn't easy to trace us, when we are apart and shielding ourselves. We will not meet until this crisis is resolved, though we will each one set our minds upon you and the task you are setting out to do."

Suddenly Morgan felt terribly alone. At the same time she recalled Dancer, jauntily zipping away on his motorcycle. The image brought her comfort and reassurance.

Coming around her desk, Coven Mistress took hold of Morgan's hands. "We will be concentrating upon you. Our strength will be focused upon you. Use them, for they will bolster your heart and your energies. Never forget that while your body may be alone, your spirit is girded about with true friends."

Morgan's eyes misted. "Thank you, Claire. For everything."

Claire stepped back and looked at her intently. "Have you another place from which to operate? If Lucien senses that you are near, as you sensed him, he will logically try to find you. Your home holds a terribly strong imprint of your personality and craft. You need to move."

Morgan thought of Dancer again. Claire caught the image in her mind.

"Ah! You have an ally!"

"Yes, I do."

"A special one, I sense."

"Very special. My knight in black leather, you might say."

Claire smiled and touched Morgan's face. "Remember your training, my child. Its cautions and its strengths. It will bring you through safely, if anything can."

They hugged and Morgan departed. Claire watched her through the shop front window, arms wrapped around herself as if to ward of a sudden chill. Though neither had voiced it, the word "Goodbye" hung in the air behind them.

CHAPTER 9

Lucien checked the street numbers. There was a blast of car horns behind his slow moving car, but he ignored them.

There!

He rolled into a parking lot that a larger vehicle couldn't have managed to fit into. The advantage of small, foreign imports. Sitting there, observing the building, he thought about Darryl Waitman's call earlier that afternoon.

He had been tense. A woman calling herself Constance Hines had come to the main office of C.C.I., late the afternoon before. She had been making inquiries about Ron Appleton. The office manager, though not privy to the secrets of the upper echelons, did know enough to inform his immediate superiors about the woman's visit.

That information had caused quite a lot of unease. Waitman had immediately set wheels in motion to track down the woman's connection to the deceased accountant. When she proved to be a close relative, one with a law degree, the situation took on ominous tones.

Although Waitman believed there was nothing incriminating left for anyone to unearth, his long habit of caution compelled him to call Wicker.

"It probably isn't anything serious," he had put forth. "We could probably disregard it entirely."

Wicker picked up on his tension. "But…"

"But I felt you should know about it. That's all. What with your unique talents, you might be able to check her out in depth, without arousing any undue suspicion.

"If she's just a nosy snooper, we we'll ignore her. But if her cousin did confide in her in regard to any wrongdoings, then that might be a problem. If she has any inkling at all of where to look… or more specifically, what to look for, she will have to be stopped. You understand?"

"Yes, I understand." Wicker could visualize Waitman sweating on the other end of the line. He was a pathetic fool.

"Of course, the decision is yours. Decide on the basis of whatever you can find out about her. We have the utmost confidence in your judgement."

"I'm flattered," Wicker smiled a humorless grimace as he cradled his phone. He recognized corporate soft-soap whenever he found it. He knew very well that Axel, working through Waitman, wanted the woman dead and the dirty work done with other hands than their own. Hands that could not be traced back to C.C.I.

Now, as dusk settled upon the skyline, Lucien tapped his long fingers on the steering wheel, waiting. His quarry wasn't home. He could sense it. But she would come.

She had spent the evening at the mortuary making funeral arrangements. This morning she visited a reference library and spent several hours researching C.C.I. He had followed her from a distance, using his seeing powers. When he sensed she was on her way back to her apartment, he decided it was time to escalate his surveillance. Perhaps even take action, if the situation warranted. But to make that determination he needed to make visual contact with his target.

He emptied his mind to concentrate his energies. An almost invisible field formed around his sports car, as he focused his talent into the proper channels.

A late model yellow Subaru sedan turned the corner and pulled into the parking lot across the street. The driver killed the engine and lights and then struggled to get out of the front seat. She was short, overweight, with that square sort of crusading jaw on a strong face that so many women were beginning to wear.

Lucien recognized her at once. It was Constance Hines. No doubt at all. He watched as she bent awkwardly to lift two bags of groceries out of the back seat. She juggled them about as she locked the door. An old man in gray coveralls emerged from the building and jogged across the open lot to assist her.

"Hold on, Miss Hines. I'll give you a hand."

"Thanks, Carl. I really need it." She handed him the larger bag and smiled appreciatively. Her face looked strained and grim in the light from the street lamp, in spite of her honest smile.

Lucien focused on her. With controlled ease, he moved into her stream of thought without causing any ripple of alarm. The woman was totally oblivious to his mental probe. In her thoughts he discovered warmth directed toward the old custodian with the grocery bag. Physical need next… her dinner was late and would be later still before she could cook and eat it.

He went deeper. There was a anguish at being so heavy, yet also an unwillingness to admit that it was her emotional disguise. Men admired big women, if at all, for their minds and abilities. There was no complication of sex or romantic adventure.

She had seen too many of her friends lose at that game. She had no intention of getting into it, ever again. Now she was plump and happy. Happy that is, except for poor Ron, who had tried so hard to help her settle in with her job and everything, was gone. And there was apprehension about his death.

Wicker probed more deeply still. Ah. Here were the complex layers of recent happenings. Appleton… agitated and frightened. A visit to her office downtown from the little man… yes, he had discovered something in the process of converting the company's information files for the new computer network. Accounts that didn't balance. Millions had been transferred, apparently from mid-air to mid-air. Her cousin's terror had impressed her so profoundly that Lucien found his seeking sense affected. He began to feel claustrophobic and he withdrew hastily. He had learned more than enough, with some left over to spare.

Now it was time for action.

The woman must be dealt with at once. But how?

Studying the couple closer, he noticed the old janitor had a half-finished cigar jammed into the right corner of his mouth. Aha. Where there was fire, there was always a way. Lucien closed his eyes and conjured up his most useful talent. He was concentrating so hard upon the effort that he failed to hear a motorcycle approach from the street behind him.

Constance Hines and Carl were nearing the front entrance to the building when the tip of his cigar suddenly flared into a red ball. The old man screamed, his mouth opening in a surprised O as he fell backward against a dirty brick wall.

The bag in his hand tilted, spilling boxes and cans. But the cigar, now a red flame the size of baseball remained suspended in mid-air, began shooting off tongues of fire in every direction. Suddenly the paper bag in his arms ignited. Screaming a second time, he let it fall, to burst into curling black shreds at his feet. A confusion of cans, jars, cartons and boxes lay everywhere.

Constance had flinched backward at the first blaze of fire. She'd tripped over a stone step and landed in a sprawl on the sidewalk. Her butt hurt like hell, but it did not stop her from moving crabwise along the walk to get away. The ball of fire, which is exactly what it appeared to be, seemed to be moving through the air towards her. Somehow, in spite of her growing fear, she managed to get to her wobbly feet and run. Now the extra weight she had courted had become a liability she couldn't afford. She pounded the street, puffing hard, too terrified to cry out.

She didn't see the big motorbike until it screeched to a dramatic stop right in front of her, cutting off her flight. She gaped at man astride it, trying to think of words to make him move the hell out of her way. He, on the other hand had no such problem, yelling at her and pointing to the pillion behind him.

"GET ON! QUICK!"

She needed no further encouragement. The heat was moving toward her back with appalling speed. Almost unbalancing the machine, she flung herself onto the back and managed to get a leg over.

As she grabbed his waist, her would-be-savior gunned the engine and popped the clutch. The bike bucked like a mad stallion, one wheel clawing the at the air. But she was aboard and her arms were securely clasped about the rider. Nothing in the world could ever make her let go.

Using all his strength, Dancer hung on and forced the front wheel down. It bit on the cement and they shot away with every ounce of speed the Harley could produce.

He felt the woman's face burrow into his back. A half turn showed him the fireball, now basketball size, was floating after them and getting larger by the second. Its heat was burning his exposed neck as the thing pursued them.

He zigzagged recklessly through puddles of street lamp glows and streams of traffic. The evening rush hour had begun and the ill-defined light and the congested roads made his task almost impossible. Zipping between cars, the glare from the unholy meteor behind them threw an eerie light overhead. Angry drivers yelled at them through open windows, only to stifle their protest as scorching heat lashed over their car tops. The growing ball was now white at its core, the continuous flares shooting forth a bright red-orange.

Dancer hunched over the handlebars and refused to let his mind wonder to any subject other than immediate survival. In and out of traffic he weaved, like a mad tinker toy gone berserk, but still managing to go on. He knew that he was running on some kind of adrenaline-charged primal instinct. He trusted it unreasonably.

He couldn't know that Morgan's spell was supercharging his mind and his body. He just knew that he had to save this woman no matter what the cost. She had to be Constance Hines and he had barely been in time to save her from disaster.

Now they were being chased through the streets of the city by a self-propelled ball of fire. There was a mad concept, on the face of it. It defied all the known laws of physics. But Dancer knew that trying to rationalize it all now would only slow him up and that would certainly mean death for both of them.

His speedometer said ninety. He gripped the plastic handles tighter, well aware that the tires were hitting the pavement only intermittently. An intersection loomed ahead, the light glowing a bright red.

Dancer bit his lip and tore through it, a prayer stuck in his throat, fighting the urge to close his eyes. A truck cut across his path. He downshifted hard, pulling the bike savagely to the left. His booted foot slapped the pavement. Constance screamed and hugged him harder.

He wrenched the handlebars to regain equilibrium, as the Harley threatened to go out from under him. They whipped around the long trailer rig and poured on more speed. Mental memo, if he lived through this, he'd write the good people at Harley Davidson one very sweet letter of praise for their wonderful products. Laughing crazily, he felt the wind sending tears streaming down his face.

The red brilliance behind them was gaining. Only Dancer's skills and lots of old fashion luck had kept them from being demolished before now. What alternatives did he have? He had always prided himself on being able to meticulously analyze any given situation with careful thought. What was required now was impulsive insight. Either he came up with something fast or there wouldn't be anything else.

A glimmer off to his right registered. The river! They were rapidly coming up to Barkley Bridge, which joined the two halves of this river-split metropolis. Water!

It was a slim chance, but it seemed to be the only one they had.

The ball was huge, now. He could tell from the awful heat on his shoulders and the glare that swallowed them from behind. From that same rear, he could hear a cacophony of screeches and crashes as motorists, avoiding the phenomenon, veered into each other in chain-reaction pile-ups. Even over the crackling of the pursuing flames, Dancer could hear horns blaring and metal smashing into metal. It was a symphony of destruction spread out in their wake.

The bridge was just ahead. He skidded into an angled boulevard skirting the water. There was a three-foot embankment that he would have to jump to enter the river.

The fireball was almost touching Constance's back and she yelled as her hair started to smoke. But she refused to loosen her grip on his torso. The darkness beneath the bridge was dispelled by the flaring light. Their shadow sped ahead of them toward the safety of the cold water.

"HANG ON!" he yelled and sent the bike up over the grass mound and out into space. For a frozen second, bike, riders and fireball were suspended over the ripples like some cartoon from the Sunday funnies.

They separated in mid-air with dreamy slowness. Dancer saw the Harley ..entirely too near! His head smacked into the front tire just before he hit the water. The impact blurred his thinking, but he could see the fiery comet racing toward him and the surface of the water.

Right on top of him!

The fireball plowed into the river with tremendous explosion that sent jets of water straight up into the sky.

The heat was agonizing. Dancer, sinking fast, thought that he had failed, after

"HANG ON!" he yelled ..."

all. Then there was a crackling hiss as water closed around the fireball and it died in a rush of steam.

Dancer struggled with the dimness in his head. His mouth filled with water and he thrashed his arms, trying to swim. He had to reach the surface. It seemed that his entire mind and body had been drained of energy and will.

He felt himself floating away from consciousness. A very bad thing to do. He had to stay awake. But he couldn't. He was just too damn tired.

His last thought was, I'm going to drown… way to go, McCoy.

CHAPTER 10

After Morgan left Claire Maxwell's boutique, she stood on the sidewalk looking about for Dancer and his bike. His plan had been to return for her once he contacted Constance Hines and made sure she was and had been warned of her danger. But there was no sign of him. No hint of the sputter of his exhaust rose above the drone of traffic. Maybe he had been stalled by that same congestion.

She thought about taking a cab and going to Hines's address, but something told her to go home instead. Dancer would call her if anything had come up. It was unlikely that he would try to reach her at the boutique after so long a time.

She raised her hand and was lucky. A yellow taxi pulled up to the curb and she scooted inside, giving the cabby her address. As the driver drove them uptown against the flow of commuter traffic exiting the city, she sat on the edge of the seat wringing her hands. The sun was well down by the time the cabby took his fare and dropped her off.

She ran into the lobby of her building and went straight for the security desk. Biff was on duty.

"Has Dr. McCoy been here?" she asked her burly friend.

"Huh, huh. Miss Rein. I ain't seen him since I come on duty an hour ago." He pressed the button to bring the elevator. "But I'll keep an eye out for him."

"Thanks, Biff. I'd appreciate that."

Her apartment, instead of being the safe, familiar haven she was used to, now seemed to be an alien place filled with an intangible dread. Scratch met her at the door. His tail was twitching uneasily. His mew sounded worried and imperative. He followed her about as she changed out of her pumps and into her softer, beat-up Nikes and put away her sweater. She replaced it with a Boston University sweater.

"What's the matter, fellow?" she inquired, bending to rub his chin. "Something wrong? Something wrong with Dancer maybe?"

The tabby stared up into her eyes. "Marrow!" His tone was so emphatic that she knew she had found the source of her own unease.

Still in her crouch, she shut her eyes and focused. A blur of fire welled up in her inner vision. Nothing else. All she could see was the brightness of flame. Yet she felt, deep inside herself, another presence.

Dark.

Angry.

Frustrated and evil.

She shuddered and opened her eyes. The entity remained hidden from her but she knew who and what it had to be.

Pray God that she was still hidden from him!

The telephone shrilled and she jumped. She picked up Scratch and sat on a bar stool as she lifted the receiver.

"Morgan Rein."

"Miss Rein... you don't know me. My name is Constance Hines." Morgan sat up straight. The woman's voice was laced with fear and uncertainty. "I'm a lawyer, here in the city…"

"Yes, Miss Hines, I know," Morgan cut in. "Are you all right?"

"Er... yes, I am... but something incredible happened just a little while ago. In the course of it, a man I've never met before in my life, came to my rescue. And he's been injured."

Morgan's heart froze. "Go on, please."

"Well, your name and number were in his wallet, when we looked for some identification. For some reason, I felt compelled to call you. Do you know anything about all this?"

"Yes I do," she willed her voice to be calm. "And you did the right thing by calling me, Miss Hines. The man who saved you is most likely my associate, Dr. McCoy. He and I are engaged in an investigation that seems to be getting more dangerous by the minute. He had gone to warn you that you were in danger. Where are you now? I'll come at once."

"We are both at Memorial General Hospital. He almost drowned in the river. I'll give you the whole story in person. I don't want to sound like a maniac. He's still unconscious at the moment."

"When I pulled him out of the water, he looked dead, but I gave him CPR and was able to get him breathing again. Guess all those life saving course at Girl Scout camp finally paid off after all. Anyhow, the doctors haven't said much since we got here by ambulance. I think he's still comatose but I can't be sure. No one has said anything and I'm still a little shaky."

"I'll be there immediately, Miss Hines." Morgan was impressed with the woman's stamina, but she didn't know how much longer she could hold up by herself. "Would you think me odd if I asked you to find a quiet spot and to keep out of sight until I get there?"

"After what I've just been through, your request sounds perfectly sane."

"Good. If I recall correctly, there's a small coffee room just off the main waiting room. If you'd go there and sit with a cup of coffee…"

"Tea. I hate coffee."

"Fine, tea it is," she liked this woman already. "And take up a magazine, preferably a large one, to hide behind so that no one can see you clearly. Can you do that for me?"

"You don't have to persuade me that I'm in danger, Miss Rein. I'll do whatever you ask. Just hurry, please!"

"I'm on my way."

Morgan looked around. The apartment felt alien, almost inimical. Her instinct told her that it was no longer a refuge from the world.

She threw some clothing and few toiletries into an overnight bag and picked up Scratch. At the door, a last backward glance awoke no misgivings in her. For now, this was no longer home.

She locked the door behind her and caught the elevator as it was about to descend with a load of theatergoers all dressed up. She stood in back against the wall, comforting Scratch. Morgan hated leaving him, but it was the wisest course open to her and she let him know that by carefully opening her thoughts. The cat licked her hand and indicated his acceptance, albeit reluctantly, of the decision. Their mutual love was based on an unshakable trust. Morgan would never allow any harm to come to Scratch and thus he always accepted her dictates.

In the lobby, she made for Biff's desk. He was just finishing a report check on his clipboard and looked up as she put Scratch on the counter above the bank of close circuit television monitors.

"Yes, Miss Rein?"

"Would you do me a big favor, Biff? Something has come up and I have to go away on a short trip, and I haven't had time to put Scratch into the veterinary clinic where I usually board him."

"You mean the one on Hollis and 46th Street?" Having been raised in city, Biff knew it like the proverbial back of his hand.

"Exactly. We're old customers and they always keep him for me when these things come up. Would you be a dear and see that he is taken over?"

"No problem," he beamed at her. "You remember my nephew, Ben? He's stopping over later with my lunch. I'll have him take Scratch over when he gets here. In the meantime, he can stay right here with me."

Biff picked up the white fur ball and Scratch immediately started mewing with pleasure; the two were old friends.

Morgan took an envelope from her carry bag and handed it to the guard. "Their number is this envelope, along with a tip for you and one for Ben. I owe you, Biff. Thanks."

"Anytime, Miss Rein. You have a nice trip and don't worry about Scratch, old Biff and him will get along just dandy."

Relieved of that worry, and supremely grateful for friends like the amiable Biff, Morgan took off for the street to find a cab. Not a single one was in sight, so she walked along toward her destination, knowing that a walk of only a mile would take less time than a long wait for a taxi. Besides, she needed the exercise to loosen her muscles. With each long stride, she was becoming aware of the emotional knot she had been tied into by her apprehensions.

Inhaling the brisk night air, she emptied her mind of everything except the feel of the pavement, the working of her leg muscles and the smell of the city around her. She never noticed the sports car that cruised past her, moving toward her building. As her aura was damped almost to nonexistence by her meditative state, its occupant did not sense her presence. That was a very good thing, for the driver was her brother, the warlock, Lucien Wicker.

Morgan reached the hospital in fifteen minutes. Constance Hines was sitting obediently in the coffee shop, her upper half concealed by a day old copy of the Wall Street Journal. The business paper went well with her gray business suit and her overall demeanor, but the witch could see that the woman was still shaken.

She went to her table and sat, smiling warmly as the nervous lawyer dropped her paper shield. Constance looked at her with relief.

"Miss Rein?"

"Call me Morgan, please," she said offering her hand.

"Then I'm Connie." They each had a firm, respectful grip. "They have him in a room, now."

She studied Morgan carefully as if sizing up the opposing counsel before the bar and then gave a positive jerk of her square chin. "You look like someone he'd know."

"Oh? How so?"

"Different, somehow. Exotic. I doubt you sell Avon."

Morgan laughed at the woman's remarkable insight. "No, I don't. You are very perceptive, Miss.. er.. Connie."

"It comes with the job. Details. Being a good lawyer means paying attention to the details. They can win or lose a case."

"Very astute. I'll remember that. And you say Dancer is out of danger and in a room."

"Yes. Would you like to go up and look in on him? The doctor I just spoke to said he's not conscious yet. That's got them a puzzled a little, since I got most of the water out of him pretty fast after pulling him ashore."

Morgan reached across the table and put her hand on Connie's forearm. It felt tight.

"I'm sure he'll be fine," she said reassuringly. "You have to relax, now."

"If I can."

"Good. We'll go up and get out of the public eye. Then I'll tell you about this thing we're looking into... and your cousin's death."

Connie's eyes widened. "My cousin?"

Morgan held up a cautionary finger. "When we're alone."

Together they rose and made their way to the of elevators in the main lobby. They caught the upward bound one, which was crowded, thus no further questions could be asked or answered. Morgan sympathized with Connie's bewilderment. She knew the woman's mind was shrewdly adding two and two and developing her own conclusions. It was clear by her expression that something had clicked into place when Morgan had mentioned Appleton. Something that now started making sense out of the entire affair.

The chief nurse at the floor station looked somewhat skeptical when they arrived and claimed to be relatives of Dancer McCoy. Neither looked in the least like him. But she sighed and let them in. Families didn't always resemble each other, as everyone knew.

There was an intern standing by the bed when they entered the spacious room. He looked up questioningly, but their calm and efficient air put him at ease.

"We're relatives," Morgan explained and the white garbed intern stepped out of her way. She bent over Dancer, touched his forehead and felt his pulse. "No sign of consciousness at all?"

The intern frowned. "No, and he should have come around by now. He wasn't in the water that long, according to Miss Hines." At that he grinned at Connie and she was grateful the room's soft light hid her blushing cheeks.

"She did awfully well," the young man went on. "Besides pulling him out, she pumped all the water out of him. There's no problem with his vital signs. He just keeps sleeping."

Morgan gave him her most disarming smile. "We'll be here for a while, if you need to tend to other patients. I have had medical training. I think it might help if we just talked to him quietly. About... family matters and such."

The would-be-doctor scratched his temple, his eyes tired from his long hours on duty. Morgan appeared both competent and cool and he had no standing orders against such visits.

He nodded. "Can't hurt. And I still have the rest of my rounds to make. Sure. Go ahead and give it a shot. I'll be back in a half hour or so to see how you're doing."

After the intern had gone, Morgan turned to Connie. "I overtaxed Dancer's energies," she explained, her tone regretful. "He evidently had to overcome something terribly intense. I know you will tell me about it, in a bit, but right now we need to bring him out of his trance."

"Trance?"

"It's not unusual, when a person has used up all his strength, and more. Here, give me your hand."

Without hesitation, Connie put her plump hand into Morgan's. Those strong fingers closed over her own confidently.

Morgan closed her eyes. The witch's other hand touched Dancer just over his heart. A tingling tension filled the air and the scent of crisp ozone breathed faintly through the room. At the contact, his body twitched. He moaned and moved irritably. The two women stood motionless, focusing all their attention and strength on him.

He opened his eyes and looked up.

"Ahhh!" Morgan opened her own eyes, loosed Connie's hand and folded her own together in a protective gesture.

"There you are," she joked. "I didn't think, when I set that spell on you, that it would overextend your energies by so much."

"That kiss, right? That's when you did it to me."

"Yes. It is used to enhance sensory perceptions and quicken physical reactions."

"So that's why I felt like Superman, dodging that damn fireball. Thanks. You saved our lives."

Connie looked from one to the other, her eyes wide. "Spell? Enhanced perception? What on earth are you talking about? And how did you bring him out of that coma when the doctors couldn't do it? I haven't understood a single thing that has happened since I got out of my car at home, this evening."

Dancer struggled to sit. Morgan reached over to help him, and when he was upright, he stretched.

"You'd better tell her, Morgan. Right now I feel like I've been put through a pretzel maker. Every muscle in my body aches."

Morgan slid a straight back chair over to Connie and motioned her to sit. Then, taking a deep breath to collect her own memories of the past two days, she launched into her story.

She started with the bizarre death of Ron Appleton and how she and McCoy had gotten involved with the mystery. With all the persuasiveness she could muster, she described her witchcraft and all that entailed. Especially all things she could do using her strange powers.

To this she added her conversation with Claire that afternoon. She also revealed her belief that it was her own long-lost brother who was behind the supernatural aspects of the case.

Constance Hines was a hard-nosed businesswoman, as well as a highly skilled lawyer. She prided herself on her judgment of people. She trusted her own assessment of truthfulness. To her credit, she required only a short time to come to the conclusion that Morgan was telling her truth. She admitted that it might have taken longer if she had not had, in the forefront of her own thoughts, the searing fireball that had somehow had her name on it.

Allowing Morgan to finish her tale, Connie bit her lower lip and waited her turn to speak. "After this afternoon's little chase, I have no problems believing every word of your story. And I now suspect I know why someone wanted to barbecue me."

"Your cousin," Morgan jumped ahead, "did find something damaging on C.C.I."

"Yes, and just as you've already surmised, it most likely caused his death. He told me a few weeks ago that he had found massive evidence of malfeasance at C.C.I. Now you say that five others involved with record keeping have died in past half-year.

"That can only mean foul play. There is large-scale fraud, embezzlement and malfeasance going on here. But, to effectively discredit a firm as big as C.C.I. would entail bringing down half a dozen third world governments and numerous U.S. government officials as well. Now that's pretty scary stuff."

Dancer was now sitting upright, getting ready to get out of bed. "But did Appleton give you any hard evidence? Papers, tapes or any such?"

"No. He intended to put together a coherent file of what he'd found, but he never got the chance. He obviously did not suspect they were on to him until it was too late to save himself." There was hurt in Connie's face. She had felt the loss of her cousin deeply. She balled her fist on her lap and her voice grew hard. "Look, if we can find those records. Get affidavits from former employees or anything else solid, I can go to the U.S. Attorney General. With that kind of real proof, his office could institute an in-depth investigation."

Morgan and Dancer exchanged looks. Neither appeared the least bit intimidated. Dancer scratched his stubbly chin.

"I'll call the lab and tell them I'm taking some vacation time. That shouldn't be a problem. Besides, like Connie, I've got a personal score to settle with those people. So count me in."

Morgan smiled. "A good choice of words. Now do you suppose you might count me in? If my brother is behind these manifestations, then he's bound to come looking for me, once he becomes aware of my involvement. My apartment is no longer safe."

"You need a place to crash."

"I do. If it won't be too much of a bother."

McCoy managed to keep a straight face. "Well, it'll be a bit crowded. Scratch may not have his own room. Still. I suppose we can make it work, if we try.

"Temporarily, of course."

"Of course."

Dancer swung his bare legs over the side of the bed. "Okay, that's settled. Now would one of you ladies be so kind as to get me my pants out of that closet so we can get out of this place. I hate hospitals." His grin was boyish and charming.

As Morgan complied with his request, Connie studied both of them and wondered just what kind of adventure she had gotten herself caught up in. She was scared but at the same time she was inwardly glad they were involved. She had a strong feeling that if anyone could see this thing through, and survive, it would be these two.

CHAPTER 11

Lucien Wicker sat, frozen with fury and astonishment, as his quarry sped away on the back of the sleek, black motorbike. His fireball fled after them. He had centered all his energy upon Constance Hines and he knew it would pursue its assigned prey to the end, wherever that might be.

Yet it had never entered his calculations that any agency whatsoever might interfere with his plans. Or, for that matter, could possibly know enough to try. That undeniable fact staggered him, momentarily. He was not accustomed to having his schemes thwarted. Anger began to swell within him.

His gaze was fixed on the old janitor, who now sat on the curb, moaning and nursing his burnt hands. But Lucien wasn't seeing the old fool. No, he was seeing something else... with his inner eye. He was seeing a beautiful face... the face of his sister, who was no longer a child but a grown woman. Morgan...?

Was it possible that she had not only survived but had somehow managed to acquire the training that would enable her to challenge him? And why was he sensing her here and now?

He cast about with his seeking sense for anyone who possessed powers akin to his own. Who might have engineered Hines's flight. He thought of the dark haired man on the motorcycle but instantly ruled him out. Had the stranger been a fellow practitioner of the arts, Lucien would have sensed it immediately. No, the would be rescuer was a powerless pawn. Still, no quiver of recognition came into his mind as to who was countering his actions.

Only that comely visage, about which hung an aura that was inimical to those dark powers he courted.

"Yes, it makes sense," he muttered to himself. "She would be the White."

Convinced of his casting, there was no time to waste. He started the engine, made a U-turn across the street and drove past the injured old man without giving him a second thought.

"There is only one group in this city," he said aloud. "I sought them out as soon as I arrived. Why didn't I sense her then?" His anger was threatening to overcome his reasoning faculties and he grimaced, squeezing the steering wheel tighter. He could not to let his passions run wild. That kind of reaction made him vulnerable to Morgan and her coven sisters.

As the sports car sped through the now dwindling traffic, he gradually regained control of his feelings. Calmly he re-examined the situation and the answer to his question became readily available. There were several astral shields the coven could easily have conjured to keep her presence hidden.

"That's it," he resolved smugly. "And that woman who leads them will know..."

Claire Maxwell's boutique had been closed for some time when he pulled up along the empty sidewalk and looked through the window at the richly dressed mannequin. The plastic grand dame posed in furs with a diamond watch draped across her hand, as if she were timing the hours of the long, slow night ahead. The interior night-light gave off enough illumination to tell him the store was deserted.

But a corridor leading to rear of the establishment had a dim glow as if a back office might still be in use.

Lucien glanced up and down the street. A police patrol car turned the corner and was slow-dragging the avenue. The two officers were methodically eyeing stores to either side as they rolled on by. He knew he would look suspicious if he remained there any longer. Slipping the car into gear, he pulled away from the curb and drove around the corner. There he parked in front of an all-night café and killed the engine.

He slumped down out of sight, closed his eyes and sent forth his mind to seeking out the boutique's office. It was now located directly to his right, at the rear of the block of buildings. If the woman he wanted to find was there now, he would soon know.

She was. Fortunately she was wrapped in some kind of paperwork. Her PC was on and its tinted blue light battled with the yellow cast of the desk lamp. Beside the keyboard was an open ledger and a woman was busy referencing numbers. Thus occupied, her mental defenses would be negligible. Deftly, he proceeded.

The intricate texture of her aura was painful to his perceptions. That kind of witch was always uncomfortable to come into contact with in any way. Yet this had to be done. Without warning her of the contact, no less.

Lucien locked himself into concentration. The rest of the sensory world about him ceased to be. Working his way through the casual shield around Claire's mind, he took extreme care not to wake any alarm in her.

His task was difficult on several levels. He had always felt such contempt for the followers of the other discipline that he had never bothered to probe any one of them before. That had clearly been a mistake. And this was a mother of a coven, the strongest of her kind. No wonder his core being was repulsed.

He was too secure in his arrogance to realize what he was seeing, so he fought down the unease and nausea. Cautiously, he sorted through the woman's thoughts, saw through her eyes.

He found Morgan there. Very near. Very recently. In that room, facing that woman.

Lucien's face contorted with effort, but he couldn't get at the subject of their conversation. Claire was too well controlled for that. Yet he found something almost as good. Morgan's name beside a telephone number was scribbled on a sheet of paper at the witch's elbow. He could see it plainly. A thrill of triumph shot through him.

His target moved suddenly, as if she sensed something amiss.

He began to withdraw for now Claire was alert. Back in the car, his body sweated with effort as Lucien mentally backtracked. The woman gave no further indication that she had detected him but he maintained a slender thread attuned to her during his delicate retreat. Finally, with a sigh of relief, he fought clear and opened his eyes.

Suddenly a voice at his elbow asked, "You okay, mister?"

Lucien blinked, startled. When he lifted his head, he saw a policeman bending down to into his window. He put on a friendly grin.

"Just waiting for my wife to get out of work," he answered, pointing to the office building behind them. "I just closed my eyes to catch a little nap while waiting for her."

The cop chuckled. "Ha, I hope she's not like my wife. She never gets anyplace on time and if she did, I'd likely keel over from the shock."

"Women," Lucien mimicked the man's mirth. "They're all alike."

"You got that straight. Well, good night."

He waited as the officer got back into his patrol car and moved off. Then he grabbed the car phone by his side and dialed his assistant. He had ordered her to standby.

The number rang only once. "Yes," she said expectantly.

"It is I."

"What do you desire, master?"

"Get into your computer and find me the address that goes with this telephone number." He rattled off the numbers he had seen on note pad and waited. Two minutes later his agent had the address he required.

Lucien replaced the phone in its plastic cradle, started his car and pulled out into the westbound artery. He turned at the first set of lights and pointed his vehicle toward the downtown street where Morgan's apartment house was located.

The same street... the same building... where the late Mr. Appleton had once resided. They were neighbors! Morgan and Appleton were neighbors. There it was! The connection that had lured his sister into his web after so many years. Yet how could she have associated him with the drowning?

She would have known, of course, that it was caused by an exercise of craft power. Even at a distance, that would be evident to one of her talents. But she couldn't possibly know that he was involved.

Could she? As unlikely as it seemed, he could not be sure. And to proceed without an answer to that one question would incur unacceptable risk to his entire scheme.

He arrived at the appropriate address and drove into the half-filled parking area to the right of the building. As he was climbing out of his vehicle, a teen-age boy raced by on bicycle. Strapped in a basked over the handlebars was a glaringly white, angora cat. Lucien stopped cold as the animal's awareness locked with his for a fleeting second. Scratch cried a warning, his claws extending as he twisted against the bonds that held him. He wanted nothing more than to launch himself at the warlock and claw his face off.

"Hey, what's the matter with you?" the boy queried. "You see a mouse in that alley or something?"

Lucien watched the lad pedal off down the street and pulled a hand over his jaw. The cat was her familiar. It was bathed in her essence and its rage at him confirmed the bond beyond any doubt.

Quickly he continued on into the lobby. There was a guard, of massive girth, seated at a security desk engrossed in a paperback novel. Lucien always took pains to look completely respectable. Indeed, he looked distinguished enough in his expensive, tailored suit to soothe away the suspicions of any doorkeeper in the world.

He nodded cordially as the big fellow looked up from his book and then dismissed him. It was so easy. People only saw what they expected to see. Give them that and they leave you alone.

The seventh floor corridor was deserted. He went to the door marked 751 and touched the knob. The design of the lock, the proper sort of key was imprinted on his mind in an instant. He sorted through his key ring and found one that was compatible. He inserted it into the lock and it turned, sweetly and silently.

Five minutes after entering the building, he was standing in Morgan's living room.

He snapped on the lights, knowing there was no one present. The place was filled with white. Pale tones struck his eyes with an unpleasant glare, as he looked around him. The cat-familiar habitually slept on the blue chair. The sofa held strong emanations of power. She must sit there a great deal.

The bookshelves were filled and the rows stacked on top with books. Those books repelled him with their very look and smell.

She had fled hurriedly. A magazine lay on the rug beneath the coffee table and a discarded sweater was draped carelessly over the back of the couch.

Something had alarmed her. Sent her to cover.

Was it knowledge of him? Maddeningly he kept coming back to the same question. It was a thorn he could not remove.

The frustrations built up over the past few hours overcame him at last. Using his psychic powers, he attacked the book shelves with a vengeance. Simply by his willing it, books sailed from their resting-places and struck against the walls and the door. One knocked over a tall lamp, with a crash of broken pottery. Another sent a long crack up and down the glass door to the balcony. But it wasn't enough. His fury demanded more.

Lucien went to the bedroom and jerked the door open. He tried to enter, but the room was filled with a stifling atmosphere that stopped him at the threshold. Suddenly he felt as if the very walls were closing in on him. He was being smothered! His old claustrophobia descended upon him in a cloud of panic. He retreated, stumbling back into the living room. That other discipline had been practiced in the room for so long, so strongly and concentratedly, that his kind could never enter it. Or survive for long after doing so.

His anger swelled again like a rising tide. One day, he thought cruelly, he would bring his dear, sweet sister in to his own special sanctum. There, the black emanations would snuff out her puny powers as easily as water snuffs out flame.

He paused. Water. Flame.

He had not doubted that both the Hines woman and her would be rescuer had long since been burned to cinders by the fireball he had sent after them. But had they?

The man on the motorcycle… he had moved quickly, with such unhesitating precision. He had known exactly what to do and had done it with swift efficiency. Could it be possible that he had managed to save the woman, after all?

Lucien dropped onto the sofa and tried to relax. He had to start thinking clearly again. With Morgan involved, nothing must be left to chance. Every facet of his plans had to be scrutinized closely. Nothing could be taken for granted. To do so would only create opportunities for his enemies. Opportunities Morgan would be quick to take advantage of.

He rubbed his fingertips to together as his mind meticulously plotted his next step. He had to confirm Hines's fate. Luckily for him, she possessed a truly strong personality. He could identify it, now, among all the others inhabiting the city, if he set his mind to it.

Drawing a deep breath, he spread his perceptions across the city below the balcony. Like a mist, it spread, thin but sensitive, through the places where people gathered or sat alone. Through a hive of thousands, he sought on one individual soul.

And failed to find her. His scanning found absolutely no trace of Constance Hines. It was as if she had never existed. Only death signified that kind of absence.

Lucien smiled. He had succeeded. Constance Hines was dead. He looked about the shattered apartment with grim satisfaction masking his face. If his sister did return for any reason, this would shake her confidence.

She had not been able to stop him. That was a good thing to know. Morgan had never posed a threat to him as a child and it was apparent nothing had changed on that score.

Whistling, he re-locked the door behind him and exited by a back stairway. He would report his success to Waitman in the morning.

Then there would be more to plan and to do. His trap was set now. He was certain that both Waitman and Axel would step blithely into it. He would deal with them and then when he had achieved his primary goal, there would be time for Morgan.

He couldn't wait to see his dear, sweet sister again.

There were so few things in this world to savor. Often anticipation was the spice of life.

CHAPTER 12

The whir of the electric clock interrupted the stillness. Around Claire Maxwell, the office seemed frozen. Even the random street sounds seemed silenced, for the moment.

She kept her gaze on her ledger. Her pencil moved lightly along the lines of figures, until she was certain that the intruding personality was no longer present. She had not often experienced the intrusion of another mind. The metaphysical invasion had shaken and angered her.

She glanced at the clock. The hour was getting late. Her gaze then fell upon the slip holding Morgan's telephone number. She had taken it from her PC file and jotted it down when she had called her earlier in the afternoon. It lay on her desktop like a dozen similar notes scattered before her. Claire picked it up and wondered.

The mind prying through her own had not, she was convinced, been able to force its way through her mental guard. But it could easily have read the numbers on the sheet of paper simply by seeing through her own eyes. It was not an impossible feat for seasoned practitioners of the craft.

But what mind could it have been? The question was not a hard one to answer. All one had to do was eliminate the options logically. None of her own sisters in the coven would have approached her in such an unconscionable way. There was a bonding loyalty among her group and information flowed freely. There was never any need to act maliciously or in secrecy.

No, she mused, there was only one outside force she could think of that would have recourse to utilize such a technique. That person was Morgan's warlock brother, Lucien. It made sense, considering the events of the past few days.

She was starting to believe that Lucien had intuited the presence of his sister, as she had originally perceived him. Such things were often reciprocal, Claire knew. Still, he would not be able to find her by using his talents, for her apartment was shielded, as all their homes were. Thus far, nothing had happened to alter her faith in that magical net of protection.

On the other hand, if he had felt her existence, he would also have discovered, almost simultaneously, that she was not involved in the black arts he embraced. Rather, just the opposite. To an adept, searching for the coven, Claire realized that her own identity would rise to the surface, no matter how carefully she kept herself in the background.

Like a fox on the hunt, he would come to her, assuming that she would know Morgan, if anyone in the city did. And, alas, it appeared he had found what he was after, through her own carelessness. She had been used like a puppet and it rankled every fiber of her being. But there was a more pressing matter than her self-indulgent recriminations. She could wallow in her self-pity later. Right now, Morgan had to be warned that Lucien was getting closer.

She tried calling her but when, after four long rings, Morgan's answering machine started to kick in, Claire slammed down her phone to cut the connection.

It would be unwise to leave any kind of a voice message that could be intercepted by unwelcome ears. But there were other ways to send a warning.

Claire switched off the desk light and sat quietly in the eerie blue nimbus of her computer monitor. She sent her thoughts winging like invisible arrows toward Morgan's home. A probe could not enter there, but a warning could.

She concentrated fiercely, blanketing the familiar rooms with a layer of unease. A palpable sense of danger.

After only a short while, she sensed Morgan's presence. In a bit more, she felt her leave the building. Good. The girl was safe, for the moment. From her sure and quick exit, it was apparent to the Coven Mother that her friend had a destination in mind. A safe harbor to ride out the coming storm.

As relief overcame her, Claire ended her scanning. She leaned her head in her hands and trembled slightly from the exertion. As she grew older, such sending became harder and took more energy than she could spare. She felt an anxious concern for her protégé, but knew that it was better she remain ignorant of her exact whereabouts.

If Lucien had come to her once for information, he might well come again. Even though she shielded herself strongly, who knew what he might learn inadvertently. This was one hunter who was not about to give up. Whatever his ultimate purpose, she knew it was evil beyond imagining. It was enough that she had warned Morgan and given her the chance to run. Claire had a great deal of confidence in her skills. She would continue to add her own prayers to that arsenal of goodness and light.

Taking her purse, she left her office, walking briskly through the darkness to the rear door of the shop. In the space of those few minutes, the Coven Mother had devised her own course of action. She would not return to her house or the shop until some disposition had been made of the matter at hand. She too would disappear.

No one. Not Lucien Rein, not anyone, would ever use her like that again. It was a promise to herself she intended to keep... or die trying.

CHAPTER 13

FIREBALL SCORCHES CITY! The banner headline all but jumped off the morning newspaper atop Darryl Waitman's desk. He had just started to read the accompanying article when the intercom buzzed.

"Yes, Selina?"

"A Mr. Wicker on line two."

That was quick. He had not anticipated hearing from the man for at least a few days. "Yes. All right. Put him through."

There was a click and then Wicker's smooth, somehow disturbing voice was in his ear. "The Hines affair has been settled."

"So soon?" Waitman turned in his swivel chair so that he could look out the window across the city. Clear blue skies and a warm sun bathed the view with a majestic grandeur.

"It wasn't all that difficult."

"But you are certain? It's done?"

"Are you questioning me, Mr. Waitman." The voice dropped twenty degrees into the freezing zone.

"No, of course not. I didn't mean to imply that you aren't competent. It is just that the importance of this particular issue... if she should have known anything at all..."

"She did talk with Appleton before his death," Wicker confirmed without excitement. "I learned that he had passed along many indiscreet items, though he never gave her any usable evidence. Her legal credentials were impressive and I am sure she had the mind and ability to make problems, once she learned where to... dig. Thus I deemed it necessary to eliminate her and did so."

"I trust there will be no suspicion," Waitman pulled at the knot of his silk tie. Discussing murder made him very nervous.

"I doubt there will even be any remains," Wicker chuckled. "Unattached people disappear all the time, even lawyers. There should be no query raised about her absence, beyond the most routine inquiry. She'll simply be listed as a missing person and that will be that. End of story."

Darryl felt an overriding curiosity. "What means did you use, this time?"

Wicker laughed again. It was a sardonic sound completely devoid of any real humor.

"I would have thought you would wish to remain ignorant of such facts. However, if you must know, this time, I used fire.

"It really was a most flamboyant sight."

"Good God," Waitman choked, swinging around towards his desk to reread the morning headlines. "The mysterious fireball that disrupted downtown traffic last night! It was yours!"

There was another chuckle, deep and ominous.

"Good day, Mr. Waitman." The line went dead.

Waitman's palms were sweaty and he wiped them on his pants. Wicker was a valuable tool but he was also an extremely dangerous one. To trust the killer completely would be a grievous mistake.

The intercom buzzed. The day was starting out busy.

"Mr. Waitman," Lilith's throaty voice materialized. "Mr. Axel would like to see you in his office. Now, if possible."

Darryl smiled sourly. The old man was chomping at the bit, wanting to know about the Hines threat. Every day he grew more cautious, more concerned for his tough old hide.

"Of course. Tell him I'll be right there."

Waitman told his secretary where he would be and strolled down the executive corridor to the president's office. Turning the corner he was met by a very alluring sight. Lilith Markova was standing next to her desk examining her hosiery. She had pulled her tight gray skirt up and was adjusting her stocking top.

She was a tall, voluptuous woman with long, perfectly shaped legs. Wearing stiletto black heels and sheer, ash hued nylons, she made a very sexy picture.

Waitman's eyes traveled the length of those magnificent limbs with open appraisal. He was surprised that women still wore stockings and garter belts, what with the advent of panty-hose. Still, certain women preferred the adornments and pleasures of a more elegant time.

Lilith looked up, saw him and held her pose, unembarrassed.

"I thought I might have gotten a run in them and they're brand new."

"Er... how ah, nice." Waitman thought the woman was ravishing, which is why his stomach always tightened into a cement block whenever he was in her presence. As if reading his ineptitude, the dark haired vixen lowered her skirt and nodded to the door behind her. Her face, chiseled without blemish, brown eyes the color of amber, full, firm lips painted a wet cheery red, was all business. Not a smidgen of warmth anywhere on it.

Waitman smiled weakly and circled her, afraid of even the smallest contact.

Axel was standing before his own wide expanse of glass, gazing, as Darryl had done, over the metropolitan panorama. He turned at the sound of the door.

"Well?" he barked. "How are things going?"

"Once again, Mr. Wicker has solved our problem in a manner that eliminates any threat to us. He is a very valuable man."

Waitman stopped in front of Axel's desk, hands held clasped behind his back in a loose posture. "In fact, I've been wondering if maybe we shouldn't add him to the staff, permanently."

"Really? In what capacity?" The old man wasn't going to make it easy. But then again, he never did.

"At a top level management spot, of course. Wicker is too useful to be wasted as simply a... shall we say, trash collector. If he were intricately involved with our overall operations, it would to our mutual advantage."

Axel gazed searchingly at his lieutenant. "Hmm, it's a possibility. Still, you know I'm careful about letting anyone into the upper echelons of our little empire. I'd need to meet him, study him closely. For several days, if possible. It requires a certain type of man to milk a wild mare."

Darryl laughed politely at the old man's stale joke. Much had been made, over the years, of the dangers of pilfering from the most powerful and influential

"Turning the corner, he met an alluring sight."

conglomerate in the world. The senior board of directors was terrified of public opinion, disgrace and possible imprisonment.

Yet Darryl had examined the entire operation from its beginning. The well-oiled machinery of the embezzlement procedure was flawless and beyond scrutiny. The danger, he was certain, lay principally in the minds of the old dinosaurs that had set up the system in the first place. Perhaps there had been risk two decades ago but times had changed. Today it was a foolproof routine.

It was their own simple-minded carelessness that had brought about the current crisis. Holding onto incriminating material was stupid. Hadn't Nixon and his tapes been example enough to even the thickest moron? Perhaps old man Grimmins had been totally dependable as a head accountant, for he was in on the deal up to his shifty eyeballs, along with all the others. But he hadn't been immortal.

Someone should have crosschecked, made sure that he was destroying everything that might make a problem. Raise a flag of any sort. Of course the new computer system had been a big mistake. Not so much in its utilization as in the massive hands-on employee involvement that would be needed for data entry. Way too many eyes had been looking at long forgotten files. Waitman had warned Axel of that, but the International Board of Directors had insisted. They old fools had opened up a bag full of bones.

Darryl stood waiting for Axel to finish his train of thought, which had evidently interrupted his words. One day, he would stand on that side of the desk and when he did, there would be no hesitations in his judgments. Things would get done fast. In business, there was no other way.

Tom Axel hit his intercom unit. "Lilith? When does the yacht trip start?"

"Sir?"

"Yes, I know you told me this morning, but I've forgotten."

I need to know the date and time. It appears we are going to have another guest come along."

Waitman liked it. Once in a while the old fellow came up with a pretty good idea, still. He could size up Lucien Wicker in the context of the yachting party.

Nobody asks an assassin to such an affair. There would be nothing suspicious about the invitation. All sorts of business people were asked to these trips, year after year. Anyone who dealt in goods, services, or construction attended. It was an opportunity to make invaluable contacts.

Waitman had no doubt that the urbane Wicker would fit into this group quite effortlessly. The list included two overseas officers of C.C.I., a countess famous for her charities and her affluence in high places, four board directors and a handful of politicians and local business representatives. The usual mix of the rich and famous.

"Good thinking, Sir," he concurred. "I think you'll find that Wicker will be an intriguing addition to the cruise."

The old man pulled his chair out and sat. "Perhaps, perhaps. But I think you'll find more to interest you than a small matter like Wicker. Things are starting to look up for you, my boy. Big things. I've been watching you for a long time and have asked several members of our group to examine your company record."

"Oh?" Waitman was caught off guard. "I trust you were satisfied with my performance."

"More than satisfied. Much more. The others were impressed as well. You can look forward to a pretty big surprise in the very near future, Waitman. Bank on it."

"I don't know what to say, Sir."

"No need to say anything. But that's all I'm going to say, for now. Just be buckling up your boots, lad. You're going to jump out of them for joy."

Waitman was tongue-tied. What promotion could possibly be in the works? Unless Axel was preparing to retire and was about to name him as his successor...? It was too good to be true.

"Well..er, I'll be most anxious to find out what it is, Sir. Thank you. I'd best be getting back to work, or nobody will be impressed with me."

Axel snorted and dismissed him with a curt wave of his hand.

As he left the office, Lilith looked up from her PC and smiled at him. He blinked. The smile was real and full of promise. Enough so that he felt his ears go red. Was she privy to the old man's so-called good news? Was that why her attitude towards him was suddenly warmer? The woman was no dunce. She had to have realized he had been drooling over her, much like every other executive, since the first day she came to work for the old man.

Summoning up newly acquired confidence, Darryl stepped closer and leaned over her desk. Looking down, he was blessed with an unobstructed view of her ample bosom, barely contained beneath her starched, white blouse. The top two buttons were open, exposing creamy, soft mounds and the edge of her lacy, pink bra that supported them.

"Ah, Miss Markova. I trust your stockings were run-free."

"Yes, they were," she replied, still pecking away at her keyboard. "Thank you for asking, Mr. Waitman."

"Nonsense, a manager should concern himself with the well being and comfort of his staff." He couldn't take his eyes off her cleavage. "Especially dedicated people like yourself."

Lilith's fingers stopped and she tilted her head up slightly. "Now why would you notice someone like me?"

"Why, Miss Markova, I have always been a great admirer of your.. ah... efficiency."

She dropped her gaze to her swelling breasts then back to him. "Only my efficiency?" she teased coyly. "I had rather hoped for something better."

He took the bait. "I'm afraid I don't understand."

Lilith stopped typing, pushed her chair away from her desk and looked him straight in the face. "Do you realize that you are the only man in this entire organization who hasn't asked me to dinner?" A small, impish pout appeared on her lips. "Where have I failed?"

Darryl was at a loss to understand her bantering with him. He had heard all the stories around the water cooler about the polite but effective brush-offs she could inflict. Apparently numerous clerks and managers alike had suffered that singular, cruel fate.

But now, if he was reading the signals correctly, the woman was actually coming on to him. More or less begging him to ask her out. He wasn't one hundred percent sure why the change of heart but he wasn't about to let this golden opportunity pass him by.

"We must remedy that at once," he offered. "And we must make it soon, for the cruise is the day after tomorrow. What about tonight? I realize it's short notice, but I'd be honored to take you to Chez Mouton. It's the best restaurant in town."

"But I hear it is always booked."

"I have a reserved table there."

Her eyes widened appreciatively. That was a good sign. But would it be enough?

"And what time would you like me to join you there?"

Darryl almost stammered, inwardly shocked that she had accepted, but he caught himself. That was not the urbane front he was forging for himself. Instead, he straightened his back and smiled his most charming smile.

"How about eight?"

"Just right."

"And your address?"

Lilith frowned and waved her hand as if to shoo away a bothersome thought. "Oh, I live across the river in a maze like condo complex that is much too hard to find. Trust me, Mr. Waitman, it will be much easier if I meet you. Isn't there a flower shop across the street from the restaurant?"

"I believe so."

"Then I'll meet you there at eight sharp. How's that?"

"Perfect. I'll be looking forward to our evening."

Lilith favored him with another of her alluring looks and then went back to her work. Darryl turned and started down corridor, a bounce to his step. In his mind, he was imagining long, elegant legs encased in the sheerest nylons and how that material would feel to the touch. It was a very exciting thought.

CHAPTER 14

Lucien had discovered sex in the Paris bordellos that flourished in the arty Latin Quarter. His curiosity had taken him into darkened alleys where he could often spy on amorous couples through gapped draperies or torn window blinds.

What he saw both amused and fascinated him. There was obviously something beyond the physically awkward and sweaty act of intercourse. His ever-searching mind needed to learn that deeper secret.

He had mused on the problem, while watching with interest the reactions of the household to Morgan's strange nervous condition. He had always found it easy to work on several projects at the same time. The more his mind was occupied, the sharper it worked.

His sister was obviously ill. That had, perhaps naturally, been attributed to the recent loss of her mother. Though this reaction was unusually severe and violent. The doctors Armand Rein called in could suggest nothing but rest and care and concentrated attention by the rest of the family. Which primarily meant father and brother.

The girl became haggard. Wizened like a little old woman. She lost weight alarmingly and Armand felt the hand of the Grim Reaper falling once more on his family. He prayed fervently every waking hour for her recovery, but his hope was fading. In the meantime, he spared no expense or effort in her care.

Lucien found himself virtually ignored in the household. This ideally suited another purpose he had in mind. For the time being he would give Morgan a brief rest, while he explored another mystery.

He chose as his victim the pretty seventeen-year-old chambermaid, Celeste. She was a lithe, brown-eyed beauty with dirty-blond hair that fell to her shoulders. Lucien probed her thoughts carefully, making sure she didn't feel his prying. He persisted until he felt certain she would be receptive to his mental suggestions.

He found her to be no virgin, which suited his purposes perfectly. He needed an experienced teacher.

He set his trap shrewdly on a Sunday morning. Celeste, knowing his lazy habits, always came to his room last. This allowed him ample time to rise and be off before she came in to make his bed and tidy his room.

He had searched the bookstalls for just the right magazine of erotic pictures. He left his bed in a tangle and under his pillow, with only a corner of the cover showing, he had hidden the pornographic book.

Then he hid in the empty guest room across the hall until he heard the winsome maid enter his domain. Silently he crept to his open door and peeped inside. He grinned maliciously as he watched the girl.

Celeste had dropped onto the edge of his bed. She had the magazine in her hands and was turning the pages slowly. Her attention was totally engrossed in the images. Her eyes were the size of quarters. Her breath was quick, and Lucien eyed the motion of her bosom, rising and falling under the stiffly starched maid's uniform.

His own pulse quickened slightly. He breathed deeply, bringing his own body under control in an iron discipline that was frightening in so young a boy.

Relaxing, Lucien sent his thoughts into the girl's mind. Her vivid imagination was ablaze with sexual arousal. He encouraged her desires. Celeste was seeing herself in the poses before her eyes. She was being ravaged in those strange ways by anonymous bodies. Her blood was pounding through her veins, excited almost beyond control.

Spreading the magazine on the blankets beside her, the girl opened her legs and tugged on her cotton skirt, bringing it up over her hips. Her black stockings and white panties were exposed to Lucien's scrutiny and he felt his mouth go dry.

He concentrated on this first challenge of its kind. He began adding his own stimulus to hers, creating even more fevered imaginings. He sent vague whispers along her nerves, urging her passions to an uncontrollable frenzy.

In her current state, it didn't take long to achieve the effect he was after. Celeste began rubbing herself between her legs. She was ready.

He stepped boldly into the room, closing the door behind him with a jar. Celeste jumped to her feet. She was startled and flushed, nervously smoothing her skirt and apron. The book fell onto the carpet at her feet.

"Lucien! What are you doing here?" Her voice was thick and heavy with the fire of her blood.

He didn't answer her at once. He went to her side. His control had to be perfect or she would bolt like an animal suddenly cornered with no place to run. And she must not run. Not now, when he was so close.

Standing before her, he reached out to touch her face, which was on a level with his own. "Celeste," he whispered, "you're so beautiful."

"Lucien, please…" Her eyes darted about the room. "I'll be dismissed."

"Don't you want to do the things in the book, Celeste?"

He kept his fingers on her cheek, the contact vital. He could feel her mind spinning, almost turning aside from his control. He soothed it, smoothed it and gently quieted it. He replayed the erotic images she had entertained so vividly. Then he put the thought in her mind that she might have those pleasures for real.

Here.

Now.

Celeste reached up and took his hand. She turned it palm up and kissed it. Her lips were moist, hot. With her other hand, she began unbuttoning her blouse.

Lucien smiled, keeping the expression from turning into a grin. As the blouse fell away, he began caressing her shoulders while she unhooked her bra. As it slipped off, his hands covered her breasts. She rolled her head at his touch, moaning. Her nipples hardened under his palms. The inferno inside her, she felt, must be quenched or she'd be entirely consumed by it.

She lost no time in taking the initiative. She stripped the rest of her uniform away, letting it fall in a heap to the floor. Frantically she removed Lucien's clothing, her hands quick and warm.

Greedily she took the boy into her arms and fell onto the rumpled sheets. She seemed to go mad with lust, mimicking the acts in the book, reliving her own carnal experiences. She let her imagination take over.

Lucien, learning every instant, took over at last. She was completely his as he reveled in every moment of this first sexual encounter. Yet, while his flesh steamed and writhed, his mind was ever cool and detached. Unmoved. Even in the act of penetration, with Celeste screaming under him, he took mental notes. Here at last was the secret he had hungered to learn.

The mystery was resolved. Sex, he now understood, was the ultimate human pleasure. The girl in his arms was totally subjected by it. And pleasure of that sort meant only one thing to Lucien.

Weakness.

Control a person's desires and you control his soul. Own it. You are able to use it in any and all ways. He was astonished at the ridiculous simplicity of the thing.

When, after hours of play, Celeste collapsed, exhausted, in his skinny arms, the boy had learned his most valuable lesson in dealing with human beings. Sex was an effective tool. It was one he would learn to employ cunningly in his single-minded quest for power.

Watching Lilith Markova get dressed was much like being seduced in reverse, Darryl mused. As each item of clothing went on, concealing another part of her flawless anatomy, he found his spent desires kindling again. Never had there been such a woman! He had known many, more than his share, he knew. Not one had been like this one.

She came out of his bathroom in only her nylon stockings and panties. She was nonchalantly running a brush through her long, dark tresses. She flipped her hair about to adjust the rhythm of the brush strokes. The motion made her firm breasts jiggle.

Darryl lay beneath the sheet, propped on his elbow. His eyes couldn't leave her. He wanted very much to lure her back to bed, to make love to her again. But something in her cool and efficient manner checked the impulse.

This was a woman who did things her own way or not at all. To push her now, he knew instinctively, would bring a rebuff. It would probably cancel out any hope for a future meeting. And Darryl wanted another such encounter very, very much.

"Are you certain I can't drive you home?" he asked.

Lilith zipped her charcoal colored skirt with a neat gesture and smiled at him. It was a radiant smile. "No. Thank you. There's no need to trouble yourself. I can easily get a cab."

"I'm getting the feeling you don't want me to know where you live."

The smile didn't waver, but the eyes hardened slightly. "Look, Mr. Waitman, there are few things in this harsh reality that I value to any extent. My privacy is at the head of that select list."

"I see."

She was slipping on her bra, an act that had always seemed comical to him, before this. Now it was sensual. Graceful.

He turned his gaze back to her face. "Can't we at least dispense with such formality? I mean, now? After... this?"

"What we have done is called sex, Mr. Waitman. An act we both seemed to enjoy. But it alters nothing about our relationship as employer and employee."

"Isn't that a bit cold, Lilith?" What the hell was going on here? Their evening had been wonderful. Everything from the gourmet dinner at the Chez Mouton to their friendly rapport during and after. All leading to the incredible sex. And now she was reverting back to the cold, hard secretary.

"I'm sorry. I didn't mean for it to be." She put on her silk chemise and fumbled with the buttons.

Waitman sensed something strained in her composure. It wasn't right.

Lilith could not meet his stare. "It's just... I do like you, Mr. Wait... Darryl. More than a little. But I'm ..afraid."

He sat up against the headboard. "Afraid? Look, if you are at all concerned about our liaison becoming public, rest assured I am a person of tact. This is between you and me. You have my word on that."

For that he got a sweet smile, but the hesitancy was still there. "Oh, it's not that."

"Then what?" he threw out his arms.

"I'm not quite sure. Not exactly. Mr. Axel has been acting strange, these last few weeks. I've thought that he intends to do something to you. Something... er... well, final."

There it was. Darryl felt his chest constrict. His next breath came very slowly.

"What the hell are you talking about?" His heart felt as it were being squeezed.

Lilith drifted to the side of the bed and sat beside him. She met his stare directly.

"Mr. Waitman, I didn't get to the position I have at C.C.I. by being blind and naïve. I've suspected for a long time that some of the organization's officials act less than scrupulously."

Waitman grabbed her arms tightly. "Damn you, woman! Get to the point!"

"Very well. But let go. You're starting to hurt me."

Waitman looked at his hands as if seeing them for the first time. He released her. "I'm sorry. Please. Go on."

Lilith rubbed her upper arms. "For some time, I've noticed that Mr. Axel has been looking into your record. Your meteoric rise in the company. He's nervous about you. Maybe scared is a better word for it. It has become an obsession with him.

"He has had me draw up several reports about you. Secretly. Within the past two or three months. Those reports do nothing but confirm his obvious suspicion that you have reached a point at which you might unseat him as the chairman of C.C.I."

Darryl frowned, chewing on his lower lip. "Why that old fox. I should have known he was shrewd enough to suspect... go on, Lilith. What else?"

She looked at him as if gauging him. "Did Mr. Axel suggest that he has some specific announcement to make to you on the yacht trip?"

"Yes, he did."

"I thought so. According to plan he's had me drafting for him and the board of directors. He's going to promote you to General Manager in charge of European Operations."

"What? That doesn't make any sense? He told me only a short time ago that he wanted Hendricks, from Marketing, to take over that spot."

The woman merely nodded. She knew he would put it all together soon enough and he did.

"He wants me out of the picture! That's it, isn't it?"

She bowed her head, her expression sad. He knew there had to be more. "Dammit, woman, tell me. All of it!"

"He's.." she reached out and took his hand, gripping it fiercely and he saw the fear again. ".. sending you over there to be killed."

"What? I don't believe it!" Still, despite his words, he felt a cold lump in the pit of his stomach. He felt like he was trapped in a nightmare. Maybe that was it. Maybe he was asleep and all this insanity was just a bad dream. His world couldn't be falling apart so rapidly. Could it?

"It's true," Lilith tugged at his hand. "You have to believe me, Darryl. Axel personally chose the liaison man who will handle your transfer, when you reach Belgium. A man named Maurice Betrand. Do you recognize that name?"

Waitman's blood went cold. Betrand. Of course he knew that name. Code sheet title, The Lynx. The most trusted C.C.I. assassin in the overseas operation. Axel's favorite.

If fear could be a tangible thing, Darryl felt it now. Axel was actually going to send him off to be killed.

That crummy son-of-a-bitch!

Waitman's mind was whirling, confused. This had come at him too fast, too unexpectedly to sort out properly in so short a space.

He had felt so damn secure, so unsuspected. Yet he could believe the thing Lilith had told him, for it was his own sort of twisted logic coming back to bite him. To survive in his world, you had to get rid of those who stood in your way or posed a threat. When you lived long enough in the jungle, you became one with the other beasts inhabiting it.

Waitman was no rookie novice in the dirty tricks business. He prided himself in being ruthless when it came to his own well being. He could also recognize when he was being manipulated.

He studied the lovely Miss Markova with a newfound respect. "You arranged all this solely for the purpose of telling me this, didn't you."

Lilith reached out and let her fingers run across his chest. Her full lips, so inviting, morphed into a conspiratorial smile. "I believe in winners, Darryl."

"I see."

"Axel is an old man. I can see him losing his grip, more and more as each day passes. It's only a matter of time until he falls from his throne, no matter how desperately he tries to hold on to it. Perhaps someone will remove him before nature takes its course."

Her long nails scratched him lightly as if to underline that last statement. It sent a shiver through him that he liked very much.

"Go on."

"There are enough executive sharks in the company, besides yourself, to make that almost a certainty. Such an abrupt change of power could easily leave me on the outside of things. Something I do not relish in the slightest.

"I've worked hard to gain my present position. I've used my talents, both in and out of bed, to gain the things I want and I don't regret any of it. Now that a change is all but certain, I've decided to shift my allegiance to someone who has the strength and know-how to take the company from Axel. And win it all."

"I'm flattered." Darryl lifted her wandering hand to his mouth and began to lick her fingers.

"Don't be," Lilith sighed, enjoying his adoration. "It was a purely non-altruistic decision on my part. I read all those reports Axel had me write up. You are the person, perhaps the only one, capable of taking over and making it all work. To the point of holding on to it, once you have it in your hands.

"I decided to prove to you that I can be of use to you in that future."

She was an opportunist. He liked that. No frills. No snow job about being in love with him. She was brutal in her own self-interest. He understood that all too well. She wanted her piece of the pie and had no moral qualms to impede her drive.

He stopped sucking her fingers. "Very well. I believe you. For now. It all makes sense. But, Lilith, if you're misleading me in any way, regardless of your motivations, you will be made to regret that."

He squeezed her fingers together to make his point and she winced. "Do I make myself clear?"

"Perfectly. But it's all true, everything I've told you. I wouldn't have jeopardized my position on a whim."

"No. I suppose not. But from now on, you will take orders from me alone."

"Of course. I intended that. I said I'd be useful."

Darryl grinned. "Yes. I'm beginning to see that."

Lilith freed her hand from his grip and slid it beneath the blankets hiding his crotch. She sought out his manhood and found it easily enough. "In more ways than one, lover."

Aroused anew, Darryl pulled her to him and mashed his mouth onto hers. Her lips tasted both sweet and cold as his hands tore her blouse open.

* * * *

It was almost two a.m. when Lilith let herself into the Master's apartment. He sat in a huge velvet chair, his face lost in shadow.

A single candle burned on the end table at his left. The wavering light sat strangely on the modern décor of the living room.

She knelt at his feet. He extended a long bony hand and she took it into both her own and bent her head to kiss the ring of black onyx on set on his middle finger.

Her attitude was totally servile.

"It went as you instructed, Master." Her visage in the shimmering light was cruel. Her blazing eyes reflected the dancing glow of the candle as animal-eyes did.

Lucien Wicker put his hands together, bringing the tips of his fingers to touch his thin, bloodless lips. "Excellent, my dear. You are sure that he was completely convinced of your sincerity?"

"In every detail. He is certain his position is now tottering and that his very life is at risk."

The warlock nodded. "It will be childishly easy to maneuver him into the next step. The poor, witless fool will do exactly as I intend. And without the slightest inkling that I am the cause of all his actions." He looked down into his servant's flatly shining eyes.

"Lilith, you have far surpassed my fondest expectations. Your abilities please me immensely."

"Thank you, Master. I live only to serve you."

"Of course. There is a treat for you in the kitchen. Your reward. But do consume it tidily."

The thing that looked like a woman rose with feline grace. She glanced to her left, twitched her nose as a familiar scent reached it. She trembled. Going to one knee, she bent to hug Wicker about the knees.

"You are most kind, Master."

In the spotless kitchen, she found her prize in the stainless steel sink. The animal, small and furry, was only a short while dead. A little warmth still remained in its mutilated remains.

Lilith grimaced, then giggled. She caught up a chunk of the thing and ripped into it with her over-sharp teeth. Blood washed her chin and lips, dripping down her long slender throat to stain what was left of her silk chemise. She leaned over the sink.

The Master hated for her to make a mess while feeding.

CHAPTER 15

Father Henri Dubois said his morning mass quickly, hoping that the Lord would overlook his indiscreet haste. It wasn't often that the rectory of St. Michael's had overnight guests. Father Henri wanted to see them early.

Removing his vestments, he pushed them into the arms of Kristi, his altar girl, and made off down the corridor in a dash. For a seventy-year-old, he moved remarkably fast. His white hair fluttered in the breeze of his passage.

Father Henri attributed his speed and agility at such an age to three factors: The inspiring grace of God, who realized that Henri Dubois still had an enormous amount of work to do in his life's mission. Two: jogging two miles a day, throughout the year (even in winter boots); and the consumption of two sixteen-ounce beers before retiring every night.

The old pastor swore that the brew kept his joints oiled. The nuns in his church swore that he was really Irish and only pretending to be French-Canadian.

Several of the Sisters were already at breakfast when he arrived at the wide L-shaped combination cooking and dining facility. They, in unison, offered him cheery greetings. He waved a hasty reply, continuing his jaunt through the homey kitchen. He was intent on Sister Xavier, the senior housekeeper and cook.

Seeing him, she pointed to a tray holding cups and saucers, a silver pot of coffee and a circling array of Danish pastries and doughnuts. All were freshly baked from her own ovens. The smell was indescribable as the priest made off with the breakfast platter. The Eternal City of Heaven, he often thought, could smell no better than a bakery in the morning. Was there ever a more divine aroma? One could almost taste it.

The two guest rooms were adjoining units located to the rear of the house behind the kitchen. He chose to meet the young man first. Balancing the tray carefully, he pushed the door inward to find the lad still fast asleep. Now that wouldn't do.

Father Henri set the tray gently on the night table and nudged the fellow. He was, the cleric saw with relief, fully dressed beneath his heavy woolen blanket. He had slept in his clothes. Strange, but practical.

"Rise up and greet the day, mon ami."

The brown eyes flickered open and shut several times and then opened fully. As the old man bent to reassure his guest, he saw a look of recognition dawn.

"Good morning, Father," Dancer yawned. He sat up and ran a hand through his thick, unruly hair. "What time is it?"

"Just after seven, M'sieu McCoy."

"Do call me Dancer, Father."

"Tres bien. You slept well? You were comfortable?"

Dancer extended both arms over his head to get the stiffness out his shoulder blades. "You bet. Couldn't have been better."

His nose wrinkled. "Mmmm! What's that wonderful smell?"

"Coffee and Danish, prepared by our own Sister Xavier. You would like some?"

"Are you kidding?" Dancer swung his feet to the floor and stood. "I'm starving! Haven't had a bite to eat since we left the hospital, last night."

Dancer took a strawberry roll into his eager hands and devoured half of it in one bite, while his host poured a steaming cup of coffee for him.

"Are the girls awake yet, Father?"

A familiar voice spoke from the doorway. "We most certainly are."

Morgan stood there looking comfortably attractive in what Dancer was coming to appreciate as her look; the well worn Nikes, hip hugging jeans and a black sweatshirt. "And terribly hungry, too."

Father Dubois put another cupful of hot java into her waiting hands. "And Miss Hines?"

"She's taking a shower." Morgan blew on the hot coffee, then took a small sip. "Oh, that's just what I needed."

"Thank Sister Xavier. When it comes to making coffee, she is a veritable."

Dancer looked up, his expression mischievous. "Or a witch?"

Father Dubois cocked his head. "You make a jest?"

Dancer sobered. "Well, it just seems odd to me, Father. I mean, look at this. A man of the cloth and a self-proclaimed witch working together. If that isn't bizarre, I don't know what it is."

"Ah, oui. I see your point. I've never looked at it in that way before."

Morgan set her cup into her saucer. "Dancer, Father Dubois was a friend of my family, before I was born. He and father were very close. When I came here to live, I was fortunate to have someone who was just like family waiting to welcome me. He helped me get settled and to find my way. To make new friends and call this place my home."

The priest sighed with the memories. "Ah, it seems so long ago, now, that time when I was stationed in Paris. I recall performing the ceremony for your parents, when they married. What a blessed event. The Church of St. Mary on the Seine was overflowing with family and friends all there to celebrate the union of Armand Rein and his lovely bride, Marie Dorceau.

"It seems only yesterday, too, which seems a paradox. They were fine people, good people, both of them. Even your sweet maman, with her strange gifts, was a devout Catholic. Though that may seem strange to outsiders."

Father Henri absently took a roll and bit off a piece, chewing as his remembered. "You see, my son, although our Holy Mother the Church dislikes words like witchcraft and sorcery, it does acknowledge that some of God's children are uniquely blessed with rare and wondrous talents. Talents that He, in His infinite wisdom alone, has given them.

"We believe in His destiny, and we do not question His ways. Morgan, as did her mother and her mother's ancestors for generations, is one of those chosen souls.

"As long as she retains her faith, realizes where the those talents have their source and respects the Divine Origin, she is welcome in God's house. Always. And, as my sixth godchild, she is always welcome to my home and my heart."

Morgan put an arm about the pastor's shoulders and hugged him. She kissed his cheek. "You have always had my love, mon pere."

Father Dubois coughed to cover the sudden moisture in his eyes. "Come, come!

Enough of this maudlin sentiment! You'll have Monsieur Dancer believing we are too soft to be any use to you, eh?"

She smiled and drew back. "Thank you for putting us up, last night, on such short notice."

"It was our true pleasure. Having guests here is always a cause for celebration."

"Then I would indulge your hospitality for a while longer," Morgan suggested, nodding towards the sound of the shower in the other room.

"I take it you want for Miss Hines to remain here for a time?"

"Yes, mon pere. If you will be so kind. Dancer and I are involved in something very dangerous. Something that could possibly destroy us. Connie... Miss Hines, is a major figure in the affair. She is the one in the most danger. One attempt has already been made on her life and I am certain that others will be, if she is not sheltered from discovery."

Father Henri grunted. "She may have the security of St. Michael's as long as needed, my child."

"Thank you, Father. I knew you'd help us. Being holy ground, this is the one place where the forces battling us will not be able to find her."

The priest cocked his bushy white eyebrows. "That sounds very frightening, Morgan."

She drew a deep breath before replying, "Father, the Devil usually is."

* * * *

Morgan had formed a mental picture of Dancer's apartment. Though it hadn't been entirely incorrect, the place did surprise her. It was an expansive attic loft above the gargantuan garage housing the maintenance vehicles for the Scientific Institute of Research, his place of employment.

A rectangular skylight in the ceiling warmed the spacious open area with summer sunlight. Dancer's hideaway was a three-room jigsaw puzzle, divided by movable corrugated partitions four feet in height. Looking over their tops, Morgan was reminded of a laboratory maze in which a mouse or rat was made to perform.

The primary living area held multicolored rugs, an open sofa that doubled as a bed and thirty or more wooden crates that held everything from books to clothing.

Two of the larger boxes were nailed together by a thick plywood square that transformed the whole into a workable desk. Atop this crude work station was a sophisticated PC set-up complete with a color printer, high speed scanner and a connected telephone through which his modem logged on to the internet. It was covered with papers, pencils, scientific journals, empty soda cans and assorted other paraphernalia. To the right of this was a fancy stereo unit for playing music disks. Wires running behind his desk were affixed to two three foot speakers positioned to the furthest corners of the room. Piled on the wooden floor around the unit were stacks of plastic CD holders.

Against a back wall, beneath another window, the kitchenette had been placed. It had a counter and a sink, a stove, refrigerator and a foldaway counter fronted with two bar stools. The entire layout had been adapted around two massive wooden support posts, one of which was plastered with posters of Bruce Lee and Raquel Welch. The other beam held a steel shelf on which was another phone, this one with fax capabilities. Over this was affixed round Star Trek clock with a picture of the starship Enterprise as its face.

The two remaining units were a tiny bathroom with shower stall and a storage area. Over the former, hanging curtains from the ceiling beams were tacked to the partition to provide privacy. Whereas the latter was as exposed as the rest of the floor. In this McCoy kept his treasure of miscellany...boxes and files of potentially but not immediately useful items of various sorts. There was also a clothes rack weighed down by several suits and other articles of clothing.

Morgan felt instantly at ease there. It was so very much like McCoy. It was almost a living extension of his character, a cluttered mess, yet it was many good things coming together to form comfort and mental relaxation. One could find peace, here, and a place to restore the energies that the struggles of life depleted daily.

She walked in a wide circle, inspecting and finally approving the place. Meanwhile Dancer was on the post phone talking to his boss, Sergei at the main lab.

Their conversation lasted for ten minutes and when he replaced the receiver, he was smiling.

"He's still a bit miffed at my absence, but he won't hear of taking my resignation. The Institute is officially granting me an extended leave of absence, without pay of course, until my so called...ah, personal crisis is wrapped up."

Morgan nodded and sat, yoga-fashion, on a plush violet cushion. "You seem to work for a very good man. The one time I met him, after my lecture, I liked him a lot."

"Ditto. Sergei is a good egg. He can be stuffy at times, but he's always been loyal to his people. You can depend on him to back you. I guess I respect him more than most people I know."

He looked down at her inquisitively. He swept his arm out in a grand gesture. "So? What do you think of my castle?"

"I like it very much. Although..." she traced a dust-line across a patch of wooden floor with her forefinger... "it could use some cleaning up."

"I know. I know." Dancer fell back on the sofa and crossed his legs at his ankles. "But I don't have much time off and house cleaning just isn't a big priority. And don't suggest I get a cleaning-woman. On my salary, that just isn't practical."

He laughed wryly. "Besides, this place would scare off a maid, pay or not."

"Oh, it's not that bad. Just a little dusting here and there would help."

"Hey, enough with the cleaning tips. How about something to drink?"

"That sounds good. Do you have any tea?"

"Huh, huh. Sorry. Milk, soda, juice and coffee. I think."

Morgan smiled. She liked being waited on. Especially by a charming, handsome man.

"The coffee sounds fine."

Dancer bounced to his feet and went into the kitchen area. He set a teakettle on the electric burner and took a jar of Maxwell House instant off the pantry shelf. "I hope you don't mind instant?"

"Instant is fine."

"How do you like it?"

"Black, please."

"Yuk! I'll go without cream, but never without sugar."

"It's an acquired taste. You should try it like this. Too much sugar really isn't good for you."

"Now you sound like my mother. Tell me, Morgan, why we needed to leave Connie at St. Michael's? You told Father Henri it was some kind of safe place for her."

"Yes. It's holy ground. Lucien won't be able to find her... that is, to sense her there. His talent isn't capable of penetrating the sanctified atmosphere of the church."

"Lucien!?" Dancer put down his spoon. The kettle whistled its steamy song and he lifted it off the burner. "Just who the hell is Lucien?"

"Oh! I'm sorry, Dancer. Things have been happening so fast that I haven't had a chance to bring you up to date on what I've discovered."

He handed her a black mug of coffee, took one for himself and dropped onto another of the oversized cushions.

"Okay, so let me get this straight. You know who's behind all this... ah, mayhem and stuff? Is that what you're saying?"

Morgan blew on her coffee and tasted it gingerly. "Yes. ..Mmm... I do. It's my brother. That is, my older brother, Lucien."

"WHAT!" Dancer gasped, coffee spitting out of his mouth. "Your brother! You're kidding. Right?"

"I wish I were." She lowered her gaze and was silent for a moment. When she looked up there was a mixture of fear and sadness clouding her features. "I wish I could kid about Lucien, but he's no laughing matter, Dancer. I am quite serious. Somewhere out there, in this very city, is my brother, a warlock with gifts that may be even greater than my own. He has turned those gifts in unspeakable directions.

"He is capable of unbelievable horrors. Like Mr. Appleton's death. Lucien was behind that. Behind the fireball, too. I am quite sure he is aware that I am now involved. Just as I am aware of him. That is why it was urgent that I find another place to stay. My apartment is too easy for him to locate."

Dancer was having some trouble digesting her words. "You mean he'd hurt you? His own sister?"

Morgan laughed bitterly. "Without a second thought. You have to understand this, Dancer. He is a monster wrapped in the guise of flesh and blood. His soul... if he even has one... is not human. He has no scruples and will do anything whatsoever to achieve his malevolent ends. Whatever they are."

Dancer managed a soft whistle. "Are you sure the two of you are related? I really don't like the sounds of this guy."

"He frightens me completely," Morgan confessed. "I have personally experienced some of his methods. Knowing that Lucien is out there, working and waiting for a chance to find me, is almost paralyzing. But we still don't know what it is he is after. That haunts me more than anything else about all this.

"Whatever his aims are, you can bet every last penny that they are wicked and foul."

Dancer combed his fingers through his brown hair, reducing it once again to a bush-like confusion. Morgan took a long swallow from her mug.

He shook his head. "This is going way too fast for me. Would you mind back tracking a little bit here? Some family history might help fill in the details for me."

"You mean about Lucien and me?"

"Right. I can't play in this game, effectively, unless I know what the rules are and who all the players are. Especially those on the other team."

The white witch studied her friend's clean-cut face. She felt something akin to a sense of destiny about him.

Dancer McCoy had entered her life at a crucial juncture. He had worked himself into the pattern of their chaotic adventure without any causal effect on her part. There was some element of fate working here that she didn't wholly understand, but she felt confident she could trust it. A higher plan was evolving.

She had been given a friend when she needed one most. Perhaps something more? She pushed that idea aside, afraid she might blush if it reached the surface of her mind and what it might reveal. To both of them. After all, every woman had a right to maintain some mystery about her.

"I'll tell you, but it is a very long story. It began when my mother died. I was seven, then. Lucien was thirteen. We lived at the American Embassy in Paris,.."

As the tale unfolded, Dancer found himself entering a world of incredible happenings. Watching her emerald eyes, listening to cadence of her voice, he saw, in his mind, the course of her life.

CHAPTER 16

The Rein family quarters had become the center of frantic activity at the embassy for weeks. Morgan's room was the focus of everything. Doctors of high repute came and went with increasing regularity, watched by the curious and concerned household staff. They muttered among themselves and avoided meeting Armand Rein's worried eyes.

Morgan's father grew thinner and more haggard. Anguish painted gray lines about his tired eyes. He knew that, for all their skills, the distinguished doctors were having no success whatever with his daughter. He grew more frantic with each day that passed.

The child's small, angelic face was frozen into a caricature of fear. She had to be constantly sedated. There was a danger that, in one of her seizure-like frenzies, she might harm herself. Her body was declining and no could offer a thimble of hope.

Her father at last came to the inescapable conclusion that her only succor lay in prayer. Thus, gathered with the loyal maids, butler and old French cook, he joined them in beseeching divine intervention. A miracle seemed like their only hope.

It was mid-October in Paris. The trees were changing color, casting their leaves across the river on a wind that seemed mad with the onslaught of winter.

Lucien, safe in his room, reveled in the sense of death permeating the outside world. He knew his sister had reached the end of her strength. Only her formidable will was keeping her frail body alive.

Her inner strength had amazed and frightened him. That, alone, had been enough to persuade him of the necessity for her death. Left to mature, Morgan might rival his own talents, in time to come. Such determination was a thing he didn't want to have to face in a distant future. Once he had brought her to her doom, he need not worry about anything of the sort from her, ever again. That was the permanence of death. He thought it was a wonderful thing.

Filled with gloating, he didn't dream that his defeat was approaching through the stormy darkness of an October night. Black clouds had covered the sky all day long. With dusk, jagged bolts of lightning streaked to light the shiny-wet streets.

Everyone in the house was locked away from the fury outside, almost unaware of its savagery, except for the boy. The others were distracted by their fears of what the morning might bring. The grim reaper was near and his victory all but assured as the dark hours ticked by.

Through the chaos slid a black limousine. It stopped at the front gate and discharged a dumpy figure, bundled to the ears. Sgt. Miller, the square-jawed marine guard on duty at the entrance booth, stepped out into the rain, his green poncho covering most of his towering frame. He waved a flashlight over the unannounced arrival, blocking the gate.

"Out of my way!" snapped a feminine voice. "We've no time for such foolishness!"

Miller jumped back as if he'd been scolded by his mother. For the first time in his ten year military career, the tough marine was totally befuddled. His experience and training demanded he stop any and all visitors until proper identification could be verified. But here and now, he felt powerless to interfere with the wishes of this small, human twister that was clearly about to roll right over him.

He waved her through. "Yes, ma'am!"

The intruder hurried through the gate and up to the front door, unmoved by the thunder that seemed to crack around her heels.

Armand and Lucien were sitting beside Morgan's bed. They were silent, Armand in prayer and Lucien in concentrated effort. As his father begged for salvation for his beloved child, Lucien redoubled his efforts to pinch out his sister's life. Neither heard the big doors downstairs as they opened and then slammed shut. Neither caught the sounds of quick footsteps on the carpeted stairs.

When the door opened and a short, tweedy figure stepped into the room, both were taken aback.

The long tweed cape dripped water onto the rug. Two short, rather crooked arms flung it open, dropping it to the floor to reveal narrow shoulders and a stocky body. Rein was reminded of a troll from various fairy tales.

Yet it was the face of the woman that held their attention. She was gray-haired, her features tiny. Rimless bifocals balanced on the tip of her little round nose. Her cheeks were puffing in and out as she caught her breath.

"Hooo! Those stairs!" she gasped, without a formal greeting. "Any longer and they would reach right up to heaven itself."

Her eyes, behind round bright lenses, caught their gazes. The intense blue orbs seemed to grow larger as she surveyed the man, the boy, and the shape beneath the covers.

She stared keenly at Morgan's pale forehead, just visible above the blanket. Then she turned to Armand. "I see that I'm just barely in time. I am Mother Kalavela."

Years later, she told Morgan that she knew that Lucien hated her instantly. It was a sentiment she tried not to return… and failed. She knew that she exuded a force… a potency that the boy could feel. It was dramatically opposed to everything he was, desired, and intended to accomplish.

Shaken, Lucien felt victory snatched from his hands.

Armand rose from his chair to take Kalavela's chilly hands. "Mother Kalavela! Marie's teacher and friend! She loved you… reverenced you. I never thought to meet you under such terrible circumstances."

The woman glanced toward Morgan as she replied, "I was in Tibet when Marie died. On personal business. I was aware of her passing, although the actual news of her death reach me until a few days ago. I should have been here, at the end.

"I find it hard to accept the fact that I was not. Forgive me, Armand Rein."

Never before had he heard such sorrowful words to match his own grief. Those bluest of eyes held such tenderness and compassion that he was moved to kiss her weathered cheek with his lips. Now, at long last, he knew why his Marie had loved this woman so dearly.

"There is nothing to forgive. You are here, now. That is all that matters. Perhaps you can save my daughter. Nobody else has given her any ease at all."

She drew herself up, as if gathering her energies. "Yes, yes. That is the reason I have come. Marie's daughter will not die. I swear that to you by the things I…

and she… revere."

While his father was experiencing a rebirth of hope, Lucien felt anger exploding inside him, though he said nothing. That icy glare of blue turned toward him.

"What is your name, Boy?"

He bit his lip, setting all his strength to resisting the power of those penetrating eyes.

Armand saw his son's stubborn expression and couldn't imagine what reason there could be for such behavior. Especially at this time and under these circumstances. He was not in any mood to put up with the boy's rebellious bent. His anger vented.

"Lucien! Be respectful! This was your mother's teacher."

The son looked at his father with undisguised hostility. Rein had never seen him look like this. So alien and cold.

Alerted to the tension between the two, Mother Kalavela turned her gaze away from the boy, as if dismissing. "No," she addressed the father. "That is all right, Monsieur Rein. The boy and I… understand one another."

The blue fires flashed briefly toward Lucien again. "I know who you are. What you have done." It was not an accusation but a statement of fact and the boy was unnerved by her incredible insights. "Go, now, and leave us, please. We will talk later. Alone."

Lucien wanted to lash out with all the power he had so painfully gained, through diligent effort. But suddenly, frighteningly, he felt his rib cage constrict. Subtly, inexorably, it squeezed the breath from his lungs, bit by bit.

He flinched, knowing that he had no chance of winning any duel with Kalavela. Not now. What talents he possessed were no match for the great and finely honed powers inhabiting her squatty, demure shape. It took all his considerable self-control to admit to his own impotency and retreat.

He straightened his back, held his head arrogantly high, and moved past them into the hall. He paused beyond the door, listening to their quiet voices.

"What on earth is wrong with that boy? I apologize for his rudeness, Mother. That is not at all like Lucien."

Beyond the door, Lucien snickered silently. His father was such a pathetic simpleton.

"That isn't important. Not right now. Morgan's life is. I must see to her at once, if you don't mind."

Once in his room, Lucien kicked his bedpost and punched his fist into the closet door until his knuckles bled. Thwarted! And so near to success! He had never been bested in his short life and he hated the feeling it gave him. The thought that he could not best an insignificant old woman plagued him until his youthful anger was almost too much to bear.

"I'll destroy Morgan yet," he vehemently swore to himself. "And the old witch, too. There will be other chances. I'll never give up. And I shall grow stronger, year by year. If I can't do it now, then I will do it later… when she is not prepared. I'll finish her for good. Then there'll be no old grandmother to save her!"

He didn't know that Kalavela, even preoccupied with Morgan, was reading him fully. They didn't have to be together for that.

He also didn't think things through to their logical end, that the woman would warn his sister or that she would arm her, over those very same years. Morgan too would be schooled and, when the time came, possess the skills needed to counter his attack. Had he seen that future, his fury would have been unleashed without restraint.

But he did not know.

*   *   *   *

For three days, Kalavela nursed Morgan. The girl was comatose most of the time, seeming not to respond much, if at all.

Kalavela kept her methods to herself, convincing the servants that it was better to have only one person attending the child at a time. On the afternoon of the fourth day, Morgan began to stir.

She had been lost in an endless nightmare, a circular merry-go-round of horror that began and ended in terror. Now she opened her eyes to the light.

Her father was standing at the foot of her bed. He smiled at her… a smile so full of love and gratitude that it warmed her emaciated body through and through.

He, too, looked ill and worn. She wanted to ask why, but her throat was so dry she couldn't utter a sound.

Another adult was sitting in the low-slung chair beside the bed. The girl looked closely, turning her head with difficulty to examine the newcomer. What a beautiful face! she thought. Old and wrinkled and wise…a soft hand wiped her brow with a cool cloth. Morgan felt a safety that she had known only with her mother.

"Maman? You have come back?" Her voice was the merest whisper but her smile was as radiant like a blossoming flower. Her intuition told her that, in some esoteric way, her mother had returned.

Kalavela nodded her head in understanding and looked to Armand Rein with renewed optimism. "The worst is over, Monsieur. Our little princess will live."

Armand sat down on the corner of his daughter's bed and began to cry. "Merci, mon Dieu, merci."

From that moment, Morgan recovered with astonishing speed. She improved so quickly that the family doctor and his colleagues could only marvel at her improvement.

"It is a medical mystery," they all agreed. They persistently ignored the strange old woman sitting unobtrusively in the corner while they examined the child.

"Almost miraculous, if one believed in that sort of thing." It never occurred to them to credit that cure to the old teacher who had been devoting twenty-four hours a day to the girl's care.

That was a matter of indifference to Mother Kalavela. Her sole agenda was Morgan's complete recovery. Once that was irreversible, she went to Armand with a startling proposal.

"I would like, Monsieur Rein, to take Morgan home to Scotland with me. It occurs to me that this city may not suit her constitution, and that country life might help her to become strong and well."

Rein had been working in his downstairs office when Kalavela approached him. He sat, put aside his papers and gave her his undivided attention. Now his reaction to her request was one of true surprise.

"But she is doing so well. You said as much this morning at breakfast. Are you afraid of a relapse?"

"I am not certain that she might not begin failing again, once I leave her."

"I see." Rein began tugging his chin as his mind accepted her worries as his own.

"In a way, she identifies me with her mother. To lose that comfort again might have terrible effects. Besides that, I hope to teach her my craft, as I taught her mother. If that is all right with you?"

"But of course, Mother. It was always Marie's fondest hopes to have you tutor Morgan in the ways of your... shall we say, unique talents. I support that with all my heart."

Kalavela smiled. "Then will you agree to my offer?"

Armand dreaded the thought of losing his little girl, even temporarily, but her illness had frightened him badly. He was also well aware of the monumental debt he owed this woman.

"If you had not come, Mother, I would have no daughter now. She would not have lived through that terrible night." For a second, his eyes mirrored dark shadows and he shook them off to be replaced by a comforting awe. "I can see that she thrives when she is with you, and she wilts when you are away, even for only an afternoon.

"Very well, then," the ambassador clapped his hands together and rose from his chair. He walked around his desk and took both of Kalavela's hands in his. "I can only agree, if she chooses to go with you. Although I have no doubt what her answer will be, knowing the joy she derives from you. In some way, it seems right. I know my Marie would be happy, as well. Yes, she may go."

True to her father's prediction, Morgan was ecstatic when told. She all but screamed her approval of the idea and hugged both her father and Kalavela repeatedly. Part of her knew she would miss her papa, but this new Mother had come to fill the empty space in her heart left vacant by her mother's death. The thought of living with this kind woman and learning her many skills overwhelmed her with joy.

While arrangements were made for her departure, Lucien lurked on the fringes of all the hustling activity. He was not surprised at the news, when his father related it to him. Somehow he had been suspecting such action.

It was clear that Morgan was being taken beyond his reach. For now. But there would eventually be another opportunity, here or elsewhere. A day of reckoning. He vowed to himself that when that day arrived, he would not fail.

Mother Kalavela came to his room on the morning of their departure. When she opened the door and entered, she knew it was to face a mortal enemy. They both understood that, with their deepest instincts. Like a cornered animal, Lucien backed far away from her, his arms held rigid at his sides. His hands were balled into tight fists and ready.

She saw the fists and sneered. "I have come to offer you the chance to redeem your soul, Lucien Wicker. It may well be your only chance, for you are already old in evil."

"You have nothing I want, old woman!"

"You are wrong. I hold the chance for you to avoid your fate. The way you have chosen leads only to death, Boy. You are well along that path. But there is still time to save yourself. Only just. A bit farther and you will be lost for all time."

She held up a finger to the scowling boy. "Listen to me. God forgives almost anything. Almost."

Lucien spat at her feet. "Witch!" he yelled. "Leave me alone! My way is none of your affair!"

She stared into his eyes. The twin circles of blue seemed to swallow him up. He struggled to draw his gaze from hers, but he could not manage it. Once again her craft was beyond his scope.

"Then you will go where you will go." Her voice was infinitely sad. Without another word, she turned and left him standing like a stone statue.

Ten minutes later, she and Morgan had said their good-byes to Armand. Doors slammed shut and the black limousine that had brought her only weeks earlier pulled away down the narrow street. A swirl of dead leaves whipped up behind the retreating tires.

Lucien, from his balcony, watched it drive out of sight. Before it turned the corner, Morgan stood on her knees on the back seat and looked out through the rear window. Straight at her brother.

It was the last time they would see one another for twenty years.

*   *   *   *

An hour had passed. Several cups of coffee had disappeared by the time Morgan ended her tale.

"So I went off to Scotland with Mother Kalavela and learned the myriad skills of witchcraft."

"And you never saw Lucien again?" Dancer sat with his back against the sofa, totally captivated by her narrative.

"No. My father was killed in a car accident six months later. I didn't even go back for his funeral. Believe it or not, I had chicken pox at the time. Mother told me the news and let me cry in her arms. When I was finished, we both said a rosary for the repose of his soul. As hurt as I was by the loss, Mother assured me that Papa was now and forever with Maman in heaven. That image did much to comfort me in the days ahead.

"As for Lucien, he simply vanished after Father's death. Even Mother Kalavela couldn't trace him. Not that she didn't try. She was very apprehensive about him and remained so for the rest of her life."

"She sounds like an incredible person. Like a character right out of Dickens."

"She was that. And lots, lots more. Believe me."

"Were you as worried about your brother?"

Morgan shook her head. "Not really. I was so young and so much had happened in such a short span of time. For me, it became as if he had never really existed. Like a make believe I'd had. As time went by the memory of my brother grew fainter. It was hard for me to believe that I had ever known him at all or that any of those dreadful things in Paris had actually happened to me."

McCoy rose and, going to kitchenette, began filling the sink with warm water. He dunked the stained mugs into the soapy pool. When they were clean, he turned to face her again.

"But that's no longer the case, is it? Now you believe he's here."

Morgan, still sitting on the plush cushion, wrapped her arms around herself. "Oh, Lucien is here. In the city. And he is active. I had a vision of him, several nights ago, not as a boy but as he must be now.

"He killed Mr. Appleton. I haven't the slightest doubt of that now. But there is no tangible proof any court would ever believe. He also sent that fireball after you and Connie."

Dancer wiped his hands on a towel and threw it on the counter. "Then I owe him one. So? What do we do now?"

"We have to find him before he acts again. Meaning, kills again. And he will kill. Claire senses him and his purposes, though vaguely. She confirms that much."

"Okay. Then we have to locate him. Where he is ..and by that I mean physically. Any ideas?"

"Well, we know he is associated with C.C.I. Their offices are over on Hanover West. As that is our only lead, I'd say we go and start with them."

"That's logical. Thomas Axel is the big cheese over there. We can check him out. Try to find some kind of connection. See if brother Lucien is on any employee rosters."

He looked up at his Star Trek clock. "I knew my stomach was growling for something. It's after twelve. You hungry for some lunch?"

Morgan stood up and stretched. "Famished."

"Great. I know where we can get some super steaks right around the corner from here."

"Sounds wonderful, Dr. McCoy. Lead the way."

He started to walk past her to get his jacket but the way she was just standing there stopped him. There was an anticipation when their gazes met and held. Without being conscious of his own movements, Dancer turned and put his arms around her. He wanted to say something... anything... to let her know how he felt but his mind went blank. Morgan sighed and her lips parted in silent reply. There was no need of words. He lowered his head and they kissed.

Her lips were warm, soft and accepting. When he felt her hands tighten on his back, he was emboldened. Her mouth opened and he touched his tongue to hers. Exploring. She responded.

Then she stiffened and pushed herself from his embrace. He immediately cursed himself for being too precipitate.

"Morgan. I'm sorry.. I shouldn't.."

She put her finger across his lips. "No. Don't be. Please. It's just that it's too soon. I'm not sure what I feel and we haven't the luxury to wait and sort things out right now. A few days ago I didn't even know you."

"Point taken."

She held up her hand. "Please, there is a whole other level to all this. I know that you don't accept what I am. The idea of witchcraft is still new to you."

Dancer shrugged. It made him look like a guilty teenager. "What can I say to that? I am a scientist, after all. And a damn good one, I might add."

"But Dancer, all your training persuades you that my kind of skills can't exist. But they do, whether anyone wants them to or not. We are locked in a situation that is going to make serious demands upon both of us. On your courage and determination and on my ..energies."

McCoy frowned. "Morgan, what's your point?"

"Do you recall how completely exhausted you were after that wild ride with Connie? How drained you felt?"

"As if all my stuffing had gone out of me."

"Exactly. That happened because I had arranged for you to have access to unusual sources of energy, at need. Sources that most people cannot reach. And, because of Lucien's attack, there was the need. That was just normal energy use, stepped up a bit.

"Now try and imagine the energy it takes to make things happen with only your mind and will?"

Comprehension dawned on his face. "So when you do your thing..er craft, you're saying it takes a whole lot out of you."

"Exactly."

"Mm. Makes sense. Even jives with the laws of physics. I can see it would have to be true. Okay. I understand the principle. What next?"

Morgan started pacing in front of him. "For the time being, it is vital I retain all my energy. When I face Lucien, and I will face him, sooner or later... I must be at the absolute peak of physical strength and emotional stability.

"Strong emotion, including sex, is a drain. They used to think that a witch lost her powers if she married or took a lover. They were almost correct, but for the wrong reasons. A witch must know when to love and when to control her emotions. In order to do her work, she has to time it correctly."

As she finished her monologue, she stopped in front of him and waited for his reaction.

Dancer ran his fingers through his hair and gave a queer smile.

"Do you see what I mean?" Morgan blurted on the verge of being frustrated by his lack of response.

"Oh, yeah. I think I get it. But ..."

"But what?"

"Morgan, I'm a virgin."

She took a step back, her mouth popping open like an oven door.

"Okay, go ahead and laugh, if you must."

She regained some semblance of composure. "You're not kidding, are you

"No, I'm not."

"But, I ...you're so..." she was having a hard time putting words together. Then a peculiar look came across her features and he understood it immediately and laughed.

"No, I am not gay. What I am is just an old fashion guy who happens to believe sex is meant for the marriage bed. I also think credit cards were the economic ruination of our society, that abortion is a sin against God and a crime against nature, and that the greatest television show of all time was the Lone Ranger with Clayton Moore and Jay Silverheels."

He finished his mini-speech and bowed at the waist. Morgan felt the giggles coming on. "Is that it or is there anything else I should know about you, Dr. McCoy?"

For his answer, he took her into his arms again. She did not resist. "One other small item, Ms. Rein. I think I may be falling in love with you."

"I know," she acknowledged in a soft voice. "Me, too. In time. But for now you are someone very dear to me. I want to get to know you better and better. Can you give me that time?"

He squeezed her and chuckled. "I told you, Green Eyes, I was in this to the end. Beside, we make a good team."

"Yes. We do."

"Well, all right! Now that we've settled this romance thing, let's go get grab some food before I say something else totally stupid."

CHAPTER 17

The yacht Seaspray was nosing her way out of Sussex Bay. Lucien Wicker, at the rail of the upper deck, felt the salt spray against his skin. Dressed in custom made, three piece, charcoal gray silk suit from Hong Kong, he looked the perfect picture of dapper executive excellence. In the crook of his left arm, he carried a black umbrella with an ivory handle.

The day was overcast, though the sun peered through a tangle of cumulus clouds, every now and again.

Most of Axel's guests were inside the lounge, coping with their sea-legs with stiff shots of Cutty-Sark. Lucien didn't particularly like the open air, but it was more bearable than the close confines of his cabin. His claustrophobia made itself a nuisance, at times, his deep revulsion at being confined in enclosed spaces causing him to seek discomfort rather than panic.

He stood there, morosely enduring the motion of the vessel and the heaving of the waves. Behind them the harbor buildings and docks were shrinking behind the boat's foamy wake.

Waitman found him there. C.C.I.'s vice-president was equally natty in a blue blazer, white trousers, and baby-blue deck shoes.

"Ah, Lucien. I've been looking for you."

"Indeed," Lucien was taller than Waitman and now he looked down at the smaller man with conscious superiority.

"Well, yes," Waitman reiterated, grabbing the rail as the vessel took a particularly nasty wave. "That damn captain must have been a New York cabby!" he said crossly.

Wicker returned his attention to the horizon.

"Lucien, we need to talk."

"I am at your disposal, Mr. Waitman," Lucien replied, looking over his shoulder. There was an odd note in his voice. Not quite sardonic, but not far from it.

Darryl tried to peel away their veneer but Wicker's face was completely stoic. "Good. I knew I could depend on you. Lucien, I've had alarming news. It may require drastic measures. I wish to discuss it with you in detail. Shall we meet here after dinner?"

"If you like."

"Good. It will be more private on deck. The others will be too busy partying to notice us. This must be kept secret, just between the two of us."

"I understand fully, Mr. Waitman." Again there was that odd, indefinable tone.

"Fine. I'll see you then."

Waitman wavered across the heaving deck. Lucien watched him go with a smile that held no amusement at all. Very soon, he thought. It is all going to come together. Waitman would have his rendezvous, but the results would not be to his benefit. Wicker would see to that. After all he was the real game-master here and Waitman had yet to realize his true role; that of a mere pawn. When he did, it would be a sour revelation for the pompous idiot. At that thought, Lucien's smile grew noticeably warmer.

* * * *

Morgan and Dancer had decided, while feasting on delicious steak dinners, to invade the precincts of C.C.I. posing as a writer and photographer from Business Daily Magazine. This was a rather obscure publication, which nobody would be likely to query as to their bona fides, as it was situated in Chicago.

They returned to his apartment loft for a quick change of clothes. They dressed in what they hoped would be passable disguises, then took a cab downtown.

Their fabricated excuse for their visit was a proposed article on the effect of current economic problems on construction and raw materials procurement throughout third world countries. This got them past the guards, the receptionist on the ground floor, and into the upper reaches of the firm's lofty management enclaves.

After they were passed so far, they went from secretary to secretary, higher and higher along the chain of corporate command. By three o'clock, they had reached President Thomas Axel's outer office. There they confronted Lilith Markova.

Morgan, attired in a navy blue skirt, matching jacket and white silk blouse, was the Vogue-perfect model of an enterprising professional. Whereas McCoy, following close behind her, wore black slacks, a gray T-shirt beneath his leather jacket and wrap-around shades. About his neck dangled an expensive Japanese camera and he kept a hand on it at all times, posing as the ever vigilant shutter-bug. Approaching Markova's station, they gave off an air of cavalier self-assurance common among journalists.

For her part, Markova heard them coming out of the elevator and turned from her PC monitor to face them. As they neared her desk, she rose gracefully to greet them. She was inwardly pleased to see McCoy peek over his sunglasses, as he drank in her statuesque physique.

"Good afternoon," Morgan began, missing her partner's reaction to the beautiful secretary. "We were sent to you by the girl at personnel. Miss Wright said that you might be able to help us."

"Ah, yes. It's Miss Rein and Mr. McCoy, isn't it?" She flashed a plastic smile at them. "Miss Wright just called to say you were on your way up."

"Right. I am a feature writer for Business Daily Magazine. McCoy is my photographer. We were hoping it might be possible to speak with Mr. Axel today?"

The artificial smile became regretful. "I'm sorry, Miss Rein, but surely you must realize that such a visit without a proper appointment is impossible. Mr. Axel's responsibilities do not allow for spontaneous interruptions."

"My apologies, Miss …ah?"

"Markova. Lilith Markova." Her eyes darted playfully to McCoy.

"Miss Markova. We had hoped to set this up accordingly, but only this afternoon were told that our deadline for the piece had been moved up. We have to finish our interviews and fly to Los Angeles within the next forty-eight hours."

Markova opened her hands in a gesture of hopelessness. "Alas, Mr. Axel left this morning for a weekend cruise with the Board of Directors and their guests. He won't be back until late Monday evening."

Morgan scratched her chin reflectively. There was something about Lilith

Markova that tickled her sensitive intuitions.

She allowed her inner sight to take over, masking her identity internally, lest the woman was someone whose powers might match her own. She had a marked feeling of danger.

"I see," she answered verbally. "Perhaps we might see Mr. Waitman then?"

"I'm sorry, Miss Rein, but .."

"He is also on the cruise."

"I'm afraid so. It is an annual event and most of the executive staff is in attendance."

Morgan decided to push. If her instincts were right, she would feel any reaction to her next words.

"I guess it's not our lucky day. What about Lucien Rein? Would he be available?"

Lilith's control was nearly flawless. Except for a tiny twitch at the corner of her mouth and an infinitesimal blink, she gave no sign of the surge of feeling that ran through her. Morgan, however, recognized it instantly. She had struck a nerve. A big one.

"I'm sorry," Lilith continued calmly. "There is no one on the executive staff by that name."

"Oh, I see. I must have misunderstood my source. Well, regardless, thank you for your time, Miss Markova. Maybe we can schedule an appointment with Mr. Axel the next time we are here for a future piece."

"Certainly. Simply be sure to call at least a week in advance. That way I'll be able to fit you in."

With that the meeting ended and Morgan and McCoy left. Markova gave Dancer a parting smile and went back to her PC. As the two reached the elevator, Morgan nudged him lightly in the ribs.

"Try to keep your mind on the job, Romeo."

McCoy blushed. "Er, of course. It was just a smile."

"A spider's smile, my dear Mr. Fly." The elevator doors opened and they walked in.

McCoy hit the lobby button.

"She knows Lucien."

Dancer looked back at the closed doors as if he might be able to peer through them with x-ray eyes. "Her? Are you sure?"

Morgan put her hands on her hips.

"What am I saying? Of course you are. But how? Is she an accomplice? An ally?"

"That's all I could pick up," Morgan frowned. "Just the fact that she in some way emotionally involved with him."

"Huh? You mean like.. lovers?"

"No. Lucien doesn't know what love means. There is something different. Bizarre. Miss Markova isn't at all what she appears."

"Is she a witch?"

"No. Of that I'm sure. But there is an aura of something unnatural about her. I just can't get a clear picture. Still, she's dangerous. Very, very dangerous."

"What? That girl?"

"Men! You are so easily deceived by outer appearances. A beautiful face and lots of cleavage and you go all goofy."

"That's a generalization and it's not fair."

"Look, Dancer, whatever else you might think, believe this. There is something unholy and deadly about that woman. We must find out what it is. What she is."

"Damn, but I don't like the sound of that. But you've convinced me." The lobby indicator blinked and the doors started to part. "You think she's a direct link to your brother?"

"Yes. I do." They emerged into the crowded ground floor lobby and Morgan lowered her voice. "If I'm right, she is a key that will help us unlock this entire business. And lead us to Lucien."

Dancer slipped his arms through hers and whispered, "So what's our next move?"

Morgan spotted a coffee shop across the street from building's front entrance and nodded towards it. "We'll stick around and follow Miss Markova when she leaves for home."

Dancer grinned, clearly enjoying the intrigue. "As Sherlock Holmes liked to quip, 'The plot thickens.'"

They made their way through the revolving doors.

Meanwhile, back at her desk, Lilith let the phone ring five times. Then she hung up, frustrated in her attempt to reach Lucien. Too late. The Master must have already left for the yacht.

She tapped her long nails on the desktop nervously, thinking about the Rein woman. Lilith had not been able to read any scent from her. That in itself was unusual. She had no idea who the woman was, but anyone who knew the Master's name could pose a threat to him.

As he was not available to deal with the problem, she was resolved to handle it herself. The Master might be angry, but if she succeeded, he would know fully how worthy she was of his trust. She knew she had special talents.

He had given them to her, himself.

* * * *

Darryl steadied himself against the railing as he moved through the darkness on deck. Lanterns set at intervals against the main bulkheads offered some illumination, but the inky night and the blackness of the waves seemed to swallow it up.

Stars peppered the visible bits of sky, and a half-moon scurried between wind-blown clouds, offered almost no light at all. Waitman was almost upon the silent figure on the foredeck before he saw him.

He almost uttered Lucien's name before he saw that this was not Wicker but Axel. He was gazing out over the waters of the Atlantic, lost in his thoughts.

"Why, Mr. Axel."

"Oh. Hello, Darryl. What's the matter? Get tired of the party crowd like me?"

"Well, yes, Sir. I also wanted to get a bit of air. It was so stuffy down there. I couldn't breathe."

The president glanced at him in the dim light, dismissing the answer with a shrug.

"Whatever. I'm glad you're here. It gives me the chance to talk to you about the matter I was discussing before in my office. This is important, Darryl. Very important indeed."

The old man reached into his dinner jacket and pulled out one of his Cuban cigars. "How about a light?"

Waitman found his gold-plated Ronson and stuck the flame under the tip of the expensive cigar. Through the tight mist, the light showed the scars and wrinkles cross-hatching Axel's weathered face.

"What is it you want to tell me, Mr. Axel?"

Axel puffed his cigar until the tip was glowing then blew out a cloud of smoke. "Have you been giving much thought to your future, Darryl?"

"No, Sir," he lied. He gritted his teeth and hung onto his self-control. "I can't say I have. I like what I'm doing."

"Hmm, I see. Well, you should." Another puff of smoke drifted up from his nostrils. Waitman coughed as the smoke whirled around his face.

"Sir, you, of all people, know how busy I have been of late. I just don't have the time to worry about tomorrow. I'm confident the future will take care of itself. It always has."

Another waft of smoke came at him. "All well and fine, but it's high time you did, my boy. The future is coming at us faster than you can imagine and there is a major role in it for you. You see, Darryl, I have plans for you in the organization. Big plans."

Here it comes, Waitman thought. He's leading me to the slaughter with all this mumbo-jumbo bullshit. As if I were some mindless sheep. Like Appleton. The old bastard!

He felt his blood growing warm, his heart speeding up. When Axel flung a heavy arm about his shoulders, Waitman felt a surge of anger. He wanted to shrug off the arm but he continued to keep himself in check. It was getting harder by the second.

Still, it was best to let him spell it all out. First.

"What sort of plans?" The question sounded curt, but it was the best he could manage at the moment.

Axel failed to notice. "We've been giving the European theater of operations a careful scrutiny lately. Things haven't been going so well over there as they did during our initial start-ups a few years ago. Some of the old Communist block countries are supporting nationalized construction outfits. Some are starting to protect their raw materials from outside takeover. Once they got a taste for democracy, its hard to get them to play along anymore. We're losing control and our stock holders aren't at all happy.

"The Board and I feel that we need a new Chief of Operations over there. A firm hand at the helm, as well as someone cultured in diplomatic circles to deal with the army of bureaucrats involved in all this."

Waitman was cold and unmoving. "I see. And you think that I'm the man for the job?"

"Exactly." Axel squeezed him like a favorite uncle. "What do you think, my boy? Big enough to fill those shoes?"

Waitman had all he could do to maintain his composure. He wanted to say something noncommittal, but his fury was bubbling up inside his chest. It would be smart to make some meaningless reply. One that would allow him to back away without a confrontation at this point in the game. One that would give him the time to assess his options. Sincerely and desperately, he wanted and intended to do just that, when he finally opened his mouth.

He was as shocked and stunned as Axel at what came from his lips instead. "I think it stinks to high heaven, you old fool!"

"What… did you say?" Axel's mouth opened like a fish pulled out of the water, gasping. He was clearly off balance by what he had just heard and was doubting his own ears.

"IT STINKS!" Darryl spat out. "That's what I said."

He pushed the arm from his shoulder and felt, at the same time, illogical panic welling up inside him. He was the one who was always in control. Mr. Calm and Collected. Yet here he was shouting, losing his temper. Blowing everything because of a sudden fit of primal anger, rather than playing it cool and crafty as was his trademark habit.

It had to stop before it was too late to repair the damage he had inadvertently caused. There was still time if he moved fast.

His mouth opened and once again betrayed him. "I'm not going to Europe! Not now! Not ever!"

"Darryl! What in the hell has gotten into you?" Axel's voice sounded breathless.

"A little touch of good old common sense, you bastard. I know damn well why you're shipping me off to Europe."

"What does that mean?" The old man's face was contorted with confusion.

"It means I have my own sources in the company. Sources loyal to me. I learned all about your little scheme to get me out of the picture."

Thomas Axel leaned back against the wet rail, trying to get as far from Waitman's fury as he could. The young man had gone mad. It was in his face and particularly in his eyes. They were large with lunacy! Suddenly the president of C.C.I. was scared.

He tried to reason with Waitman, at the same time slowly moving away from him physically. "Waitman, I suggest that you get control of yourself. You've obviously had too much to drink. Get hold of yourself before you say any more. Some things once said cannot be ignored."

He raised a hand and pointed a warning finger at Darryl's chest. It was false bravado. "Shut your mouth and get away from me. I don't put up with this kind of behavior from my subordinates! Another word and I'll.."

"What? Going ahead, say it, if you have the balls, you gutless wonder. You'll have me taken care of? Like our friend, Mr. Appleton and all the rest? Is that your threat?"

Waitman felt his head throbbing and his face growing hot. "Well, for your information, Boss Man, that isn't going to happen to me. I'm not some trusting stooge to be pushed aside as if I didn't amount to anything. I can damn well take care of myself. "And when someone pushes me, I push back!"

Axel bolted. He tried to push Waitman aside and get around him. "You're crazy, Waitman! Out of your freaking mind! Get out of my way!"

"NO!"

Everything fell apart. Waitman felt his last vestige of control dessert him.

"A piercing shriek emerged from his swollen lips."

His body went on automatic, leaving his helpless mind to boggle at what was happening.

His hands grabbed hold of Axel and threw him hard against the railing. The old man groaned. Waitman punched him in the face.. again.. and again. His first blow sent the cigar spinning into the black void beyond the rail.. a tiny spark of fire across the roiling darkness below.

Axel grunted in pain. The next blow smashed into his nose and the third collided with his temple. He tried to raise his arms to ward off the pummeling, but he was too late. Waitman was beyond stopping.

In his mind, Darryl was attacking the only obstacle in his path to power. All the violence of his unconscious drives was focused into the rain of blows that brought grunts of pain from the older man.

A cut appeared over Axel's right eye and it gleamed with seeping blood in the dim light. It stimulated Darryl as nothing ever had before. He felt a warmth in his loins. A perverse sexual thrill moved through him, as he let his basest and suppressed urges have free rein. His vision blurred with red, whether Axel's on his own, he neither knew or cared.

Axel's legs buckled beneath him and he started to fold. His head was a bloody ruin. Angry that his beating was ending, Waitman dragged him back up against the rail. He was so weak. So weightless in his grip.

Waitman laughed, jerked his victim up over the rail and flung him away like a discarded piece of junk. In the second before Axel cartwheeled into the beckoning deep, he realized his immediate end looming below him. A piercing shriek emerged from his swollen lips.

His body turned twice in mid-air before hitting the salt water. It splashed into the murky sea and was lost at once in the heavy wash of ship's twin propellers.

That was how easy it was to kill someone.

Waitman leaned against the slick rail, panting, his heart thudding heavily, his erection going flaccid as his adrenaline high came down in a beat. Killing Axel had given him an orgasm. He peered into the ship's wake but could see nothing. The darkness and the heavy swells were all there was to see.

The mad glow was subsiding. The euphoria that had gripped him was quickly releasing its hold.

"My, my! What a horrible accident!" The sardonic voice from behind spoke without any warning. Darryl jumped and spun about, his heart nearly freezing in mid-beat.

Lucien Wicker stood just behind him.

"Wicker! What are you doing here?"

"Why, we had a meeting set."

"Ah… yes, right." Wicker tried to straighten his tie. "Where were you?"

"I was unavoidably detained," the tall man said. He stepped beside Waitman and looked out over the Atlantic.

The ship was moving along steadily at twenty knots. The place where Axel had gone into the water was irrevocably left behind.

"What... did you see?" Waitman's voice was a raspy croak, barely able to pronounce the words. His heart had become a lead weight in his chest.

He had killed a man. Before a witness!

His stomach lurched and he fought down nausea. The taste of bile was foul in his mouth.

Wicker continued to look at the sea. His voice was insanely untroubled. "Why, Mr. Waitman, I saw exactly what just happened."

"You did!" Waitman held on to the rail.

Wicker turned to him. "I saw Mr. Axel come out on deck. He seemed a bit under the influence. He did drink a lot of wine at dinner, as I recall. He was unsteady on his feet.

"I think he may have felt ill, for he bent over the railing. Too far, I'm afraid. It was such a horrible accident. The ship heaved and he just pitched overboard. Just like that." Wicker snapped his fingers in front of Waitman's face. "It was over in a second."

The two men stared at each other through the dimness. Neither needed to say anything else for the moment. The understanding was clear enough to Waitman and at last he nodded in approval.

"Exactly, Wicker. Exactly what happened. We must tell the Captain at once."

Lucien chuckled. "Shall I go? You still seem to be... quite shaken. Especially after you tried so valiantly to save the poor man."

Darryl heaved a sigh of relief. "Yes. Go ahead. Do that. And Wicker..."

"Sir?"

"I won't forget your assistance. Your aid in this terrible tragedy will not go unrewarded."

The voice seemed amused as it drawled, "You are too kind." The thin figure moved away toward the cabin. "I'll find the Captain, now. Shall I?"

"Of course. Do that. And hurry!"

Wicker almost laughed as he walked off. The thing was done. His dominance over Waitman's mind and body had been masterful.

Yet it had required only the slightest nudge from his will to loose Waitman's long suppressed instincts. The years of careful control had been blown away like tissue-paper. And Waitman would never know that it had not been his own will that had murdered Thomas Axel. No one would ever know.

Wicker chuckled quietly. Waitman would be so grateful to him for this night's work. He would be putty, now, in skilled hands. Useful, for the time being.

Until it was time to move up another peg.

Wicker grinned into the darkness, his face a mask of satisfied mirth.

It was a fine night. A very fine night, indeed.

CHAPTER 18

It was almost six when Lilith came out of the C.C.I. complex and headed east through the pedestrian traffic. She was moving at fast clip. Concealed in the mass of people behind her followed Morgan and Dancer. They stayed a good distance behind for safety. Markova's height was helpful as McCoy had no problems keeping the top of her dark head in sight.

At the same time, Morgan opened her inner sensing and allowed her perceptions to define their quarry. This accomplished, she was confident she could home in on the woman anywhere in the city. Thus there was no real need to shadow her too closely.

That became a very crucial asset in short order. Keeping her march steady, the mysterious secretary rushed across a four lane intersection and down a subway ramp. In a flash she had disappeared into the bowels of the concrete tunnel.

Morgan and Dancer raced ahead, reaching the bottom of the stairwell just as the east-bound train was loading. They spotted Lilith entering a car. Quickly the pair hurried onto the platform and climbed into the one behind it.

They rode silently, the rocking of the car a background symphony to their private thoughts. Ten minutes later they were at the Kingsborough station. Markova, amidst the press of weary, anxious commuters, disembarked and went with the human flow towards the exit portal.

Once back in the open, she led them into a new high-rise condo complex, a very classy and lushly appointed modern day palace. Dancer was both impressed and puzzled as he and Morgan entered the lobby. It was filled with potted plants and mirrors and gave off tropical atmosphere. A three-tiered fountain at the center of the main concourse completed the garden illusion.

"Wow. This place is too much. I didn't know executive secretaries made this kind of dough."

Shhh!" Morgan hissed. "She's certainly in one of those elevators. I've got to concentrate to discover which one and then see where she gets off."

That was going to be a good trick, Dancer mused, looking at the row of six elevator doors. By the indicator lights, four were in motion; three of them going up. Markova had to be in one of those. Morgan closed her eyes and took a deep breath. Dancer felt a familiar creeping sensation at the base of his neck. No matter how hard he tried, he would never get used to this sort of thing. Ever.

Morgan's eyes opened. "Twenty-second floor. Room 22C. Let's go."

He sensed her edginess as the rode up the next empty box. Thankfully they were alone and could talk. Morgan seemed tense and wary. Almost frightened.

"Have you figured out what it was about her that bothered you? The thing you couldn't quite put your finger on?"

She shook her head. "No, and it's driving me wild. Stay on your toes, Dancer. Things may happen fast and furiously. Promise me."

"I promise, Princess. After that ride with the fireball, you don't have to tell me twice. I'll do whatever you say, any time and any place."

She smiled, though grim lines still tugged at her mouth. "I just want you to stay alive."

"Not a bit more that I want for me to stay alive. On that we are in complete accord."

They arrived at the right floor. Cautiously they moved along the carpeted corridor until they located the door to 22 C.

Morgan rapped sharply.

There was a short pause. Then steps sounded on the other side and the door opened a crack. Lilith Markova peered out at them through the space allowed by the chain.

"Miss Rein! What are you doing here? What do you want?"

The white witch was pleased. The woman was genuinely surprised and off balance. Now she had to appear both innocent and persuasive. "I'm so sorry to bother you again, Miss Markova. I realize this is a tremendous imposition."

"That's an understatement," Markova's stare went from Morgan to McCoy, sizing them up.

"Yes, I know," Morgan concurred readily. "But we need to talk you privately. It's urgent we do so."

Lilith thought for a moment, her long eyebrows coming together. Then she smiled and loosed the chain. Suddenly she looked insufferably smug, Morgan thought. The spider and the fly analogy came back to her again. Only this time they were actually entering her parlor.

"Very well. Come in. Would either of you like something to drink?" The polite cordiality was almost convincing.

As they stepped past her, Morgan saw that Lilith was dressed the same as they had last seen her, except now she was in stocking feet. She gave the apartment a cursory glance and saw that it was richly furnished as one would expect. Lots of valuable furniture, original paintings and other priceless adornments. Miss Markova was well kept.

McCoy took note of Lilith latching the door behind them. Looking at her, an alluring, sexual creature, it was difficult to understand why she should suddenly appear menacing to him. His imagination was working overtime.

"Thank you, but no," Morgan answered for both of them. "We need to ask you few questions about your work at C.C.I."

"I thought we did that this afternoon," Markova said, taking a stance between them and the door. She folded her hands over her chest and stamped her foot on the floor. "There's really nothing else I can tell you."

Morgan and Dancer faced her, shoulder to shoulder. The time for chicanery was over.

"We have some questions about your personal connections with certain people at the company," Morgan fired back.

"What? Now you go too far. My personal affairs are no concerns of yours or anybody else for that matter."

"Not even when murder is involved those affairs?"

Lilith didn't even blink. "Murder? What on earth are you talking about?"

"Oh, I think you know exactly what I'm talking about, Lilith. I think you have a complete understanding of what has been going on at C.C.I. for a long time now."

As she talked, Morgan moved in closer. Dancer wished he could feel as calm as she looked. There was a strange atmosphere in the room.

Morgan pressed her attack. "And I think you know where Lucien is. In fact I think you know him quite well."

Lilith's face contorted. "See here! I told you that I don't know anybody by that name!"

Morgan stepped up and slapped her hard across the face. "LIAR! You reek of his foulness!"

Lilith's head snapped around. Her eyes narrowed, the pupils contracting into yellow points of hatred.

"Witch! How dare you speak the Master's name!"

Like a maddened beast, she leapt at Morgan, long nails extended. With a blinding swing, those nails raked a track across Morgan's neck and she screamed. Lilith grabbed a handful of her hair and with super-human strength propelled her backwards into McCoy. Caught off balance, they fell backwards. Lilith laughed. As Morgan tried to get off her dazed companion, Lilith once again took hold of her hair and pulled her up. Her face had started to change, skin darkening, eyes blazing and her teeth were all becoming needle sharp.

"What's the matter, witch!" she snarled. "Cat got your tongue?"

Fighting her pain, Morgan reached out and took hold of the woman's shoulders to steady herself, at the same time bringing her right foot off the floor with all the force she could muster. Her knee slammed into Lilith's jaw, causing her to loose her grip on Morgan's hair as she rocketed backwards into the front door. It cracked at impact.

On the rug, McCoy heard the sound and looked up in time to see Markova, or more precisely the thing she had become, spring off the damaged wood and fly back at Morgan with lightning reflexes.

"MORGAN! LOOK OUT!"

Morgan jumped to her right as the creature hurtled past, and drove a hard backfist into her ribs. The were-cat somersaulted in mid-air and landed in a crouch, her arms waving before her in frustration. The nails were now claws, as tufts of fur materialized along the forearms. They were matched on her feet as well, where they ripped into the rug for purchase.

Morgan gulped. She put aside her fear. There was no time for it now. Only defense and survival.

The Lilith-thing started to move around the alcove, circling. Morgan did likewise, skirting a huge, leather sofa. The she-cat monster hissed between her teeth, head swiveling in search of an opening. As Morgan moved backward, Lilith suddenly swept a plant from a hanger beside her head and hurled it straight into her face.

Morgan went tumbling over the sofa and out of sight.

For a second, the beast was elated with her throw. Stunned, the meddlesome witch would now be easy to finish off. But she had forgotten the man. She twisted about, her rage returning.

Dancer, still stunned, was in a crouch, getting to his feet, when she came at him. He'd seen Morgan go down and was doing his best to come to her rescue. Suddenly the world exploded in front of him in the form of the slashing she-cat.

Her nails aimed for his eyes and he shot up an arm to protect his face. Claw like talons ripped into his leather sleeve. They razored through the thick material and cut the skin beneath.

Grimacing, he threw her off and looked down at his torn jacket. He could feel the blood on his arm. Then she was at him again, as if she had bounced from the floor like a rubber ball. Her feline eyes were glaring, now. They were complete yellow slits.

Slash after slash, she came on, panting. Her mouth open, her lips curled back, her tongue sliding over feral teeth… God! Her tongue was forked!

A black-belt in karate, McCoy lashed out with a side-kick that caught her in the stomach and doubled her. Then, before she could move, he brought the same foot back and connected with her head. She went down in a sprawl and he took a breath. Then she screeched and was up again. This kitty had lots more than nine lives. But he didn't.

He backed off, hands up to block her next assault.

"Bastard!" she hissed. "I am going to rip your heart out and eat it slowly."

Something in McCoy snapped. That was the last straw! First the fireball that chased him through city streets. Then a dunk in the river where he nearly drowned. And now this two-bit horror-queen with claws! Enough was enough. He turned his shoulder to her, ducked his head low, and drove into her like a football tackle.

The collision knocked Lilith temporarily off-balance. Enough for him to wind up his right arm and punch her squarely in the face. It was his best shot. It should have knocked her out cold. Instead it only jolted his ego and bruised his knuckles. The blow didn't even rock her.

The nightmarish face contorted with laughter. One of her hands came up and caught his throat. With no apparent effort, she lifted him off the floor. Steely fingers tightened, cutting off his wind, as he fastened his hands onto them. Frantically he tried to pry them loose but all his strength could not budge them.

He brought his knee up hard into her stomach but this time she was ready. She slapped it away and maintained her hold on his throat. He kicked again with the same results. He knew her vice-like fingers would crush his larynx, unless he could shake her off. Deprived of air, his vision began to blur and he felt a pounding in his temples. If he didn't get air into his lungs, it would be all over. The claw tips cut into his flesh.

But Dancer wouldn't give up. His third kick hit her chest and thrust her back. Her hand opened and he fell free. Gulping air, he tried to clear his sight. Everything was a haze of fuzzy shapes. Something hard slapped his side. The camera! Hastily McCoy pulled off the camera that was somehow still slung around his neck and spun it over his head like a sling.

Come on Kitty-Goliath! Come and get it!

When she came at him again, he swung the camera into the side of her head with all his remaining strength, plus the centrifugal force added by the swing. Good old physics!

She screamed! He had actually hurt her. Good.

Suddenly her hands shot forth with terrible speed and jerked the camera from his hands. It went flying and something out of sight crashed with its impact. Oh well, it was a good idea while it lasted.

The claws were at his jacket again.

This time they left ribbon cuts down his chest. Dancer fell backward and went down, the beast on top of him.

Morgan, all but forgotten, pulled herself up, using the sofa for bracing. Her legs were wobbly and her left cheek and her forehead were bleeding. The rivulets of blood stained her neck and blouse. Dancer, on his back and fending off the enraged cat-fiend, was startled by her appearance.

"LILITH!" Morgan cried. "Come after me."

The creature's head twisted around at the sound of her voice.

"I challenge you! My powers against yours!"

The thing that had been Lilith Markova sprang off Dancer and landed on its feet, perfectly balanced. Dancer coughed, the pressure off his chest a blessed relief.

The she-cat threw back her head and roared, then she lunged at Morgan with her uncanny speed. Even seeing it, McCoy couldn't believe anyone could move that fast. It was impossible. But she did.

Only this time Morgan was ready for her.

The witch's hands wove a pattern in the air between them. Lilith ran into it at full momentum, stopping with shocking suddenness, spread-eagled against what seemed to be nothing but air. An invisible wall seemed to have sprung up in front of Morgan.

The witch made another pattern, this time different. Then she pointed both her index fingers at her adversary.

"Return to the unholy elements that formed you! Go back, Beast.. to nothingness!"

Lilith's golden eyes widened. Her body began to convulse wildly. So violent were her gyrations that it looked her bones might crack from the strain being inflicted upon them.

"NOOO!" She jumped toward Morgan again, only to be repulsed even more dramatically than before. This time there was a loud slapping sound, as if her body had hit a giant, transparent pillow. She began caterwauling in a frustrated tantrum.

A wisp of smoke rose from her skin. All the skin that was exposed started turning blue and chalky colored. Lilith stopped screaming and looked at her smoking arms and legs. More smoke rose from her pores. Blisters began to form. She seemed to be burning up from the inside.

"Wickedness formed you." Morgan's final exhortation was unforgiving. "Now return to bodiless evil."

Lilith's clothing began to smolder, then burst to flames. She ripped her blouse off, her skirt.

Dancer rose onto one elbow and shook his head, sure he was hallucinating due to the choking he had just endured. None of this tableau before could be real!

The beast looked up at Morgan through the fire that was quickly consuming her. The warped mouth opened. Words tumbled out. "The Master will destroy! He will find you, Witch, and you will die! You cannot defeat him. YOU WILL DIE...!"

Patches of the body were blackening. A stench filled the apartment as the thing began flaking, crumbling. The creature tore at its own skin in agony.

Turning its head toward the window, it laughed madly and ran full-speed toward it. Some of the unholy quickness she had used before sent her charred body into the thick glass with shattering force. The noise was tremendous and the cat woman was lacerated by hundreds of broken shards as she crashed through. So much that her body leaked streamers of dark blood as it hurled to its doom, far below on the street.

Dancer rose slowly. He looked at Morgan, the empty window, down at his ripped leather jacket.

"Well, there goes my desire to ever see CATS!"

CHAPTER 19

It was midnight by the time the Seaspray returned to her berth. Waiting for her were representatives of the Coast Guard, Homicide Detectives and dozens of TV and print reporters. The crowd on the dock looked like a festive reception gathering awaiting the arrival of some superstar or foreign dignitary.

The executive members of the C.C.I. Board of Directors were not at all pleased with the publicity. It was obvious that an enterprising someone, either at Police Headquarters or the Coast Guard station, had made a few dollars tipping off the press about the tragic drowning accident that had claimed the life of Thomas Axel.

Jack Conover, the senior director, took charge immediately upon learning off Axel's loss, while they were homeward bound. Calling an impromptu meeting in the luxury craft's main lounge, he cautiously suggested that everyone remain tight-lipped when getting back to the city. He, and Darryl, would handle the police and whoever else would be waiting for them. Second guessing the possibility of the news-hounds being on the scene, Conover also put together a small, formal statement that would suffice until there was time to regroup and assess the company's position in the aftermath of the president's death.

This business quickly settled, Conover then took Waitman aside and privately informed him that for the time being, he would be in charge of day-to-day operations. He was told, in no uncertain terms, that the Board was counting on him to pull this off.

Although bolstered by these words of encouragement, it was a shaken Darryl who later met with the police officers in the same lounge, once they dropped anchor. Although he was not suspected of causing Axel's death, he quivered internally all through the questioning. One of the detectives mentioned having taken Lucien Wicker's eyewitness account and went as far as to call Waitman a hero of sorts. It was at this point that he started to relax, realizing that with Wicker's corroboration, his story had been accepted as fact. He had gotten away with murder.

Yet the thing had happened too fast. Too irrationally. At the center of his life and character had been firm control of himself and his environment. That maintenance of propriety had been shattered in a single act of reckless abandonment. One that could very well have cost him everything. His position, his ambition, and goals. Even his very life.

Not until he was safely inside his own apartment did he have the time to wonder at Lucien Wicker's instant willingness to cover for him. Perhaps the man, being really nothing but a hit man, for all his class and aloofness, had feared for his own well being. With the knowledge he possessed of Wicker's crimes, it was to the man's best interest that he remain uncompromised and free. Was he afraid of what Darryl might say to the authorities if he were apprehended and have recourse to plea-bargain?

No. Waitman dismissed that thought at once. Any testimony he might give against Wicker for the Appleton and Hines murders would sound like the ravings of a madman. Wicker was well aware of that. No, whatever his motivations, that was not one of them.

He poured himself a tall glass of whiskey, threw a few pieces of ice into it and then, returning to his den, turned on the giant, 60 inch television. Even though his set was always tuned to the headline news channel, he was jarred when the digitized image clarified into the face of Thomas Axel. Darryl almost gagged. Then he realized it was an old photo being used as a backdrop while the attractive, brunette anchor was rattling off the news of his sudden death at sea.

Darryl dropped back into his over stuffed lounge recliner and, using control knots set in the lamp table to his right, he slowly brought up the volume.

"…Axel then was the company's third C. E. O. since its creation thirty years ago. His strong hand and astute business savvy made him one of the most powerful men of our times."

A video clip taken at the pier smoothly replaced the image of former C.C.I. president. There was Jack Conover talking with the press and Coast Guard people, giving them his prepared statement. As the camera shot panned the room, Darryl saw himself standing in the rear with several other board members. He took a sip from his strong drink and grinned. He didn't look too bad on the tube.

Granted he looked a bit shaken, but not overly so. Just a bit out of tune, like a good, loyal vice-president should look at such a sad occasion.

As Conover was wrapping up his brief comments, he promised that C.C.I. would make announcements as to the now vacant chair as soon as the board had chosen and confirmed the right candidate. That made him laugh aloud. There was no question that he was the only viable choice. No one else was as involved with every day operations. No one else knew the entire scope of C.C.I.'s vast world wide interests and manipulations. To elect someone else would have been folly. Conover had suggested as much when they'd parted.

"Go home and get some rest, Darryl. You're most likely going to need it in the days ahead."

His meaning had been subtle but clear. Once the formal protocols were dealt with, some kind of public memorial service for the old man, and a vote by the governing board, the door would be open to him to step up.

He swished whiskey around in his mouth to dampen it. "Darryl Waitman, President of C.C.I." Now didn't that sound sweet.

As the sports news came up, he switched on the mute button. He suddenly had the urge to share his euphoria with someone. There was only one person in the world he could do that with, other than Lucien Wicker. Lilith. Yes, he could talk with Lilith.

That would be safe.

As he picked up the receiver on the stand, he wondered if it was too late to see her. It was well past one a.m. as his fingers dialed her number. She'd probably be annoyed at being awakened. But, that would change when he told her what had transpired. About the awful accident, that is. He had no naivete about speaking over the telephone. A veteran in the world of industrial espionage, he never took anything for granted. Including the security of civilian telephone lines.

Her phone was ringing. For a second he remembered their last encounter and the idea of seeing her became stronger.

But the phone kept ringing. After the fifth jangle, he heard the distinct click of her answering machine. Then her taped voice came one, instructing the caller to leave the usual information bits. He dropped the phone back in its cradle, dejected.

Where was she? Had she turned off her ringer so that the machine would take calls and still allow her to sleep undisturbed? Or was she out somewhere?

She's a beautiful girl, he thought. And it is Saturday night. There is no reason for her to be at home on a Saturday night. That's unreasonable to expect.

On the giant screen clips of several baseball games flashed on and off. Suddenly the phone, still in his grasp, rang and he jumped.

Could it be her? Recovering, he picked it up and again.

"Hello?"

"Waitman." That was Wicker's voice. The 'Sir' and the servile note were gone from it. Why was he calling?

Agitated, Darryl cleared his throat and steadied his voice before speaking. "Yes. What is it, Wicker?"

"I wanted to make certain you reached home safely and are not having any.. delayed reactions… to your shocking experience. I also wanted to ask you to name me your vice-president after you move into top spot."

"What? What are you saying?"

"That would be a convenient thing for both of us. Don't you agree?" The threat behind the words was not audible, but Darryl's guilt made it ring through brazenly.

He bit his lower lip and turning his head, looked out the window. Lights glimmered on the skyscrapers across the street. The night was moving as if in slow motion, so long did it seem to him now. The caller on the other end wasn't making it any faster for him.

He gripped the receiver until his knuckles ached. He wanted another drink. "I suppose.. so. That might be sensible. I haven't had time to make definitive plans yet. You must understand, I can't move too fast. But I had asked Axel to take you into the company."

"Is that so?" There was a mocking note present.

"Yes, it is. I always felt that your unique gifts had a lot to offer us. That we, the company that is, use you most profitably. Haven't I demonstrated that in our previous dealings?"

"Yes. You have." The voice was now amused. "Then I will see you on Monday morning. At C.C.I. Sleep well, Mr. President."

Darryl shuddered. He didn't know quite why, but he felt chilled, full of renewed dread. He tried to reason that it was only a normal reaction to his action on the boat. But that didn't really help. There was something about Wicker that bothered him. He was more than a cold-blooded killer. That was something he would prefer to leave alone. Some secrets were better left untouched, if a person wanted to stay healthy.

Darryl finished his drink and was starting to get up to make a second when the news program flashed the picture of a city street filled with police cruisers and throng of night citizens. Curious, Waitman reached down and reactivated the sound.

"..victim supposedly went through her plate glass window and fell to her death. Police have yet to reveal the name of the deceased, pending further investigations into the incident."

Gruesome, Waitman thought. It certainly was a night for foul play. He chuckled at his own sick joke and went into the kitchen to refill his glass. Hopefully the alcohol would help him fall asleep. It was what he needed now, more than anything else. He was tired of the myriad thoughts floating around in his head. The images of Axel spinning off into open air before plunging to watery end. His high pitched scream slicing over the water. Darryl wanted it all gone. Out of his thoughts forever.

If he had to get drunk to do that, he would. Then, perhaps, he might be able to sleep. A long, peaceful repose. Without dreams.

CHAPTER 10

Morgan Rein realized she and McCoy had very little time to exit Lilith's apartment before the police arrived. Hurriedly she shoved him into the plush bathroom and, using a wet face cloth, cleaned up most of the visible scratches on both of them. There was a bottle of disinfectant and she threw it into her purse. Their next stop was the bedroom where Morgan hastily rummaged through a long walk-in closet and found a light blue pull-over sweater. Removing her jacket, she tugged the garment down over her shredded blouse. Meanwhile McCoy's own scavenging paid off in a large, dirty green laundry-bag into which he stuffed his ruined leather jacket.

Morgan caught his look of resignation as he tightened the neck of the bag then hoisted it over his shoulder with one hand.

"You can always get another jacket," she reminded him.

"But not another life," he finished. "Okay, let's get the hell out of here!"

The witch would have liked to stay and give the place a complete search. She knew the secret of Lucien's whereabouts had to be here somewhere. But to risk being apprehended would be foolish. They would just have to find her brother another way.

Once in the hall, they took the elevator and rode down to the third floor.

"No sense going out the front door," McCoy explained as he ushered her off. He looked about and found the door leading to the stairwell. "This way. Come on."

The stairs led them to the rear of the hotel and an empty back alley. As they moved out towards the main thoroughfare, they heard the wail of approaching police cars. Coming out from the darkness, they beheld a large crowd of pedestrians all gathered over something hidden from their view. Morgan wondered how much of Lilith Markova was still recognizable. She could imagine the puzzle her remains would pose to the authorities. It wasn't every day a real live.. er, make that real dead, cat-woman ended at the city morgue.

Within seconds two black and white patrol cars arrived and the uniformed officers dove into the crowd, barking orders and trying to create some semblance of order. The first cop to push through the crowd and view the body took a half step back and gasped, speechless. One of his buddies joined him and exclaimed, "Holy shit! What a mess!"

"It don't even look human?" the first cop finally found his voice. "Better get a blanket from the car and cover it up."

As his friend went to comply, an ambulance pulled up and the medics were quick to move into action although there was very little for them to do. The police quickly set up a cordon to keep the onlookers away from what was now an official crime scene. Hopefully detectives would be on their way to take care of matters from here. The last thing the blues wanted to do was to have to deal with news reporters and TV crews. Of course the crowd continued to grow as the commotion grew more complex with each passing minute.

It was the opportunity Morgan and Dancer had been waiting for. They walked past, along the outskirts of the gathering, showing only what they hoped was normal curiosity. No one paid them the least bit of attention.

Once down the street a few blocks, they took to the subway again. Luckily the car they boarded was deserted and Morgan was able to use the disinfectant. She dabbed some on a handkerchief in her purse and applied it liberally to her neck wounds. Dancer had a few deep scratches where Lilith had choked him. Satisfied with her rudimentary first aid, she capped the bottle and rested her head back. Ten minutes later they were safely back at Dancer's hideaway loft.

It felt like a refuge. Morgan flung her purse onto one of the box-cupboards and turned to Dancer, who was already putting on his ever-ready kettle for coffee.

"We've got to clean those cuts again," she advised. "With something really strong this time. Do you have any carbolic?"

He fished in one of his boxes and brought out a brown bottle.

"I keep it handy. Sometimes I handle really strange stuff. I like to make certain that I don't bring any infection home with me. Here."

They stood under the strong light in the kitchen area while Morgan went over his face, chest, back and arms. She swabbed deeply into the cuts with the abrasive chemical.

It wasn't any fun at all. Dancer squirmed and cursed beneath her touch and she smiled sympathetically.

"You'll have your chance for revenge in a minute. Just grit your teeth. I'm almost done."

Next Morgan peeled off the sweater and torn blouse to allow McCoy access to her own cuts. Standing before him, her torso naked except for her bra, she was suddenly very self-conscious.

Dancer looked from her eyes to her bosom and actually blushed.

"Kindly keep your eyes where they belong. I am not a corrupter of virgin males."

It was just enough to break the awkwardness and Dancer laughed as he began washing her cuts.

"I'll bet you're something in a bikini."

"Like I'd ever have the nerve to wear one." She winced slightly.

"You don't have a bikini! I'm shocked!"

"Having dirty old men ogle you when you're at the beach is an experience I'd just as soon forego, thank you very much."

"How about dirty young men? I"m a great ogler. Really!" He pulled his hand away and dropped the cloth on the counter to signify he was finished.

Morgan reached up and kissed his cheek. "I'll keep that in mind. Thanks."

"My pleasure. How about some coffee?"

"At this hour, I shouldn't. But who can sleep! Okay. But not too strong."

As McCoy started spooning instant coffee from a jar, Morgan went to change into something comfortable. By the time he had poured the hot water and set the cups on the counter, she was back wearing a black sweatshirt and loose fitting jogging pants of the same color. She added sugar and milk to her cup then sat down on the sofa, stretching her long legs outward in a relaxed posture. Dancer took his own mug and sank into a chair facing her.

They sat with smarting wounds, drinking quietly. For a long while neither said a word. They enjoyed a companionable silence, relaxing, mentally reviewing what had happened.

McCoy finished his coffee and set the cup on the floor. He leaned forward. "So where do I start here? I've got so many questions and don't know which one to ask first?

"I haven't had time to really think about what's been happening. Been too busy just staying alive. But now, after that ...cat thing... I need some kind of answers."

"Of course you do," she agreed, putting down her own empty cup and curleding her legs up beneath her. "I am surprised at just how well you've been able to deal with things to this point. Without craft knowledge or training... it's remarkable. I suspect you have some inborn instinct."

"What? You mean ..like yours?"

"Dancer, I believe everyone with a soul has some magic ability. Whether it be a strong imagination or intuition. Whatever you want to call it. Yours seems to be an inbred adaptability, which is really very rare."

"Really. I prefer to call it gut fear."

Even though he tried to mask it with his humor, Morgan respected his modesty. "Anyway, ask whatever you want. Our discipline doesn't inhibit inquiry, as the Dark one does. We appreciate other seekers after the truth and actively encourage sincere studies. Although we do tend to keep a low profile, as you can probably understand.

"So what do you want to know?"

"That waving stuff you did with your hands? How did you learn to do that? Tell me how you were taught. About the things you do and believe in. And while you're at it, how about a little more on Lucien and his kind of magic. How's that for starters?"

"Fair enough. But make yourself comfortable. It's a long story."

"My favorite kind. Beside, after tonight's bout, I'm too keyed up to sleep."

"Me too. Okay. It really all started in Scotland, where I went to live with Mother Kalavela....."

Dancer sank back into his chair and let her words carry him along.

* * * *

Scotland was very different from Paris. Mother Kalavela lived in a cottage that was tucked into a hillside above a swift burn that tore along to its adjoining loch below. Though the spot seemed remote, and there were no close neighbors, it was only a short drive from the bustling town below, where several of the witch's fellows lived and worked.

Around the cottage was a well-fenced garden. There Mother Kalavela had brought rich soil from many locales. Some of her beds of herbs and flowers were tucked against the stone wall surrounding the garden. Many less hardy ones lived inside a plastic encased greenhouse.

Now, so late in the year, the outside beds were blackened and dead-looking, though Kalavela assured the city-bred child that the plants would rise green from the soil come spring.

"... Mother peered through her glasses and told the child it was her talent feeding the hot point."

Morgan loved the greenhouse. Inside its warm, humid walls grew climbing vines, vegetables for the table, and a profusion of multi-colored flowers. There were also odd little plants that Kalavela seemed to tend with unusual care.

"The edibles are delicious. The flowers are all very well. But these are part of the stuff of my… our …craft, child. Those less strongly gifted than your family in the dramatic forms of witchcraft turn to gentler things."

Mother, in a weathered cotton apron and wearing soft leather gloves, pointed to individual stalks with consummate care that her pupil not miss a single fact.

"Look. Here are angelica, sweet basil, and betony. See how unassuming they are? Like weeds, almost. Yet they form a part of our armament against sickness and evil. It is important that you understand these things, Morgan."

Wide eyed, the seven year old bobbed her head in assent. She did not want to ever disappoint Mother.

"Good. In time you will learn all about them. And about many other things besides."

Thus she had. Through long days, she studied in the parlor that Kalavela had turned into a combination library and study. It was soon apparent that the girl had a thirst for knowledge and she drank it up like an greedy sponge. Languages, history, the beginnings of several sciences, mathematics.

But most of all she studied logic. Clear seeing and clear thinking were necessary for the arts she must master. Over and over, Mother Kalavela stressed the fact that practitioners of the darker arts wanted nothing so much as for all the world to think unclearly. They wanted people to be muddled by prejudice and self-interest. On the White trod the pure and difficult path of rationality.

One rainy afternoon, while drinking herb tea and knitting in her thick, oak-wood rocker, Mother waved her silver needle about like a conductor's baton as she lectured.

"Many make the mistake of thinking that faith in God requires no thought, only an emotional commitment. That may suffice for those who aren't capable of much thought, but for one who intends to work for good, who must put life itself into jeopardy time after time, battling against what is cruel and destructive, that is simply not enough!"

Her bifocals had slipped and she nudged them back over the bridge of her nose before continuing. "One must understand what he or she is doing. Why she is doing it. Without distraction from the selfish or the prejudiced or the inhibited sides of her nature."

She held up her needle before Morgan's face and suddenly the tip began to glow like a tiny branding iron. The girl was instantly mesmerized. Behind the golden glow, Mother peered down at her through her glasses and told the child it was her talent feeding the hot point.

"Thought is our greatest weapon! Logic is the thing that sharpens our thought to its finest edge." Just as quickly, the glow faded and the needle was once again dodging in and out of the yarn like a dancing bee. "Remember that, Morgan. You must keep the blade free of soil."

The talents she had inherited from her mother's family were grasped eagerly at the teachings of the elderly matron. The girl took to these sessions with enthusiasm, feeling immediately at ease with her own inner gifts. She quickly absorbed every nugget of information and instruction Kalavela had to offer. All too soon she matured, filling out both physically and intellectually with knowledge and understanding.

As fast as her body grew, in those teen years, her mind and will kept pace. She toiled at her books, worked in the greenhouse among the spicy scents of herbs and the heady fragrance of the exotic flowers. When she walked along the steep path beside the burn, or over the moors in the uplands, she mulled over the things she was learning, chief of which was the person she was becoming. It was a ferociously exciting time in her life.

Yet the first time there was a coven held at Kalavela's home, Morgan was terribly nervous. Almost afraid.

So many new things had come into her consciousness that she felt herself to be a kettle boiling over with half-cooked ideas. She was afraid of seeming ignorant to the practiced witches.

And deep within her evolving mind there was a remnant of fear... fear of another sort of witchery. A deadly kind that had been aimed at her with fatal intent.

Kalavela understood much of what she was feeling, Morgan knew, as she stood beside the old woman, welcoming their guests. It was evening. Early summer had warmed the day, but dusk, in the high country, was cool.

Both of them were wrapped in tartan shawls, as they waited behind the grilled gate in the stone fence, watching figures toil up the crooked path. Though a good road led to the rear of the cottage, nobody ever drove to meetings of the coven. Winter or summer, they walked, so as to remain as inconspicuous as possible. It was their way and such traditions were not held lightly.

Morgan thought that nobody could have found a more innocent seeming group of people. There were four stout women of middle age, whose demeanor breathed the very air of homely comfort as they greeted their hostess and went into the house to relieve themselves of their burdens of homemade bread and pots of preserves and still-warm plumcake.

There were three men, obviously brothers, whose names Morgan didn't hear. Yet she watched them all evening with something akin to wistfulness. They reminded her of her father.

Two young women, hardly more than girls themselves, brought with them light laughter and the scent of cologne as they moved through the garden. They smiled at Morgan openly, as if recognizing in her the bonds of youthful sisterhood, a kindred spirit. It made her feel wonderful. Accepted.

Last of all came a very old, extremely stooped man. He struggled up the incline with the aid of a cane as crooked as he was.

Forgetting her shyness, Morgan ran down the path to meet him and help him with the climb.

"Could I lend you my shoulder, Sir?" she asked, a bit timidly. She stared up into the age-tested visage beneath his wide hat brim.

She was startled when her eyes met a pair of vibrant, young eyes, sparkling with vitality in a face that was a roadmap of wrinkles. So odd was the combination that she stood, staring openly, forgetting what she had come for.

There was a dry chuckle. "Thank you, Lassie. Yes, a young shoulder under my hand might make the way a bit easier at that. I be Andrew. Andrew Wyatt, at your respectful service, Ma'am." The eyes were teasing her.

Morgan felt herself blushing. "I'm Morgan Rein. Mother Kalavela's student, Sir. I'm sorry if I was rude. You are so young, it surprised me."

He laughed heartily. Then he set his hand, rather heavily, on her shoulder and got his stiff legs into motion once more.

"Aye, Lassie, I be young, indeed. A pity these old bones of mine don't know it. But inside, I be made up of springtime and sunshine for sure. 'Tis not so many young ones would notice that."

Obscurely complimented, Morgan trudged sturdily uphill. Indeed, she could feel through her shoulder that he was being helped by her presence.

Kalavela turned to walk with them from the gate to the house. "Greetings, Andrew," she welcomed cordially. Beside the oldster, she looked positively spry by comparison.

"I'm happy to see you out, this chilly evening. I had feared you might not be up to it."

"Ha," he snorted. "And let you hold the coven wi'out me? Tcha, Madam! Ye ken that as long as I am able to set one stubborn foot before the next, I'll come. When I canna, ye'll know to pray for my departed soul."

Kalavela stopped before the front door and touched his arm, very gently. Almost reverently, Morgan thought. "And then, Master Andrew, we will pray and rejoice to see you so well on your way, free of the burdens of the flesh. But it will be our loss, make no mistake."

She turned to Morgan. "This is my own teacher, Child. Just as I taught your mother and now you, Master Andrew enlightened me, when I was scarcely more than a sprout. A very bewildered one at that, with talents she could not hope to fathom and that no one about her would admit could even exist."

She sighed at the memories. "I know in a very painful way what it is like to go untutored for too long, with the world as it is. Master Andrew untangled my fears, with gentle ways. He set straight my misunderstandings and dispelled my confusion by putting the strands of knowledge in order and then setting them into my hands.

"I wanted for you to meet him, for he is, we believe, the greatest warlock of the White persuasion in our times."

Morgan looked again at the frail old fellow still holding on to her shoulder and cane for support. Anyone less like a witch of any sort she had never seen. Then those merry eyes twinkled again and he cackled with a robust laughter.

"She be thinking that I dinna look to be any sort of magician," he said to Kalavela as if reading Morgan's thoughts. "Little do I blame her. But, Morgan Rein, let this be a lesson to ye. Dinna judge by the outside o' the package. What's inside it may often surprise ye."

Morgan responded with a polite nod. She was too young to know just how well that lesson would come to serve her in the years ahead.

Once all were in the cottage, the group sorted itself out into a round dozen. "Thirteen is the number of the Dark," Mother had explained to her protege. "Twelve is the number we use. Come, now, and sit with us."

Much that was said that night, Morgan didn't understand until years later. The meeting reminded her, more than anything, of Report Day at her Paris school. Each of the ordinary looking members of the coven gave a brief resume of his or her doings for the past several weeks. They made no great thing of their achievements. They merely put them on the record, as things to be checked off as completed, of no more concern to the group.

Yet as the girl listened, it became increasingly clear to her that these normal-seeming people were living on two levels. On the first, they had families, work, and all the ordinary interests of other folks.

Yet added to those, superimposed on them, so to speak, were the activities of the second level. These were tasks and missions that their peers in the small community didn't dream of in their wildest imaginings. Subtle, important things like the healing of minds that had been touched by sickness or the Dark. And they did these things without those they helped ever being aware of what was done to them.

Beth, one of the two young women rose. "I have completed my assigned task," she began. "The child-killer in Edinburgh has confessed his crimes to the police and is now in custody." She turned to her lovely colleague and smiled. "I had the help of Rose, here, and of Master Andrew for the concentration of Power. We managed it without having to make the long trip to the city."

Morgan was stunned. She had read in the newspapers that Mother received of the terrible things happening in the capitol metropolis. There had been dreadful apprehension in Edinburgh for months. Three children had been found strangled, one after another, in the same four-square-mile district. The horror had captured her fearful attention and she'd followed the daily news accounts with morbid fascination. She had seen, in her fertile mind, the frantic terror of the helpless victims and the grief and devastating shock of their families, even through the carefully impersonal wording of the articles.

Now this delicate young lady in a flowered frock claimed to have made that murderer surrender to the authorities. Without altering in the slightest her normal, daily routine!

It was an exciting and life changing thought. Up until this moment, Morgan had never contemplated too deeply the ultimate uses of her skills. The fascinating tricks were enough for her childish fancy, to justify learning them. Now a new dimension of her talent opened up before her like the parting curtains of a theater.

One could play an important, if unacknowledged, role in the world. Things could be made to happen that would alter people's lives for the better.

Thus inspired, she concentrated hard on each succeeding report. Not all were so dramatic, of course. Some merely smoothed the aches and pains of the old or calmed the anxieties of young. Some corrected small errors in direction of local society. But every one revealed helpful activities that were a normal part of the coven's purposes.

From that night, Morgan's dedication to her craft as a profession was insured. She was shown a practical use for what she was and what she knew and could learn. She never forgot that zeal in the time to come.

At the end of the low-key meeting, Kalavela stood and moved to the center of the circle of chairs. With her back to the crackling fire in the hearth, she said,

"I have a certain need, my friends. It requires your aid in a thing that closely concerns the child, here."

All eyes turned to Morgan. She smiled timidly.

"Her brother is at large in the world," Mother continued without pause. "He is old in wickedness, as I have told you before. I, alone, cannot discern him. No matter how finely I cast my nets across the world.

"Will you lend your strengths to my own for the purpose of discovering him? I would like to know where he is and what he is doing. Rest assured, he is a threat to his sister for as long as he breathes the air of this earth."

Pirouetting slowly, Kalavela registered silent acceptance from her peers and nodded her head in gratitude. She took Morgan by the hand and led her to the center of the circle. Sensing her apprehension, she softly patted her cheek.

"I want you to stand here, Morgan, and be perfectly still. I promise we will not hurt you."

"Yes, Mother. I know that."

"Good, child." She took her chair again and addressed the others. "Morgan will be our focus. Being of the same blood as Lucien, her presence will hopefully help us form the connection. If such a thing is possible. Let us proceed."

As one, they leaned forward and laid their fingertips lightly upon the hem of Morgan's skirt. Their eyes closed and Morgan felt her own eyelids grow heavy. Something powerful thrummed along her veins. An electric tingle grew inside her blood and bones.

For the first time in her life, the young witch felt a concentration of the Power.

Her mind reeled through space. Much was darkness. Some was spangled with brief flashes of light. She hadn't the training to read the scurrying signals that overwhelmed her. She stood still and let the adepts work through her.

It seemed a long time before the fingers withdrew from her dress. The mind flickered away, one by one. The blackness dissolved into the warm light of the fireplace.

"He is beyond our power to find him," said Andrew at last. His wrinkles were twisted into a worrisome mask. "If he is still among the living, then he has grown verra strong, for one so young."

He scratched his chin as the others digested his words.

"I never doubted that for a second," Mother agreed. "But where do we go from here? I am afraid this lack of knowledge will leave us vulnerable."

"This be a thing to think on," Andrew continued, his voice rising with his own convictions. "If he be dead, then well and good. He is gone beyond harm to any. But if he be alive, and strong enough for this…hiding, then we had best watch well, over the next few years. He will be a peril for sure."

"Do you mean Lucien is going to try and hurt me again?" Morgan asked, unable to keep silent a moment longer. "Is that what you're all talking about?"

Andrew reached out and motioned for Morgan to take his hand. She did so and he squeezed it tenderly but with firmness. His eyes bored into hers.

"Lassie, you must arm yourself verra strongly. If he lives, yur kin, then yes, he will try to harm you. Of that there can be no doubting."

He turned to Mother. "Kalavela, ye must gi' the lassie your best. Nothing less. And I will gi' her what I'm able, old as I be, if she will make the trip to my house.

Together, we must try to gi' her the armor she will need, one day, to save herself from that spawn o' the Dark."

Thus was the covenant between the orphaned girl and Scottish coven sealed. Mother and Sir Andrew had, indeed, done their best, as they had sworn. All the others had helped as well, each providing the young witch all the strengths and skills they believed she would need, although they all hoped they were wrong and that Lucien was in fact deceased.

In the months and years ahead, they came to form the family she remembered best. Her true family. Lucien, though he had sprung from the same blood-line that produced her, held a fatal flaw that removed him from any real kinship with anyone who practiced the white arts. So she came to understand that either dead or alive, he was truly lost to her forever.

CHAPTER 21

The apartment loft was silent as Morgan's voice stilled. Lights from the few cars moving along the nearby street arched across the ceiling. The Star Trek clock was indicating the time to be minutes shy of two a.m. A horn tooted off in the distance as McCoy sat stretched, his body aching from sitting too long in the same position.

"So you really can't know how Lucien got his training, or who gave it to him?" he asked.

For a moment he thought Morgan may have dozed off, for she did not reply immediately and the kitchenette lighting left her in dull shadows before him. Then her voice came to him, sure and steady as ever.

"Not precisely. Not in specific detail. But there has never been any shortage of those who work and teach the ways of Darkness. I have been taught what I need to know of those and their ways."

"Watching you in action, I can believe that."

"Still, I'd prefer not to get into that subject. Not because it is any great secret, but because to speak of them feeds their potencies. It is always better not to talk or even think of such matters, except when you need to combat them actively. Even when you are armed to resist them."

"That old saw," Dancer mused knowingly. "Speak of the Devil?"

"What?"

"There's something to it that when you speak of the devil, you somehow put yourself into his power of influence?"

"More than anyone outside the disciplines could possibly imagine," Morgan admitted.

The telephone shrilled and Dancer fumbled through the semi-darkness to reach it as he mumbled. "Who the hell is calling at this hour?

"McCoy."

"Oh, thank God you're there!" Connie Hine's voice was sharp and staccato in his ear. "I'm sorry if I woke you.."

"You didn't." McCoy ran a hand through his hair while mouthing the woman's name for Morgan's sake. "Morgan and I were up."

"Oh?"

"Discussing battle plans. We ..ah..went to C.C.I. headquarters this afternoon and then later paid a visit to Tom Axel's private secretary. With results that I'd rather not discuss over the phone."

"You know Axel is dead, right?"

"What!"

"A boating accident early this evening. He supposedly fell off his yacht at sea and drowned. It was on the late TV news."

Dancer shook his head in wonderment and Morgan sat up straight on the couch.

"Connie, hold on a second." He covered the mouthpiece and turned to Morgan. "Thomas Axel drowned early this evening, during that cruise Lilith told us about."

Morgan bit her lower lip, her face becoming a mask of sharp consternation. "Damn," was all she said.

"Connie, was there anything else on the news?"

"Well, yes. Come to think of it. Someone fell to their death from a high rise apartment. The Hampshire Towers, I think. Why?"

"I can't tell you right now. What exactly did you hear?"

"Well, let me see. The police found a window smashed on the twenty-second floor. A body of some description. They wouldn't confirm if it was human or animal, was dead on the sidewalk below.

"Meanwhile the tenant has disappeared and there was sign of a major struggle in the apartment itself, with blood everywhere. The news reporter was speculating that whatever it was on the pavement may have attacked the missing tenant before it fell."

"And there were no names mentioned in all this?" McCoy was keeping his hopes up. Inwardly praying he and Morgan had left no incriminating clues behind.

"They've given out zip. No names or any real facts yet."

"Good."

"Well, Axel drowning was the big news flash anyway. This other thing was a secondary feature."

"Right."

"From what little there was, I gathered the police are really puzzled by all of it."

"Ha. If they knew the truth, they'd know what the word puzzle really means."

"So you and our friendly witch were there?"

"Connie."

"Okay, I know. Not over the phone. All right. I get it. Look, none of this is why I called. Although Axel's death does obviously figure in somehow. But we'll figure that out later."

"Right. What's up?"

"I sent that list you gave me to an associate of mine. His name is Harold Springer and he does good work. Don't worry, I didn't go out. I sent via e-mail.

"Well, he just got back to me. It seems we've got enough to interest the DA, already. More would help, but there's plenty now in just that hit-list. All those people died suddenly. No previous illness. Several seemed like heart failure, but there are too many to be a coincidence."

"Then we were right all along." Dancer gave Morgan a thumbs up sign.

"Yes. Add to the fact that my cousin's death was so outre that it caught the attention of a lot of people in high places. That certainly helps us."

"Umm. You think, then, there's enough to move ahead, as is?"

"I do. Still, is there any chance you two will come up with anything else?"

"Connie, whatever Morgan and I came up with now, no DA in the world could possibly use in a court of law. It's something akin to that fireball we dodged. Really wild and hairy stuff so far-out that it would make us all sound like madmen."

"That sounds dangerous?"

"No argument there. Still, we've gone this far. It would probably be more dangerous to stop now. As long as we've got the other side on the run, let's not give them a chance to retaliate."

"Okay. That makes sense to me. What do you want me to do next?"

Dancer repeated the question to Morgan.

"Let me talk to her," she said as she bounced off the sofa and came over to take the phone from him. She swept back her long hair to expose her left ear to the receiver.

"Hello, Connie. Morgan, here. You and your associate keep digging. Go into that list and get anything else you can run down about C.C.I.'s financial dealings. Swiss bank accounts, those kinds of things. If there is any way to trace them down. Things like that. I'm sure there miles of paper trails if you look in the right places."

"Gotcha. What about you and McCoy?"

"We've got to go visiting a bear in his den, I'm afraid."

Dancer suddenly snapped his fingers. "Hey, I just thought of something? Ask Connie how she's fixed for expenses. This must be costing her a bundle?"

"Did you hear that?" Morgan asked, putting the receiver back to her ear.

"Huh, huh," came the reply. "Not to worry. My cousin left me his sole beneficiary. He was a thrifty man and made quite a sum before his death." She sounded as grim as Morgan felt. "I'm going to put every penny of it into solving his murder, if that's what it takes. There should be more than enough to get the job done."

"But you shouldn't have to bear that burden by yourself, Connie."

"Look, Morgan, you and Dr. McCoy saved my life and are the only two people in the whole world who give a damn about what happened to Ron. As far as I'm concerned, I'm the one who owes you. And if I haven't said before, thanks."

"You're welcome."

"Besides, it wouldn't surprise me," the councillor added as an afterthought, "if this case didn't make me famous, as a lawyer. My practice is a good one, but nothing spectacular. Being the lawyer who brought down C.C.I. could make it that overnight."

Morgan heard her wry chuckle and she grinned. She really liked this spunky little woman.

"Good enough. On Monday, Dancer and I go to C.C.I. If we're never heard from again, at least you will know where we disappeared.

"And we just might, Connie. You keep your eyes open and stay with Father Dubois until it's safe to come out of hiding. Understand?"

"Will do. Take care.. you and McCoy. I'm going to worry sick until I hear from you again. God bless." The phone clicked off.

"So, we're going back," Dancer echoed in the semi-darkness as she put the phone back in its wall mount. "I sort of guessed that would be your next move."

"You understand the need, then," she confirmed. "I'm glad. I was trying to think of how to tell you before Connie called."

"Oh, I get it. We have to go after brother Lucien ourselves. It wouldn't be safe for anyone else to do it.. or for us, for that matter. I'm hoping that you have some sort of protection plan against what he might do to us. Pinch out our hearts or whatever?"

"Yes, I do. And I'd better see to the lesser part of my armament right now." She began rummaging in her suitcase. Her tall shape looked almost ghostly in the dim light. From the pocket of the case she took two vials.

"Snap on the light, will you?"

He complied. Then he watched, fascinated, as she took envelopes of stuff from the pocket and took pinches from three of them. She sealed the dry-looking stuff into still other vials.

"What's that?" he inquired as she handed him a vial.

"Sweet basil, bramble, and mugwort," she identified. "All basic defenses against evil. They can't protect you alone, but in the hands of a witch or in the possession of one protected by a witch, they can be pretty powerful."

She stared down at the glints of light in her hands. "This should, with the proper ritual, protect us from having our internal organs disrupted."

"Really?" Dancer suddenly looked sick. "Disrupted organs. How lovely."

"It may even deflect his fires a bit, if he forgets himself and throws that sort of thing at us."

"Fire! Oh, joy!" The memory of the runaway fireball was fresh in his mind.

Morgan put her hands on his shoulders. He was tall, but so was she. Their eyes were almost on a level.

"Dancer McCoy, we are about to do a madly dangerous thing. It's not just the risk of death... you've dealt with that, and very nicely, too... without losing your never. This will be much worse."

"Kalavela believed, as long as she lived, that Lucien is more than just your average warlock. She thought he possessed fantastic psychic powers that he did not realize originated from inside his own mind, instead of the demons he courted. He chose the evil way, not because he was in touch with the Dark Ones, but because it was a true part of his nature.

"Everything he did, that I know of, as well as everything she read inside him in Paris, pointed to that conclusion."

"Which means exactly what? That he's not really a witch at all?"

"Oh no, Mother never claimed that. Lucien is a warlock. The thing is, she thought that he had never truly touched the dark forces. Instead all his magic was really the product of his wild talent.

"She would, she knew with some certainty, surely have detected the stink of the lower orders on him, if he had really touched the Black Ones."

Morgan let go of McCoy and took a breath. Now she hugged herself and he knew the worst was coming.

"That's all changed, hasn't it?" he ventured.

"Yes, it has."

McCoy snapped his fingers again. "Lilith! It was Lilith! No mere psychic could have created her out of thin air."

Morgan's eyes flashed. "You never cease to amaze me, sir. That is exactly right. Lilith was a construct. The stench of demonic power was all over her being. It appears what Mother Kalavela feared the most has come to pass.

"My brother has made communion with the Dark Princes."

"Which will make him that much tougher to bring down."

"You mustn't joke about this. We are about to confront things that even your worst nightmares cannot envision."

Dancer smiled and wrapped his arms around her. "Then, I'd suggest you and I try and get some sleep. It looks like we are going to need all our wits about us and right now I'm about to start counting sheep right where I stand."

"You're right. It's so late and all of a sudden, I am bone weary."

Dancer pointed to the closed off section of his loft. "The bed is in there."

Morgan shook her head. "No. The couch will do me fine."

"What?"

"Don't argue. I live by an old tradition that says it is wrong to deprive a host of his or her bed. I'll take the couch."

"Okay, have it your way."

"I usually do." She closed her eyes and tilted her head for his kiss. As their lips met, she felt secure. Maybe for the first time in her life.

"Good night, Green Eyes."

"Good night, my dear Dancer."

Ten minutes later both were asleep dreaming of each other.

CHAPTER 11

Lucien Wicker woke early on Monday. Anticipation, which he had thought lost with his long-ago youth, rippled beneath his solar plexus. Today began his real ascension to corporate power.

Jumping from his bed, he hurried into the kitchen and gulped a half glass of cold orange juice. The sweetness pleased him and he smacked his thin lips before wiping them with the back of his hand.

Back in the living room, he parted the curtains to the new and harsh sun. A creature of the night, he knew this day would be the one marvelous exception to his normal attitudes. With success ready to be plucked, he could savor even the pure brightness of daylight.

Dropping to the carpeted floor, he began a series of calisthenics established to keep his body trim and fit. As he worked through a routine of push-ups, his arm muscles contracting to bear the weight of his body, he could not help fantasizing about the hours ahead.

Victory was such a satisfying taste.

As the new vice-president of C.C.I., he would have access to their entire worldwide computer systems. He had learned enough from reading Appleton's mind, before he killed him, to know there were unlimited funds available to anyone with the secret of access. More wealth than any single human had ever controlled before.

Standing up to complete a dozen jumping-jacks, the thin Lucien looked like an emaciated scarecrow come to life. Still there was compact toughness to his sparse physique. He was thin but never weak. That he would never allow.

In the hot, scolding shower a few minutes later, he continued to mentally muse over the coming day's events. He now had the president of the corporation securely under his thumb, like a bug under glass. The long training, the battle to conquer his unusual gifts, all those were about to pay off handsomely.

He dressed conservatively. He combed his black hair and donned his silk tie with meticulous care. To his faint disgust, he was beginning to look faintly satanic, thanks to his thin, arching eyebrows. That was a thing to be avoided.

In the business world, image was everything. He had to look innocuous. The ultimate capable young executive, earnestly striving to make his way up the ladder of the American Dream. Someone with neither the time nor energy to devote to anything malevolent. Harmless.

Which is exactly how he looked when he came strolling into the company's top floor and greeted Darryl Waitman's secretary with a huge, friendly smile.

"Miss Ellett. Good day to you. I am Lucien Wicker, the new vice-president. Did Mr. Waitman inform you that I was coming?"

Emily Ellett was rather pretty, if somewhat washed out, a blonde on the wrong side of thirty. She looked up from her PC, her face slightly pink.

"Yes, sir. First thing this morning, in fact. You'll excuse me if I seem flustered but what with Mr. Axel's passing and all, things have been rather crazy around here."

"I quite understand," Lucien looked sympathetic. "It was such a tragic shock to all of us. He will be sorely missed."

"Were you with another branch of the company?"

"You might say that. Tell me, is Mr. Waitman available? There are several matters he and I have to go over."

"I'm afraid he is still with the detectives."

"Detectives?" Lucien flinched. "I thought they had finished with him Saturday night after taking his statement."

Miss Ellett's eyes doubled and she paled. "Oh, dear. You haven't heard the other bad news."

"What other bad news?"

"About Mr. Axel's secretary, Miss Markova."

For a second, Wicker felt the room spinning. "What about her?"

"Well, they really don't know. That's the awful part of it all. She's missing."

"Missing!" His voice was sharp. In his surprise, he almost said Lilith. That would have been a foolish mistake. No one suspected their involvement and he had no intention of changing that fact.

The blonde nodded somberly. "Something dreadful happened in her apartment Friday night. There was blood all over the place. At least, that's what I've heard.

"Mr. Merkel, from Personnel, was called to the police station yesterday afternoon, as nobody knew any next of kin. He said something that looked like a hairy monster had fallen through her window onto the sidewalk and been killed. When the police went up to her apartment to investigate, they couldn't find her. No body, nothing. Not a single trace. They're afraid she might have been murdered and her body taken away."

Lucien tried to filter through the girl's words to find the kernels of fact amidst the speculations. He disliked getting his information so haphazardly. He also did not like having the police prowling about. This, coming on the heels of Axel's demise, would look funny. It would invite closer scrutiny. Suddenly his perfect day was turning sour all too swiftly.

"And the police have no clues to go on?"

"No, sir. From what Mr. Merkel said, they are at their wits' end. We are all worried sick. Especially Mr. Waitman."

"Yes, I'm sure."

"Did you know her?" It was an innocent question.

Lucien had himself under control, now. "I met her once or twice. She seemed a very capable woman. Axel certainly depended on her."

He composed his expression with even more care and looked at his watch. "Look, will you be a dear and check to see who will be taking her desk for the time being?"

"Oh, it's Deborah Perkins. Personnel sent her up as soon as Mr. Waitman came in. He was very upset by the news."

"I'm sure. Please call Miss Perkins and tell her I'd like to see Mr. Waitman as soon as he is done with the police."

"Yes, sir. Right away."

"Until then, hold all my calls. I don't wish to be disturbed except for Mr. Waitman."

"I understand, Mr. Wicker. You can count on me."

Lucien stepped into his new office. Unlike Darryl, he paid no heed to the plush décor.

The lively watercolors that replaced the lush oils in Axel's office had been Darryl's pride. They might as well have been flower prints from Wal-Mart, for all Lucien noticed. He sat in the swivel chair, mindless of the fact that it was rich Russian leather. His mind was elsewhere.

He put his fingertips together against his thin lips and frowned. His non-seeing gaze zeroed in on the Chinese vase atop the walnut bookcase beside the door. A green and yellow dragon twisted its scaly form around the smooth pottery, like the venomous thoughts that slithered behind his eyes.

Something had gone wrong!

Only another power… one antithetical to his own… could have dealt with Lilith. Nothing normal could have driven her through her own window. In her own lair, she was well-nigh invincible. He knew that because she was his creation. His masterpiece of metaphysical demonology.

What could have destroyed the changeling? A chill moved along his spine, thinking of what that power might be.

Lucien closed his eyes and rubbed his temples. The face of Morgan hung there, behind his closed lids, just as he had seen it before. MORGAN!

He shivered with anger at the memory of his greatest failure. Now it was the time he had waited for so long. The time when he would avenge that shameful humiliation he had suffered under the old witch's hands. He would find his sister and bring her life to an end. A very bitter one, he hoped and expected.

CHAPTER 13

The crosswalk light turned red and Dancer McCoy eased down on the brake pedal of the cherry red Jeep. Morgan kept fidgeting in the passenger seat, once again looking ready for action in her jeans and sweatshirt. A far cry from their last visit to C.C.I.

A group of pedestrians, hustling natives and curious tourists, ambled across the busy thoroughfare as McCoy twisted his hands about the steering wheel trying to hide his anxiety.

"It was nice of your friend to loan you the Jeep," Morgan said, only to break the silence. "Although I wouldn't have guessed him to drive a Jeep."

"Sergei Antonovich is a man of many sides," he related warmly. "He loves the outdoors. Told me he grew up in the Ural Mountains as a boy and this Jeep was one of his first purchases when he came here to work for the Institute.

"Any chance he can get away, he loads this sucker with outdoor gear, fishing rods etc. and heads for the wild."

The light turned green just a harried housewife made it across with her brood of three small children, the youngest in a stroller. Morgan looked at her wistfully.

"I wish that was where we were going now."

He let off the brakes and started forward again. "Yeah. Me too."

* * * *

After waiting a half hour, Lucien received his summons to Waitman's office. He wasted no time getting there.

As he entered the office of the soon-to-be new president, he was met by a frantic, totally frightened man. Waitman jumped up from behind the ornate desk and rushed to Wicker, his eyes wild with fear.

"They know!" he blurted. "The police! They just left here and know!"

"Know what exactly?" Wicker demanded. He was tired of Darryl's lack of character. Normally he would have quelled his own annoyance and endured it. But today, after the surprise of Lilith's defeat and death, he was off-balance and now had the beginnings of a king size headache.

"About everything! About Axel and us and Appleton!" Waitman was talking so fast, his face reddened and he stopped to inhale as if he were running a marathon, before continuing. "They asked all kinds of questions!"

Wicker's gaze bore into Waitman's eyes. "Calm down! Now!"

"Calm down! How the hell can I calm down? It's all going wrong!"

Enough was enough.

SMACK! Wicker hit him with a hard back hand that rocked Waitman's head. The pain broke through his fog of confusion and, as he felt tears welling up, he touched the red welt on his face.

"I'm sorry," Wicker picked up, taking control of the situation before the fragile executive lost it again. "But you've got to calm yourself. You're ranting and it isn't helping anything. Do you understand that?"

Waitman blinked back the tears and coughed. "Yes, I do. Forgive me, Wicker. This …this whole mess has got me rattled."

"What you need, my friend, is a drink." Lucien went to the well stocked bar against the wall to his right and found a bottle of Club Royal. He poured a glass full and handed it to his employer.

"Take it."

Waitman took a small swallow, then another.

"Better?"

"Yes. Thank you."

"Good. Now I know about Miss Markova's disappearance. Is that why the police were here?"

"Well, yes. But they asked about Axel too." Waitman took his half finished whiskey and returned to his desk. "They thought it was a strange coincidence that she should vanish within hours of the old man's death."

"Which is a perfectly natural reaction on their part."

"But they asked about Appleton too." Waitman sat back in his chair and took another drink. "They wanted to tie it to the other events."

Wicker leaned over the desk, his face a hard front. "But they can't. Right?"

"Well, no. I suppose not. I told them as much. I mean, that I was as much in the dark as they were."

Lucien smiled. "Good. Then they were only fishing about."

"Perhaps. But still, it was unsettling. They just kept mumbling about people dying right and left who are connected with the company. Their implications were loud enough."

Waitman loosened his tie and finished the last of the whiskey.

"Relax, Darryl," Wicker said in his most charming voice, stepping away from the desk. "They don't have a thing. As long as you maintain your composure, they have nothing…"

His forehead wrinkled. There was something in the air.

"Wicker? What is it?"

"It can't be.. can it?"

"What?"

Lucien's head turned, his nostrils flared as if sniffing for an elusive scent. Ignoring Waitman altogether, he spoke to himself. "She's coming."

* * * *

As Morgan and Dancer entered the main lobby, the first-floor receptionist was touching up her makeup.

Morgan made a small gesture with her fingers. The woman didn't glance up as they walked across the lobby, but continued to freshen her lipstick. It was as if they were invisible to her.

Reaching the bank of elevators, Dancer hit the up button and the door nearest them whooshed open.

"That was a neat trick," he commented as they rode up to the executive level. "Sort of like a Jedi in the Star Wars movies."

"Only our Darth Vader is for real," Morgan reminded him.

The elevator was a fast one; soon they were stopped and getting out. The corridor was empty. There was a murmur of voices from a partially open doorway halfway down the hall to their immediate front. Girls talking.

Morgan touched Dancer's arm. "Wait. It's Lucien. He's here!"

"Where?"

Morgan turned and pointed to the aisle going leftward. "That way."

"Well, let's go before we both lose our nerves."

They started off, shoulder to shoulder.

Morgan continued to sense her brother's presence. "He's with someone. They're emotionally upset. That much I can feel."

"Good. But does he know we're here? Can he sense you as well?"

"Oh, yes. At this nearness, it would impossible not to."

They rounded a corner to the president's office. The same reception area they had visited only days earlier. Miss Ellett saw them and put down a folder she had been reading.

"Can I help you?"

Morgan was tempted to use the same spell she had worked on the receptionist but thought better of it. The closer she came to the door leading to their goal, with Lucien on the other side, meant any use of her abilities, no matter how minimal, would warn him of her nearness. Even if he were aware, as she suspected, there was no need to start sounding the battle trumpets just yet.

"Hello. Miss Rein and Mr. McCoy to see Mr. Waitman." She was grateful for Connie's Saturday night call informing them of the change in C.C.I.'s hierarchy. Asking to see a dead man would have been tres gauche.

"I'm very sorry, miss, but Mr. Waitman is not seeing anyone today." The poor girl looked totally beyond her depth. "Mr. Wicker just went in and I'm certain they do not want to be disturbed."

Morgan felt sorry for the young woman. The change in position had obviously come too fast for her to adjust properly. As much as the witch hated to take advantage of the girl's timidity, she had no other recourse.

"That's most fortunate. We need to see Mr. Wicker, as well." Wicker, indeed! Thought Morgan. He might have been a bit more subtle! "We'll just go in. You needn't announce us."

Without further preamble, she swept past the secretary's desk, opened the heavy oak door, and, with McCoy at her heels, marched into the inner office.

* * * *

For the first time in twenty years, Morgan faced her brother Lucien. They stood only yards apart, each recognizing the other immediately. For Morgan it was a revelation, as she realized for the first time that what she had harbored in her imaginings all those years was the picture of a boy. The boy she had subconsciously hoped to find and save one day.

The reality of the gaunt, dark man before her instantly demolished that fantasy.

Behind her, she could hear a babble of inept apologies from the flustered secretary to her new boss. Before she could come in, McCoy politely but forcefully closed the door in her face. Then he took his place behind Morgan's left shoulder and waited to see what would happen next.

"So Lucien. You are now Mr. Wicker."

"I thought the name had a certain panache. Don't you agree?" His voice was as cold and lifeless as she remembered.

"And the new vice-president of Consortium Cross International, no less. I'm impressed." Her emerald eyes were sparkling with reckless bravado. She dared not show him any hesitancy.

Darryl Waitman had watched the exchange from his chair. He was clearly irritated by the interruption and stood, pointing a finger at Morgan.

"Now see here!" he exclaimed. "I don't know who you people are, but you have no right to come barging into my office unannounced and without an appointment."

"Relax, Darryl," Lucien ordered without taking his eyes off his sister. "This is a family matter."

But the edgy Waitman was not to be placated. "I don't care if they're your long lost cousins! Things are bad enough without this sort of intrusion. I want you people out of here before I call security and have you bodily ejected!"

Morgan took her eyes from Lucien and regarded the yelling chief officer. She moved her hand and the man's teeth seemed to glue themselves together in his jaws. He went silent in mid-sentence.

"Be quiet, Mr. Waitman. Quite obviously, my brother has you in his snare. Thus you don't really exist, any longer. Nothing you could say would be of any importance to any of us."

Waitman, horror stricken, stumbled back into his seat and began struggling with his recalcitrant mouth. Morgan returned her full attention to Wicker.

For his part, the Warlock stood as if he were frozen. He felt the aura of danger around the two intruders and now he knew how dangerous Morgan had become. He turned his gaze towards McCoy.

Morgan smiled. Having anticipated his reaction, she had shielded her companion from Lucien's reading. Wrapped in a cocoon of protection, nothing of his intimate self could escape into her brother's perceptions. So far she and Dancer were holding their own.

Recognition flared in Lucien's face. "I remember you. You're the one on the motorcycle, who interfered with my plans for the Hines woman."

"Sorry I broke up your party." Dancer tried to sound flippant.

"Oh, I've plenty of tricks left in my bag."

McCoy's face went stony. "No thanks, I still owe you for the last one."

"Leave him alone," Morgan said, interrupting their verbal duel. "Your fight is with me, big brother."

Lucien's smugness evaporated. Black eyes met green eyes. A visible, audible spark of electricity jumped between the two. It met at the mid-point between them with a sharp crack. McCoy flinched but held his ground. All of Morgan's earlier warnings echoed in his head. Be prepared for anything.

"Well, little sister, you have learned a lot, it seems. No doubt from that old witch who stole you away from my tender loving care."

"Is that what you called it? How original. I'll have to remember that the next time I'm working a crossword puzzle. A four letter word for attempted murder: love."

"The actions of misguided youth," Lucien explained, clasping his hands together, feigning supplication. He opened them palms out as if he were making a peace offering. "Surely you can't blame me for experimenting. How else was I to learn without using my newfound skills? You know what they say about the omelet and breaking a few eggs."

"Enough of your chicanery!" she snapped. "Your lust for power has not diminished in the slightest over the years. And you're still playing your perverse little games. Such as making demonic constructs."

Wicker's eyes narrowed. McCoy saw the look and prayed Morgan knew what she was doing, goading her brother like this.

"Lilith Markova was a nice bit of work, in a nasty sort of way."

At the mention of Lilith's name, Waitman tried to stand. Stifled noises came from between his locked teeth. His eyes, now wild, kept shooting from Morgan to Wicker. He was slowly turning a pale blue.

"Did the police ever figure out what she.. ah, it was?" Morgan needled. "Or have they filed it under the heading of unsolved mysteries?"

Lucien drew himself erect. "So, it was you. You actually destroyed my little cat-woman all by yourself. Bravo, Morgan. I didn't think you had it in you."

"You would be surprised at what I am capable of these days."

Lucien shook his head. "Perhaps, but I'm afraid neither us will have the opportunity to explore such things. You see, my dear sister, I've no intention of letting you leave this office alive."

Dancer knew it was going to start.

"It doesn't have to be like this," Morgan pleaded. "We are of the same blood, Lucien. Doesn't that mean anything to you?"

The thin man shifted his weight to balance himself.

"Oh, it means everything to me, my dear. Everything!"

His right hand moved.

Morgan's right hand drew a pattern in the air. There came a faint scent of ozone. Lucien's forehead began to sweat.

The air in the office became heavy with tension. McCoy could almost feel in his own flesh the strain that was building between the two combatants, warlock and witch, Dark and White.

They were locked into a motionless conflict.

He felt as if his hair were trying to stand on end, his skin to crawl. Electrical potential was being generated in some uncanny way his scientific mind could not possibly understand. And it was rising fast.

There came a crack of sound. A streak of black (if Dancer could have accepted the notion of black lightning that would have described it) darted between the brother and sister.

Morgan staggered back a step. Lucien's face, rigid in concentration, eased a fraction.

Another discharge. Another bolt of blackness. Morgan trembled.

Dancer moved to her side and took her hand, hoping that by establishing physical contact, he might lend her some kind of aid. Be it energy or moral

"Smoke started rising all around them .."

support, if nothing else. The moment their hands touched, millions of bee stings raced through his nervous system and he gasped. But he did not let go.

She was terribly pale. The jewel-green eyes burned in her oval face with a reddish glow and her black hair streamed outward as if a wind were blowing through the closed and air conditioned office.

Dancer felt as if he were being battered, in the midst of a hurricane or a tornado, buffeted by an element that he couldn't see.

Waitman screamed, a muffled but desperate sound. McCoy looked toward him and saw flames shooting from the back corner of the office where the floor met the wall. With all the rampant electrical charges going off all around them, he was not surprised by the fire.

He tugged at Morgan's sleeve and for an instant, her focus slackened. She glanced aside and saw the flames near enough to scorch the incapacitated Waitman.

Her forehead wrinkled, just a tiny bit. Waitman shot from his chair and raced toward the door.

"Fire!" he shouted. "Help! Fire!" He disappeared from view, the door shutting behind him.

Morgan had already forgotten him. Flames were now eating toward her brother. Two fires moved toward the center of the room, where the embattled pair stood. Neither was willing to move in spite of the new, fiery threat. Smoke started rising all around them like an intangible corral.

Dancer suddenly felt his heart give a great thump. Hastily he checked himself, scared that the warlock had somehow reached into his chest and touched the pumping muscle. But he was all right. If that had been Wicker's doing, there would have been some kind of harm done. No. He realized it was simply sheer terror.

Feeling the increasing heat of the blaze, he caught Morgan around the waist and tried to pull her toward the door.

With spectral suddenness, Lucien winked from sight. Morgan went limp in Dancer's arms. The rug was blazing. A searing tongue of flame had leaped between them and the door. Their escape route was effectively cut off.

Morgan moved. "No! Not the door. The window!" She sounded exhausted, but he did as she said regardless.

While Morgan stood against the desk, Dancer pulled back the heavy drapes and looked for the lock hinges. The plate glass windows opened outward. Quickly he unlocked them and pushed them open. Cool air slapped his face at the same time tendrils of gray smoke began snaking towards the opening. He knew the fresh air would only feed the fire that much faster.

Morgan stumbled to him and he held her steady. She looked out. The streets looked like they were a mile below. Across from them were other buildings. All of them were shorter and from their vantage point, they could look down on their roofs. For all the good it did them. They were just too far away.

"Dancer!" she looked at him with desperate earnestness. "I think I can save us. But you've got to believe. Really believe. Not lip-service. Sheer faith. Can you do that?"

He looked at her and then the doorway now engulfed in flames. "Princess, I've got to. If you can get us out of this, go for it. But don't wait too long. This place is going to make like a giant firecracker any minute now."

"We're going across.. to that rooftop, across the street. See it?" She was pointing toward the building directly opposite, whose roof held a maze of pipes, conduits, electrical boxes and the top of an elevator shaft.

"On what?"

"On faith, Dancer. On pure faith."

"Right. A magic carpet ride. Only without the carpet."

She touched his face. "Listen to me. You can do this. And I won't leave you here. You've got to go or we'll both die. Here and now. And Lucien will have won."

She meant it. Every single word. Her eyes were full of determination. She meant it and Dancer knew he could not doubt her.

He took a deep breath. Good-bye scientific method. Good-bye, lifetime of training and convictions. Or else, good-bye Dancer McCoy.

"Okay, Princess. I'll go. If I don't believe in you by now, I'm too obtuse to live, anyway."

Morgan gave him a small kiss and then took hold of his hand.

"What do I have to dooo..."

Dancer had no time to wonder or to worry. At one instant her hand touched his. The next instant, he felt himself slipping sidewise... or sliding endwise.. or something.

He opened his eyes, which he didn't recall closing. He was floating upright through the air, the city far below his feet. Still clutching his hand, Morgan was beside him, her face serene, as they moved along weightlessly like leaves falling in an autumn breeze. It was every childhood dream he had ever had. Flying. They were flying! Then he saw the cluttered roof below them and all too quickly their journey was over.

Feeling his stomach heave, Dancer closed his eyes, sure they were both about to break every bone in their bodies when they made contact with the roof rushing up at them. Air rushed out of his lungs and he waited for the impact.

It never came. Instead he opened his eyes and found himself staring across space at the billow of smoke coming from the top of the C.C.I. structure across the street. He looked over at Morgan. The witch was lying on her face on the tarred roof. Out cold?

He knelt and gathered her into his arms. Her eyes fluttered open, but their bright green fires were damped to the faintest of embers.

"Morgan. You did! We made it!"

She felt cold. Limp. Almost as if she might be going into shock. He had to get her some help.

There was a sound behind him and he twisted his head back. Lucien Wicker leaned against the elevator doorway. He too appeared completely drained of strength. His legs were wobbly and he was having trouble maintaining his stance. Thank God for little favors, Dancer thought.

"Little sister," Lucien croaked. "We will meet again. I promise you. Both of us cannot exist on this single planet. Not at the same time. If only I had succeeded, long ago."

"Shut your face!" McCoy cried. "It's you who don't deserve to breathe the same air she does!"

The warlock studied McCoy and then his pasty white face grinned. It was a sick smile, as if a new notion had just crept into his awareness.

"You insignificant worm," he retorted at last. "You don't get it, do you? You are her greatest vulnerability. I should have seen it all along."

"What are you saying?"

"Only that without your involvement, Morgan might have easily beaten me. When I teleported out of the fire, she could easily have done the same. It is apparent to me, now, that her talents are far beyond those of a normal witch. Perhaps even greater than my own.

"By choosing to stay behind and save you, she had to double her efforts in guaranteeing your safety. That she accomplished it at all, and still lives, is absolutely amazing."

Dancer looked down at the dazed woman in his arms and tried to guess where Wicker's hypothesis was going.

"So she is stronger than you after all," he challenged. "That's what you're admitting."

Regaining his color second by second, Lucien stood, his posture began to straighten. "Maybe it is. But as long as she has to protect you every moment, she will continue to waste her energies and thus weaken her own defenses."

Dancer mopped his hair back off his forehead. He was confused, whereas Lucien was truly enjoying himself.

"Don't you get it, you thick-headed worm! You are her Achilles heel. Her one weakness. By all means, hero, stay at her side. In doing so, you will guarantee her defeat at my hands. Ha, ha, ha."

Lucien's laughter rose in volume until it drowned out every other noise around them. Finally, holding his ribs, he stopped and wiped his eyes with the back of his hand.

"What a pity that I have nothing left in me. I would finish you here and now. That would be doing her a favor, don't you think? But, alas, I will have to kill you both later. Adieu, worm. Do tell Morgan, I'll be waiting for her."

Wicker waved his hands in a semi-circle twice, up and down and then flickered from sight.

Kneeling on the rough tar, Dancer held Morgan tenderly and pondered Wicker's accusations. Boiling hot anger began sizzling through his veins.

Perhaps it was true that Morgan had endangered herself to save him. In the warlock's viewpoint, that had been foolish. But what did he know about love or the self-less caring of others? As he gently rubbed her brow, Dancer swore to himself that Morgan would never have a reason to regret her act. He would not be a hindrance to her. Somehow, someway, he would contribute to this battle everything he had to offer.

Still Wicker's laughter echoed in his heart and he could not dispel the doubts that had taken root in it.

Morgan stirred and sat up. "Ow, my head feels like it weighs a ton."

"Go easy," he cautioned, still supporting her. "You really pulled it off, Morgan."

"Did I just hear Lucien?"

"You did. He's gone. Vanished. But not before saying he would be waiting for you."

Before Morgan could comment, the door to the elevator shaft opened and a middle-aged man in coveralls stepped out onto the rooftop. When he saw them, he nodded pleasantly.

"Up here to see the fire, heh." In the distance the shrill wail of firetrucks could be heard. The janitor wiped dusty hands on a red rag from his hip pocket and pointed to the column of black smoke rising out of the C.C.I. building. "Good place to see it from."

"Yes, it is," Dancer agreed. He helped Morgan to her feet and guided her to the door the fellow had left open. They left him staring at the spectacle across the way.

CHAPTER 14

Lucien broke his long-held habit of entering his apartment in a normal fashion. He had always avoided doing anything the least suspicious that might attract undue attention among the other tenants. He did everything the way ordinary people did. If he could.

That was impossible now. He had no stamina left for walking or taking elevators and unlocking doors. He had to content himself with the belief that few people ever took notice of their neighbors' comings and goings, anyway. Such was the protective anonymity of big city living.

He teleported, using the very last of his craft's reservoir of strength, to his balcony and entered his bedroom through the glass-doored wall. He collapsed onto his bed, exhausted beyond anything in his experience. It was infuriating. What should have been his moment of supreme triumph instead had become a humiliating defeat.

He had been right all along in fearing his sister. In those long-ago Paris days, he had been entirely correct. But that was little consolation for the way he felt now. Only with the most tremendous effort had he maintained his fire charges and his own balance in the storm of her fierce attack in Waitman's office.

Now that office was a smoking ruin. She had escaped it... taking along with her the unknown man who was her ally. That galled him the most, despite his cocky words to the stranger in their rooftop confrontation afterward.

Lucien made himself dismiss the thought. He wasn't at all certain that he, with all his abilities and power, could have carried another at that point in their encounter. Now he refused to consider anything that might erode his own faith in his superiority over Morgan, or anyone else for that matter. Still the doubts were there and he would deal with them by committing himself to her total destruction.

For now, he had been warned and that was a good thing. Now he truly knew the mettle of his adversary. The next time they met, there would be no further mistakes on his part. Now he would know exactly how to deal with dear, sweet sister Morgan!

The telephone rang, jarring him free of his reverie. He groped for the extension beside the bed.

Before he could speak, Darryl Waitman's hysterical voice rattle at him, the words coming like machine gun bullets. "Wicker! Wicker, what in God's name went on in my office? I think I'm losing my mind! Who were those people? Especially that woman! The police and the firemen have asked me all sorts of questions that I can't possibly answer. How can I? I don't know what happened."

"What did you tell them?" Lucien sat up, his mind once again sharp and alert.

"Well, I described those two people who did this. As best I could. I didn't exactly say what started the fire or anything about my not being able to talk or... hell, man, it all happened so damn fast! One minute we were talking then the next they showed up and the place was on fire. Just like that!"

"You mustn't say anything else. Do you hear me, Darryl?"

"I couldn't move, Wicker! I couldn't even speak. What the hell did she do to me. You have to tell me what happened up there or I'll go crazy."

The idiot! Lucien shook his head. It would all fall apart if Waitman wasn't brought under control.

"Listen to me! There are certain things that cannot be explained. What you saw this afternoon was one of them. If the authorities continue to hound you, tell them I accidentally threw a cigar in the waste basket. Just make something up."

After a pause, Waitman was back on. "All right. I get it. But I want answers, Wicker. And I want them soon!"

"Very well. When you get home, call me. We'll deal with this together. Right now, I am tired and need to rest." He hung up the phone without giving the rattled Waitman any time to argue.

Lucien sagged back onto his pillow. His carefully laid plans were tottering. Waitman, as always, was the key to his future in C.C.I. Oh, how he would have loved to pinch the man out of existence. The temptation was so great. The mousy business man had seen too much, knew more of Wicker's affairs than anyone alive. He was a very real threat. But he was still necessary.

Once again he saw Morgan and the dark haired man.

Damn them! Their timing could not have been worse! If they had waited a week, seven pitiful days, he would have had key personnel in his palm. He could have been prepared to take over Waitman's position without any bother. But to be shaken from his path on his very first day as vice-president… that was something he could not have foreseen.

It was obvious now that he had become lax and overconfident. And of for it he had paid the price. Never again.

Blackness flowed toward him, easing his racing mind. His last conscious thought was of Morgan. Soon. The end would come soon.

There was another thought, if only fleeting. He must rid himself, as well, of every practitioner of the Old Religion in the city. They were all a threat to him. He would be forced to call upon forces that he was wary of waking, but there was no other recourse. He would summon the major demons.

He felt asleep in the middle of that delicious thought.

CHAPTER 15

Connie Hines paced the guest room of St. Michael's rectory, biting her finger nails. Eight paces across. Twelve paces length-wise. She couldn't do a diagonal on account of the twin beds.

She felt like a caged tiger, trapped and impotent. She had spent the day here waiting. Waiting for either an e-mail reply from Harold Springer or any further news from Morgan and Dancer.

She detested waiting. Patience had never been one of her better characteristics. In fact she hated waiting. Most times, when handling a lawsuit, Connie would find herself in the courtroom long minutes before anyone else was present. She had always been a person who believed in getting on with life. Nothing useful was ever gained by being late. And waiting never produced anything of value except gray hairs and ulcers.

The morning dragged interminably. Then it was noon and still no word from anybody. She pulled up the solitaire game on her lap-top PC but eventually gave up on it because her imagination kept intruding on her. It was afire with all kinds of far-out scenarios of what had befallen her new friends. None of these images was positive.

As she was folding up her monitor, one of the Sisters padded up along the hall and stopped at her door. Connie had it opened before the nun could knock.

"Is there any news?" she blurted out, unable to contain her anxieties a second longer.

"Father asks that you come to his study," Sister Blaise said in a sing-song voice that was well appreciated in church's choir. "He has heard a news broadcast that he thinks you might want to hear."

"Then let's go." Connie followed the Sister along the divergent corridors to the open study door.

The old priest looked up from behind his desk. "Ah, Miss Hines. Come in. Please close the door behind you. Merci. Now would you sit here..shh!" He pointed to the radio on the corner of his desk.

Connie sat quickly on the sofa he had indicated just as he cranked up the volume. The voice over the speaker was professional and sounded almost bored as it announced the latest news. "...and no cause of the fire has as yet been determined. Late word comes from Fire Chief Brogan that a lit cigar, thrown into a wastebasket, has been mentioned as a possibility."

"A fire? Father, what has this got to..?"

Father Dubois shook his head and put a finger over his lips. "Listen, please."

"However," the reporter went on, "the nature of the fire in those offices is such that officials have pretty well ruled out most natural causes. Fortunately for all involved, it seems only the president's suite in the C.C.I. building was destroyed.

"A source at C.C.I. also informs us that a number of rare plants were destroyed, as well as several expensive sculptures, which were cracked by the intense heat."

"C.C.I.?" Connie's interest perked up and she leaned her head closer to the small portable radio not wanting to miss a single word.

"There has been a description issued for two intruders who appeared in the offices moments before the outbreak of the fire. The secretary in the reception area could not recall their names but describes them as follows.."

Father Dubois glanced up to meet Connie's gaze. Neither of them doubted the identity of the two so called intruders. It had been Morgan and Dancer.

The priest shut off the radio.

"Did they.." Connie's voice quivered. ".. find any bodies?"

"No, mon cher. No bodies at all. But the two were not seen to leave the building. Yet they are not there now and no trace of them has been found. Most intriguing.

"How so?"

He folded his hands tightly over his lap. "I have known for a long time that Morgan's talents included some extraordinary things. I believe that in some mysterious way she spirited them out of the fire."

"You really think so?"

"We will hear from them, Miss Hines. I am sure of it."

Connie stood, a bit unsure. "Well, thank you for sending for me, Father. Even news of this kind is still better than some of the things my mind has been conjuring up."

She started for the door. "Please let me know if you hear anything else. I have some more files I have to review, so I'd better get to them."

"If there is anything the good sisters and I can do to help you, do not hesitate to ask. I know you must feel like a prisoner here."

Connie smiled. "It isn't enough that you're probably keeping me alive? My dear sir, if I have to be cooped up anywhere, I can't think of a lovelier place for it. And your hospitality is far too gracious. Why the food alone is fantastic! You can tell Sister Xavier that she has my heartfelt admiration. And if she keeps feeding me like this, I'll have trouble fitting into my clothes within a few days."

Dubois laughed good-naturedly. "Yes, I know what you mean. She is a wonder in the kitchen. And I have a particular weakness for her Danish delights. It's a good thing I jog or I too would have the same problem."

He patted his round stomach. "Can you find your way back to your room? I can call Sister Therese for you."

"Please, don't bother. I think I can find it. I seem to be getting the hang of the place."

Once in the hall, she hustled. There was a lot to do and she wanted to get her completed work to Springer before night fell.

For most of the ensuing hour, she used the internet to further her research into C.C.I.'s history and the people who ran it. Soon she had amassed a huge data file, which she then cross-referenced with other files she had previously gathered. When she was finished, she'd found new financial threads that seem to vanish into thin air. All of which was clear indication that there were two sets of books used in C.C.I.'s accounting protocols. One for the public and the other, exclusively accessed by top executives alone.

Pleased with her work, Connie then e-mailed the entire new file to Springer with specific instructions on how to use it. She knew the fastidious Springer would do exactly as she wanted and then some. He had the tenacity of a bulldog, when he went after information. He was completely reliable and able to keep his mouth shut with superhuman discretion. He also lacked any personal ambition.

Harry Springer was the kind of man who was at his best when he was serving others. He was one of a rare breed and Connie valued him highly. She often congratulated herself on having hired him just out of law school and giving him an equal partnership in her firm. For that she had gained his dedication and loyalty.

Lifting her arms over her head, she stretched, feeling the bones in her back pop. She had been sitting too long. As she shut down her lap-top, she reviewed what she had just sent off. Most of it was conjecture and opinion. Yet if there was any substance at all to sustain her suppositions, Harry would be the one to find out. To turn ideas into facts.

She was getting to her feet when Sister Therese arrived.

"There is a telephone call for you. In the study. You know where it is?"

Connie's heart jumped in her chest. "Thank you, I think I can find it."

She hurried to the study, hoping that the call was from either McCoy or Morgan Rein. As she was entering the study, Father Dubois appeared at the end of the hall and followed her in.

"Do you mind if I listen, too?"

"Of course not, Father." She picked up the phone. "Connie Hines."

Dancer's voice was quiet but filled with a subdued tension. "Connie, McCoy here."

"Oh, thank God." She held the receiver out so that the cleric could hear the conversation.

"Take it easy," McCoy said. "We're safe. Both of us. I knew you'd be worried. Have you heard any news at all?"

"About the fire at C.C.I.?"

"Yes."

"We did. Just a while ago, over the radio. Father Dubois is here with me."

"Good, my regards. Anyway, we're both okay, though Morgan is really wiped out and sound asleep right now. We had a showdown of sorts with her brother, one Lucien Wicker. And let me tell you, he is one scary dude."

"Her brother! I don't understand."

"Morgan's older brother, Connie. I'm sure Father Dubois can fill you in." The priest nodded. "Anyhow, he's a warlock and he is dangerous. With capital letters. And get this, as of today, he is also new executive vice-president of C.C.I."

Connie's eyes registered her surprise. "VP! Dancer, can he be the person behind all the weird stuff going on with them?"

"Give the lady a cigar," McCoy confirmed. "This outfit wasn't particularly admirable to begin with; can you imagine what would happen if he were running the show? With a monster in charge, C.C.I. could virtually take over the world's entire construction and raw materials industries. Think about it! It could actually hold governments literally for ransom." He paused and Connie heard him swallow.

"We've got to lie low until Morgan is rested. She.. Connie, you're not going to believe this, but she whisked us from that inferno through space to the rooftop across the street. How she did, I couldn't tell you! We were flying! Really flying!"

"After the fireball, I'd believe anything."

"Yeah, exactly. Anyway it took a lot out of her, having to carry me along with her. Now we're at my place. We'll be here for a while, if you need to reach us."

"Gotcha. And thanks for calling. I was getting an ulcer." She grinned at Dubois, who gave her a thumbs-up gesture in return.

"I've just sent off a new file to my associate. He's a real digger. Nothing gets past him and he never quits."

"Does he know anything about the weird stuff?"

Connie laughed. "No way and I'm not about to tell him. Beside he's practical guy and practically fearless."

"I use to think I was. Okay, that's about all. I'll call you later. Our best to Father Dubois and the Sisters." The line went dead.

"Did you hear all that, Father?"

His eyes twinkled behind his glasses. "Oui. Quite clearly, my dear. God help those children. They have taken upon themselves a terrible challenge."

He looked at her, his expression turning serious. "Do you pray, cherie?"

"Not very often," Connie admitted, not meeting his eyes. "And not very well, when I do."

"There is no such thing as a bad prayer, my child."

"Maybe. Perhaps it's time to try again. Maybe it will comfort me. Possibly it may even be of some help to them. You think so?"

He smiled, his wrinkled face curiously young and innocent. "That is the very thing that makes up my life's work, ma cherie. I do think so. And it does not require practice. Only a sincere heart and a dedicated mind."

Strangely comforted, Connie returned to her quarters. She tried kneeling, but her with her weight her knees soon protested on the hardwood floor. So she sat in the chair at the small writing table and clasped her hands together.

"God," she began, "I hope you remember me. Even if it doesn't seem so, I remember you. And now I ..we need your help!"

The afternoon went in a blur of the most concentrated effort she had made in years. If God heard her, He/She made no immediate response.

CHAPTER 16

Dancer McCoy poured himself a cup of black coffee and, drinking it slowly, took a turn around his apartment. Morgan lay sleeping in his bed, still in her clothes. He had draped a blanket over her. Now her face was pale and every so often she would moan. Whatever she was dreaming about, he surmised, it was something sad.

* * * *

On a morning in early spring, Mother Kalavela failed to rise with the sun, as had been her invariable habit. Morgan, with the effortless vigor of eighteen, went about her morning chores, letting the old woman sleep.

Still, she thought it odd. Very odd. Perhaps, she decided, Mother wasn't feeling quite well.

Though this new day was bright and fresh, there had been a cold rain earlier, before dawn. Kalavela might well have caught a cold from a chill. Torn between letting her rest or going to check on her, Morgan started cooking breakfast.

Her mentor's silent call touched her mind when the eggs were half scrambled. She set the skillet aside and flew upstairs to Mother Kalavela's small room.

The witch lay peacefully on her back, her tiny hands folded over her stomach. Her small frame was covered by a patchwork quilt that the women of her coven had made for her winter use. Its colorful criss-cross pattern contrasted with the pallor of her skin.

Looking up at Morgan, she gestured toward the window. "Open the window, dear. Pull the curtains all the way back, so I can see the sun. I feel it, beaming away out there."

The girl tied back the bright fabric and touched the pane of glass. "It won't be too cold for you? It's sunny, but the air is chilly."

Kalavela shook her head. Morgan swung the casement wide, letting in the warm flood of sunlight.

"Mother, are you ill?"

Kalavela patted the mattress beside her. "Come sit here, my child. You and I must talk."

Morgan brushed back a long strand of hair and sat carefully on the edge of Kalavela's Spartan mattress. One of the veined and liver-spotted hands took hers tenderly. The old woman turned her head on the pillow, peering intently into the girl's lovely face.

"Morgan, my journey is coming to an end. No! Let me finish!" She tightened her grip on the girl's hand.

"It is a thing all must face. We, of all people, know that best. We have been trained to work within the natural ways of God. Each of us has a time to be born, to live, and to die."

"But you can't leave me! Not yet! I'm all alone, except for you!"

The loving eyes saw her doubt. The quiet voice said, "As if I could ever leave you, true child of my heart. Morgan, have you not learned the things we tried to teach you?"

Shamed, the girl lowered her gaze to the bright bedspread. "I have tried, Mother."

"And you have exceeded all our expectations, Morgan Rein. Old Andrew, before he died, told me that himself."

Astonished, Morgan looked up, her eyes wide. That was the highest praise she could imagine receiving.

"Yes," Kalavela reiterated. "He, who was by far the greatest of us all, and perhaps the greatest of all who ever lived, said that very thing!

"He was certain that if you continued your training and your discipline, you would have the ability to outdo us all and achieve things not one of the rest of us has ever mastered."

Morgan felt herself blushing. "You'll give me an ego like a balloon."

"At times, there is need for a large ego, child. You are too humble, in some ways. You must be proud of your abilities. Be confident in them. Fill yourself to capacity with character and good will. Yours is a mighty strength. Mighty indeed."

She sighed. "Few have known such strength. Except, of course on the Dark side. But you are of the White, through and through. This unhappy world has a great need for such as you."

The old witch drew a long breath and held it for a moment. She closed her eyes for an instant.

Morgan remembered the first time she had ever seen that odd little face with its tiny nose and round, lively blue eyes. Now their roles were reversed. She was the strong one, now, who must help Kalavela through this last test of all.

"Are you in any pain, Mother?"

The blue orbs opened. They were as round and blue and young as they ever had been.

"Only in my heart, my dear. I have had the best of lives. I am wrapped about with such loving memories. My heart ties me to this earth. God has been good to me."

"You have been the loveliest person in my life," Morgan whispered softly.

"Now listen to you! Blarney is for the Irish, child! I am a tough old Scotswoman, may I remind you." She sighed again.

"Be true in your vision, child. I have been His servant all my life, so I have to appear good, even with all my faults. It is the only life. Never doubt that."

When another breath was drawn, it rattled in Kalavela's throat. "Now, Morgan, there are things that you must do for me."

"Anything at all, Mother!"

"You must notify the coven. Gather them here. I would like for them to arrive shortly after noon. Go into town and ask Father Danielson if he'd be so kind as to come to see me. He has never felt entirely easy with our ways, but he knows that I have always kept the faith. He will not deny me the Sacrament of the Eucharist, one last time."

Morgan rose and wiped her eyes with the back of one hand. "I'll go at once.

But shouldn't I fetch Doctor Cairns as well?"

"His work is for the living. My malady is merely an old heart about to go to a well-deserved rest. No need to be taking him away from those patients who need him. Now off with you, before I die all alone, with my good-byes not properly said."

"I won't be long. I promise." And Morgan sped away.

By afternoon, all the coven... all those left from the original group... had arrived. Welcoming them into the cottage, Morgan realized for the first time how many were now missing.

Andrew, of course, was gone. Two years after his death, Sister Rose had died of cancer. Two of the McGill brothers had gone to America, leaving the oldest, Denby, behind to tend the family farmstead. Nancy Souci had run away to Denmark to marry an exchange student she had met in college. She and Morgan had kept in touch, but her bright face no longer graced the circle.

Now there were only seven of the original twelve left. Too few, even with Kalavela, to continue their group. Morgan knew that when Mother was gone, they would disband and look for new associations. It was the only way to survive the poignant loneliness of their discipline. They were unique people, and only those with like talents and training could be proper companions for them. Could give them the human contact that they needed.

Father Danielson had arrived before any of the others. He had given the last rites of the church by the time they had begun to assemble. He blessed Kalavela, packed his small kit, and made his way down the stairs. At the door, he offered his sympathy to Morgan, assuring her that he was ready to give any further help he could. Morgan was touched by his sincerity. They both knew what his next role would be; officiating at a funeral mass.

With the pastor gone, Morgan joined the rest of the coven in the little room. One by one they went to stand beside the bed. Kalavela had a special farewell for each.

They listened to her words with acute attention, for they believed that a dying witch's senses were heightened to an ultimate peak. That her predictions were usually accurate and to be heeded. They listened, and they remembered her words always.

Mother purposely kept Morgan for last. When she had finished with the rest, she motioned for the girl to come close.

"Sit here on the bed, dear. I have a last word for you. Always be wary, child. Examine your motives constantly. Keep them pointed straight for the goals you know to be right. The Dark can be deceptive. Never forget that."

"I won't, Mother."

"You have the ability to perform valuable service in the world. You will be such a force for good. Yet in itself, that will single you out. The other forces will identify you, eventually. They will try to destroy you. It is their way.

"You must battle force with force, knowing that the two are equally matched in most ways. But know that in the end, we hold the ultimate power... not only the power of love. Also the power of surrender."

Morgan was puzzled. "I don't understand. Surrender? To the forces of evil?

How can that be a power for good?"

"If I had time to explain it to you, you would come to understand that. But now there is no time. Just remember my words. A day will come when they will help you to win your darkest battle, to come through your most dire time of need."

Mother's eyes bored into her. "Promise me that you will remember!"

"I promise." She nodded. "I will learn to love all things, as you have taught me. And when that time comes, I will surrender my own will. Is that what you want me to do?"

The old teacher closed her eyes. Her face looked peaceful, composed.

The eyes flicked open. "You have always been my best-loved student. Till we meet again, little one. I love you always… and remember."

Kalavela's hand rose to touch her wet cheek lightly. Then it fell limp and the round indigo eyes closed, never to open again.

Morgan held the tiny hand and wept quietly.

* * * *

The village church was filled with people for the old woman's funeral. Not only Kalavela's associates came, but also many who had come to her in need. Nobody had ever been turned away empty from her door. There were people crowded into the church from all social standings, from the humblest poor to the most famous dignitaries. On this day, in this small brick sanctuary of God, a royal princess rubbed shoulders with a seamstress and a government minister from Africa shook hands with a chimney sweep from Galway. From all over the globe they came to offer their condolences and pay final respect to a loving soul who had, through her long years of living, touched every single one of them in a special and unique way. All had come to say farewell to a beloved friend.

In so doing, the multi-national throng that gathered to do Mother honor helped to ease the pain in Morgan's heart. Seeing and meeting so many of these good folk, the young witch could not help but be awed by the true power of human kindness. Mother had touched so many. She knew, with a comforting intuition, that the world had been made a better place because of this old, Scottish witch woman. Someone who had called her a daughter of the heart.

They laid Kalavela to rest in the cemetery that topped a jagged cliff overlooking the wild Atlantic coast. Though, for most of the year, the waters here were whipped to a frenzy by the mad winds, on that day, as if in reverence to the solemn occasion, the wind was only a gentle breeze.

Before the pastor had finished his last prayers over the plain wooden casket, all but hidden beneath a blanket of flowers, Morgan felt the impulse to slip away and be alone. She strolled to the edge of the rocky cliff. The sea below frothed against the rocks sending up sprays like giant fans of water waving to the lonely beach beyond. Gulls caromed off clouds, playing like children in the sky. Their merry cries pierced the silent air like musical notes sounding a tempo. The air itself, even at this height, was tangy with a taste of sea-salt. It was such a joyful day for all the senses.

Morgan, absorbing the calm and the peace, let Mother go free from her sore and weeping heart.

She had learned well the lesson that despair and loneliness are crippling diseases of the spirit. Yet she did feel alone, and it frightened her into recalling those other times of loss.

Within a single year, she had lost both her mother and father. Lucien had disappeared from her life, and though he seemed a small loss, he was nonetheless still her flesh and blood.

Now, for most of her life, Kalavela had been her mainstay. After saving her from Lucien's assaults, she had opened the doors into myriad worlds of wonder. She had ushered Morgan into an existence she had never dreamed of. But now the future once again seemed blank. Once more she was an orphan. Where might she go from here? Who would help her to conquer and to train her talents now?

"The sea is breathtaking, isn't it?" The voice was beautiful..and that of a stranger. Yet Morgan felt an instant warmth.

She turned to face a stunning woman who was dressed with quiet elegance. "Yes, it truly is. Do I know you?"

"Not yet. I am Claire Maxwell." She offered her hand to accompany her inviting smile of friendship. "From America."

They shook hands and there was an immediate bonding. Minds and spirits recognized their likeness. These two shared both talents and disciplines.

Morgan looked at the newcomer with close attention. "Oh, I remember! Mother used to talk about you often. She called you her Yankee cousin."

"That's me. Born and bred in good old New England, although I make the Big City my home now."

"I'm Morgan Rein."

"I know. Mother wrote to me about you, many times. Especially this past year, when she sensed that she was drawing near her end. She told me all about your marvelous talents. She also asked me to look after you after she was gone."

"She did?" Morgan could not hide her surprise.

"Yes. She suggested, if you consented of course, that I take you with me back to America."

Morgan was at a loss for words. Kalavela. It was a name that meant all that was dear and caring. Knowing she was about to die, she had made provision for her young ward. Even then, her love for the girl had been her primary concern.

After digesting the news for a few seconds, Morgan came to the conclusion that it seemed a particularly pleasant provision at that. She liked Claire at once. There was a lot of Kalavela in this attractive woman with the ready smile.

"America! I've never thought of going there before."

"Why not? You were born there. It really is your home."

"True, but we left when I was only five."

"Then it's high time you came home again, Morgan Rein." Claire's smile was infectious and kept striking emotional chords in her. Only seconds ago, she had been pondering a future filled with questions. Now an answer had been dropped, rather charmingly, at her feet. Was it answered prayer?

Morgan felt a surge of excitement. "Are you the Mother of a coven, too?"

"I am. But it will be a long time before I can ever approach Kalavela's caliber. She was an exceptional master. One of a rare kind." She turned her head to the assembly at the plot now just starting to break up. "No ordinary soul could have touched so many lives in such good ways. We were all blessed to know her."

"But I need a lot of training, yet. I need so much advice and..and shaking up, from time to time. Will I be welcome there? In your group?" Morgan was quivering inside with tension.

Claire shook her head, the breeze ruffling her fine wheat colored hair and the edges of her silk collar. "Morgan, you ask such a thing? It's a foolish question, and well you know it. We will be happy to have you among us. Please, say you'll come."

The girl bit her lip reflectively. She had read of the fine schools in the states. The McGills had given them a lot of information in their letters. Mother had wanted her to get a formal education, as well as her esoteric one. This sounded ideal for both purposes.

"Miss Maxwell, I'll go. I'll be happy to. Thank you."

Claire leaned forward amid rich scents of fur and perfume and kissed the girl's cheek gently.

"Then it's done. And call me Claire; after all, we're going to be grand friends from this day on."

As they stepped apart, Morgan had a heady sense of being about to go out into the world, to tackle the thing that would become her life's avocation. She felt almost intoxicated.

The breeze quickened, and the sea below was pounding with returning momentum against the shiny rocks of the cliff. Claire smiled and took her hand, turning them both away from the Atlantic.

"Kalavela was right, Morgan. I sense it, too. You are a very special person. A special sort of witch. We will learn a great deal, you and I, together."

* * * *

Dancer had finished his fourth cup of coffee. He stared into the sediment in the bottom of his cup and tried to read some meaning into it. Sort of a poor man's Rorschach test, he mused.

Perhaps if he had some of Morgan's talent, he might have made something of the brown swirls. They might carry some portent of things to come. But the only thing he could divine was the fact that it was now well past midnight, and he couldn't sleep.

Sitting there at his makeshift crate desk, beneath the goose neck lamp, he had replayed the incredible events in his mind, over and over. The things that led to this moment.

I've come a long way from Berwick, Maine, he thought.

Morgan was still sleeping restlessly beyond the crate barrier. He had hoped she wasn't having a nightmare and debated several times whether to wake her or not. But he didn't have the heart to do it. She needed her sleep, no matter how fitful.

Hell, for that matter, the entire day had been a full-fledged nightmare, in itself. Meeting Lucien Rein face to face, was like something out of his worst childhood fears of the Bogeyman.

Rein had jolted him right down to his socks. He couldn't disguise or deny that fact. Even all these hours later, he felt like nothing but a set of jangling nerves.

The thin man's final words on the rooftop continued to plague him. Was he a liability to Morgan, as her brother had declared? And if so, what he could he do about it? Abandon her? Could he do that, if it was for her own benefit? One question seem to lead to another even more difficult to grapple with until he felt his mind spinning on some runaway carousel.

He rose stiffly, hearing his knees pop. More coffee? Maybe if he drank enough of the awful stuff, he might sober up and leave those niggling thoughts behind. Fear was something he thought he had left behind him when he entered the safe and secure world of science. He despised himself for letting it get such a grip on him now.

"Mother! Mother!" Morgan was calling out aloud from her dimmed bedroom space.

He set his cup on the crate and hurried to her side, dodging crates in the process.

"Easy, Princess. It's okay." He sat down beside her on the mattress and put his arms around her. "Just a bad dream."

"Dancer?"

"The one and only. I'm here." He kissed her forehead and brushed his hand over her hair. It felt like finest silk beneath his palm.

"I dreamed about Mother Kalavela. Dancer, I miss her! I need her so much!"

She was still half asleep. The stresses of the past twenty-four hours had drawn her back into her younger, more vulnerable self.

"Sure you do, Morgan. But it will be all right. Really. We'll manage this thing ourselves."

She moved her head until she could look up into his eyes. She still was seeing partly into her past, he could tell. "I'm so afraid, Dancer. Don't leave me, please?"

The child that she had been stared at him. She seemed more fragile that he had ever suspected she could be. A surge of love and protectiveness swelled up inside him. He bent and once again kissed her forehead.

"I'm here. I'll never leave you."

The words seemed to comfort her. She put her head against his chest. He continued to stroke her hair with one hand, to hold her with the other. In a few minutes she was sound asleep again. Only this time she was truly at rest.

Very carefully, he laid her back down. Sitting on the floor beside the bed, he propped his back against a crate.

He looked into her weary face and knew he had spoken from his own deepest feelings. But were his words true? He wanted them to be. Whatever that devil, Lucien, threw at them, he wanted them to face it together. To the end.

But what if that meant her defeat? What if by staying at her side, he ultimately was the cause of her death? A shiver ran through him and he sliced his fingers through his hair.

No, he would not allow these self-doubts to undermine all they had achieved together. He could not betray her. Lucien was an agent of evil and his words were

"I'm here. I'll never leave you."

lies, intended only to confound and confuse him. That was it. Slowly, the logic of it began to assert itself and the scientist that he was took control.

He would not give into these fears, no matter how formidable. Fear, after all, was a thing a wise man heeded, but controlled.

Looking at Morgan's face, all the love he experienced came to the front and swept aside all other thoughts. He would protect her no matter what the consequences. He laid his head against the hard crate and continued to look at her. He intended to keep watch until sunrise.

CHAPTER 17

The portable phone on the desk unit buzzed. It awakened Harold Springer with rude abruptness.

He groped past the account ledgers for his glasses, somewhere in that pile before him. Grumbling, he slipped them onto his undistinguished nose and reached to silence the plastic buzz. Early morning calls were the very devil, when you'd fallen asleep over the books again the night before.

His neck was stiff and he had a dry mouth. He ached for a glass of orange juice. He had to clear his throat before he could manage to answer.

"Yeah, yeah. Springer here."

"Harry, you lucky bastard! This is Phil!"

Phil? Images coalesced in his rapidly unfogging brain. Ah, right, Philip Longley, Assistant District Attorney.

"Damn it, Phil! What the hell time is it, you asshole?"

"Six-ten. Sleeping beauty."

"What? Phil, whattinell.."

"Shut up, Harry, and listen! I'm about to make your whole damn day for you. Not to mention your entire career, while I'm at it."

Harold stretched his legs and back. He scratched his scalp and yawned widely. "Okay, okay. What is it? And it better be worth a call at such an ungodly hour."

"Did you or did you not call me yesterday with some questions about an outfit called Consortium Construction International?"

"You know damn well I did. Why? Have you found something?"

"Have I? Man, you are going to flip over this! Not two hours after you called, we had a visitor here at the office. One Donald Brunner, attorney for the late Mr. Thomas Axel."

"The guy who just drowned a few days back?"

"One and the same. The former president of C.C.I."

"And what did his lawyer want with the DA's office?"

"Don't rush me, Harry. I'm trying to tell you. It seems that old man Axel was a crafty son-of-a-bitch. He'd gotten where he was the hard-nosed way. He was scared that somebody might replace him, one day, in the same manner he got to his own position. Dirty works, if you catch my drift."

"Go on. I'm all ears."

"Well, it seems like Axel kept personal dossiers on everybody in the upper echelons of C.C.I., already prepared and ready just in case he might be the victim of foul play."

"You mean he was afraid of being murdered?"

"You got it. And knowing this, his death now comes under a very harsh new light. In spite of the so-called eyewitness accounts.

"Anyway, this Brunner comes here last evening with a huge package of folders the old fox left with him. He had instructions to deliver them personally to the DA, in the event of his employer's death by unnatural causes. Of which drowning is certainly one."

"Holy smoke, Phil!" Harold was now wide awake. "Let me guess. It fitted in with what we'd been giving you to look at."

"In exact detail, like two faces of the same coin."

"What was in those folders..the dossiers?"

"An outline of an entire system by means of which the top brass of the company have been skimming off the cream from the company's operational profits for decades. Our staff has been here all night, running everything down piece by piece.

"Your information fitted right into the middle of it. Though the old man never specified who got hit, or when, your data filled in those gaps like the missing pieces in a jigsaw puzzle. As far as I can tell, Axel and his boys have been siphoning off nearly forty percent of the profits into their own private funds." He chortled.

"Harry, we found Swiss bank accounts. Illegal stock portfolios. You name it. As nearly as we can estimate, this early, it's embezzling on a multi-million dollar scale."

Harold leaned back and ran his fingers through his tousled mop of hair. "I knew it! Once I got all that stuff from Connie, I just knew we had something big. Dammit, Phil, she was right, all along the line, wasn't she?"

"That's why I'm calling, buddy. I told the DA you and Connie were working on something related to C.C.I. I showed him your preliminary work and he asked if you can get down here pronto with anything else you might have on hand. Proven or not.

"What do you say?"

"Are you kidding? I'll run all the way if I have to."

"Great. We want to wrap this up before noon. The boss is going to call for a Grand Jury hearing and demand subpoenas for all the C.C.I. brass, before anybody, including the press, gets wind of it. Wouldn't want to tip anybody off and have them get try to leave the country."

"Not wasting any time, are you?"

"That's our job. And I'll admit that it's a real personal kick when we get to nail fat rats like these guys. Always think they're above the law because of their rank. Far as I'm concerned their the lowest scum of all. There are too many names on that hit list!"

"Amen to that. Well, it looks as if we've got them now. Phil, thanks for the call. I've got to wash and get some coffee. I'll see you in less than half an hour."

"Harry, what kind of barbarians do you think we are down town? We've got fresh coffee down here, too. And doughnuts."

Harold got creakily to his feet. "Ha. Great. Then make it fifteen minutes."

"Great. See you in fifteen."

Harry started whistling as he quickly set about putting his desk in order. This was almost too good to be true. He glanced at Connie's notes, which were spread over some of his ledgers.

He chuckled. She was going to love this. He picked up the phone again and began dialing St. Michael's. The DA could wait a minute longer.

CHAPTER 18

Darryl Waitman stood numbly beside the front door of his apartment, holding a subpoena in his hand. He looked down at it as if it were the strangest thing he had ever seen.

The unexpectedness of this development had caught him by surprise. As if from a great distance, he could hear the heavy tread of the court officer's feet retreating down the hall.

He ran his free hand down his velvet robe, wiping away the perspiration that had dampened it, all the while still staring at the folded paper in the other. This was the last straw. He had been losing control, not only of schemes but of his life, for days now. Events were rolling over him, leaving him gasping like a swimmer caught in an undertow.

His life was being dragged away and he was helpless to save himself.

But it wasn't only events. His own mind and body had betrayed him along the way. He could never forget that appalled helplessness as he found his mouth speaking words he hadn't intended to say, his hands beating Axel, pushing him overboard, while his will was unable to stop them.

For a man whose entire life had been centered around his domination of himself and his environment, that had been a terrifying ordeal. Next had come Lilith and her mysterious disappearance to further shake him. Finally that bizarre incident in his office, leading to the fire. That was the last blow to his sanity.

The confrontation between Wicker and the two strangers had been something right out of a nightmare. His suffering mind could not accept the things it had seen. It was sheer lunacy. All of it.

Thus he came to the conclusion that he was losing his mind. That had to be the explanation. But why now? Why at this particular point in his career, when he had the whole of his ambition within his grasp?

He thought of the sand castles he'd built on the beach in his childhood. So strong-seeming, those walls had been. As so quickly crumpled by one rolling wave.

Darryl was weary and frightened past enduring. If he couldn't trust his own will, his own senses, he was finished.

In his hand was the beginning of that end. A summons from the Grand Jury. That meant that the District Attorney had information enough to warrant taking such a step. He tore up the sheet and let the pieces fall out of his fingers. Then he put his fists against his forehead and groaned.

Closing the door behind him, he imagined what lay ahead. In his present state of mental deterioration, he could never withstand the sort of questioning he could expect at a hearing. His crimes would be revealed for all to see. Then would come the conviction and sentencing. And then…

He had, very simply, run out of options.

His slippers slapped against the tiles as he went into the bathroom and opened the medicine cabinet. His lips drew back in a sardonic grin as he took the razor blades… thank God he hadn't got into the habit of using an electric!

He had a mental picture of trying to cut his wrist with an electric razor and it made him laugh. He should have been a comedy writer. That was really funny.

Through the laughter, he took a single blade from the packet and tore off the brown paper. He dropped the rest of the packet into the wastebasket. He wouldn't need those, now.

Looking up at his reflection in the lighted mirror, Darryl saw a stranger. The eyes seemed blank, uncaring. He thought them pathetic and his laughing subsided.

His mouth was grinning as he raised his left hand over the sink, palm up, and sliced the blade down the length of his wrist. The vein parted beautifully. Blood bubbled out.

The pain was excruciating... and beautiful.

CHAPTER 19

"Yes. Right! We'll see you in a little while. Bye, Connie." Dancer hung up the phone and jumped into the air. Having just come out of the shower when the phone rang, he was only wearing striped boxer shots and damp towel draped around his neck. Which made his leap all the more watchable.

"Alriiiight!"

Morgan turned from the stove, where she was making bacon and eggs for their breakfast. Wearing her comfortable jeans and sweatshirt, with her hair tied back with a checkered bandanna, she was the image of carefree domesticity. She stared at him quizzically.

"Let me guess. Good news?"

"Good! It's fantastic! It's the greatest news ever!" He swivel-hipped around several crates, took her hands from the skillet and fork, and began waltzing her across the room.

"Well, there is some dancer in you, after all," she laughed.

"That was Connie. It's all wrapped up for C.C.I. Her man, Springer, just spent a few hours at court house with the assistant DA, helping them get material together for a Grand Jury.

"Connie said there was even more stuff than she had, so somebody else must have rung their bell, too. She seems pretty sure that they're really in the soup. It's just a formality to get things into motion for indictments and trials."

Morgan stopped dancing. She stood back, staring into the distance with a strange look on her face.

"Hey, Green Eyes. I thought you'd be little bit happier."

"Oh, I am happy." She saw his frown. "Really. Mr. Appleton and those other victims will get a bit of justice, now. The end of that evil organization is a thing to celebrate."

"But..?"

"Lucien is still out there. Free. And they will never find him."

"You think so? Connie said all the big shots are being subpoenaed from Waitman on down. Surely that will include your brother."

Morgan's eyes grew stern. "Are you really that naïve? Do you really think Lucien will give a damn about a subpoena? Or that he will allow himself to be taken and imprisoned?"

McCoy shrugged. A bit of the edge went out of his jubilation. The smile left his face.

"No. I suppose not. I wasn't thinking. Still, maybe if he sees he's all alone now, he'll go into hiding. Maybe even leave the country."

Morgan shook her head. "He was always alone. C.C.I. was just a toy to him. What he really wants is for me to be dead. Dead and damned, if possible. Nothing else can satisfy him at this point. If he knew this would be the last action of his life, he'd come after me."

"Sort of like the pitbull of warlocks, huh."

"That about sums it up. Nothing will stop Lucien."

Even as the words left her lips, the air in the loft took a chill. An electrical tingle moved through the air. Dancer had never felt anything like it before. One second he was comfortable and the next he was cold. Shivering.

"Morgan?"

She was standing in a defensive posture, her chin up. "He must have felt me, in the night. I was too exhausted to shield myself. Now he's tracked my aura here."

Dancer's head circled, peering everywhere. "Here?"

"Yes. He is here. Now."

Suddenly the gooseneck lamp rose from his desk and floated to the end of its cord. Then it smashed to the floor. The bulb popped like a gunshot. Dirty dishes rose from the sink like flowered bats, darting across the room toward the two of them.

Morgan stepped in front of McCoy and wove a pattern with her fingers. The wet dishes shattered in mid-flight.

"You were moaning in your sleep... all night," Dancer said. He was trying to clear a large lump from his throat.

"I must have felt him trying to sense me, from wherever he lives. And my dreams... they may have made me vulnerable to him, in some way."

"So what do we do now?"

"Nothing. It's his move, Dancer. But stay alert."

McCoy's attention was caught by something... not quite motion or quite form... that was hovering above the sofa in the middle of sunbeams lancing down from the overhead sky-light. At first he thought the rays were playing tricks with his eyes.

Enlarging slowly, the something formed itself into a giant mask. A face. Lucien's face.

The thing in the shimmering light spoke in a remote voice.

"Greetings, Baby Sister. Our time has come."

Morgan didn't flinch. "A little early in the day for one of your kind, isn't it, brother?"

"Ha, one has to make adjustments. A minor annoyance in achieving my goal."

"And what is that?"

"Why your life, of course. It is time for the final game, for the highest possible stake. Winner take all. Which is me, naturally. I would have long ago, if not for the interference of that old hag!"

Morgan stayed calm. "And if I refuse to play it?"

"Then I will squeeze out of existence a hundred people a day until you do. Beginning with him.." the baleful gaze turned to toward McCoy. "Be here within an hour. Or I will begin, and you will see death such as you never dreamed of."

Dance put his hands on Morgan's shoulders and whispered in her right ear. "He'll have all the advantage, if he chooses the place and the time. Don't do anything rash, Morgan."

Keeping her voice low, she spoke without looking at him. "I can't allow him to kill innocent people who haven't anything to do with this. And believe me, he does not bluff. He will do exactly what he is threatening to do. No, Dancer. Nobody is going to die in my stead."

She patted his hand and directed her next words to her brother.

"Very well, Lucien. I will come. Where do I find you?"

The smoke-face smiled, thin-lipped. "Come now, Witch. If I could find you, then surely you are not so weak and stupid that you cannot do the same. Follow my aura... to your death."

The fog rolled into a small ball and then it dissipated slowly into millions of dust motes. Morgan turned and faced McCoy. He was tense, worried.

She gave a hollow laugh. "Well, Sir Galahad. Here it is."

"That's an understatement."

She drew a long breath. "We have been invited to our deaths. Should we dress for the affair?"

"Come on, Morgan, don't make jokes. Not now."

"Sorry."

"Are you ready to face him? Can you win? Can you beat that creature at his own game? That's' what I want to know."

She backed away and sat for a moment on the edge of the nearest crate. "I pray that I'll be able to. I was taught all my life to meet this very thing. If I am to do the work Mother Kalavela taught me to do, then I must destroy my brother, root and branch. I must send him to join those powers he professes to worship."

She stood again, lifting her chin and squaring her shoulders. Dancer had never seen her look more radiant.

"There's no guarantees, Dancer. I can only do my best and hope that it's enough."

He put his arm about her shoulders.

"That's good enough for me, Princess. Let's go finish it."

Morgan nodded and then looked down at his shorts.

Dancer coughed. "Right after I go put on some pants!"

CHAPTER 30

Lucien Wicker had dressed himself with great care. His black robe was draped just so, its cowl covering his head completely so that his features were lost inside its black void. He drew the crimson draperies over the glass wall of his spacious living room and then lit the red candles in the iron candelabra.

Using his telekinesis, he had moved the furniture against the three walls, leaving the center of the room bare.

Lastly, he took the cup of blood he had managed to obtain, on an early-morning hunt, from the altar in his bedroom. He touched his tongue to it. The copper taste was bitter and to his liking. There was nothing like fresh spilled blood to arouse the senses. He dribbled it onto the thick black carpet, forming the geometric shapes, the esoteric symbols of his craft. This time he would be summoning a demon that would not only work his will but would also be physically present and visible.

In all his years of training, work and deviltry, he had never performed a full spatial transfer. Most minor demons were conjured spiritually and only the effects of their mayhem were discernible. But not so today.

This time, if never again, he intended to bodily call forth a creature of the netherworld and command it to do his bidding. It would take all his skills, for such things demanded the fiercest concentration and will. There could be no room for error. Any miscalculation would prove disastrous, for demons were unruly and just as dangerous to the conjurer as they were to his intended victims. They were the foul monsters of Hell who existed only to cause pain and suffering.

Lucien was well familiar with the risk he took. Ironically his dear sister should be flattered by just how far he was willing go to destroy her. He smiled at his own dark humor as he dipped his right forefinger in the blood and carefully created scarlet runes in the huge pentagram he had drawn.

"I have no weakness," he said aloud, beginning his mental exercises. "She is burdened with the restraints that those of the other order put upon their powers. I am not. I control the Dark Forces. They work through me. I have no weaknesses!"

The atmosphere of the room, with the draperies pulled shut, seemed stifling. His heart pounded harder than usual. He felt flushed. He kept looking toward the candles and the crimson star, not at the walls hemming him into this box of a room. His claustrophobia was ever present, lurking beyond his consciousness.

He sensed the approach of the pair he awaited. Kneeling away from the wet script so as not to smear it, he lifted his hands upwards and began speaking the ancient words.

* * * *

Dancer had never felt so helpless in his life.. or so useless. As they drove eastward toward the park, he glanced aside from time to time at the every day scenes around him. It was early afternoon and rain clouds were gathering to the north, although they seemed hours away.

On the sidewalks, people of all shapes and sizes moved to and fro, all caught up in their own private lives, hopes and dreams. While he was on his way to do battle with a warlock.

For the hundredth time, he asked himself why he, of all these thousands... no millions of people, had become involved in something so ...strange. Even the word seem pathetically ill suited to convey all the weird and unnatural things he had seen in the past few days.

Why me?

Mentally shrugging, since no apparent answer was about to come down out of the sky, he set himself to driving the borrowed Jeep in the direction Morgan kept pointing out. Sitting beside him, her eyes focused beyond the reality before them, she used her inner senses to ferret out her brother.

The question ebbed to the back of his mind. Why anyone, for that matter? If this was real, then someone had to deal with it.

Morgan was pointing again. "Turn right.. there! I can feel him very close, now. Ah! Over there. That building across the street."

She was indicating the brand new condominiums that had been erected by a series of wealthy east-siders.

"Your brother does himself well," Dancer murmured turning into the left lane.

She didn't seem to hear. "There's a parking area to the left of the front entrance. There!"

Dancer eased the Jeep into the parking spot and shut off the engine. He and Morgan stared up at the building.

"This is it. He's up there." She was tingling with energy. Dancer actually felt it across the space between them.

"Then let's not keep him waiting."

She reached across the seat to touch his arm. Dressed in a denim shirt and khaki Dockers, he looked almost naked without his old leather jacket. If they survived this day, she promised herself she would buy him another one.

"We must be extremely cautious from this point on."

"If we were cautious, we'd never have come," Dancer countered, his tone dry. "But what the hey, we're here now. Let's go before I start having second thoughts. And thirds and fourths."

Nothing, he thought to himself, as he climbed out of the vehicle, was less cautious than going after a mad warlock in his own lair.

Once inside, Morgan had no problem sensing the correct floor. The moments in the elevator seemed terribly long to both of them. Exiting, Morgan turned her head to the right and started off in that direction. Lucien's sanctum was the studio suite at the end of the hall. As they approached to within a few feet of the door, Morgan stopped, her face pale and her green eyes enormous. She caught at Dancer's arm and sagged against him for a brief moment.

Alarmed, he grabbed her elbow to steady her. "What is it?"

She gasped, then straightened. "He's doing something ..foul! In there!" She peered at the bronze designation before them, 11A. "We've got to stop him!"

"How, Morgan? What do you want me to do?"

She turned and looked into his worried brown eyes. She smiled. An untroubled, confident smile.

"Hold onto everything that you know is good. Believe in yourself, Dancer, and in me. Think of everything strong and fine that you know, and do not think of what he is trying to do. We MUST win!"

The door swung open of its own accord and they were hit by a pungent odor. Together they crossed the threshold and entered a stygian, oppressive darkness.

Morgan grasped Dancer's hand as if it held her to the real world. She stared around the room, looking for Lucien, but in his black robe, against the blacker rug, disguised by swirls of incense smoke, he was almost invisible. The sparse candle glow provided only the barest illumination.

Lucien's arms opened to them. "Welcome, dear sister, to my humble domain. You and your friend are just in time to meet out guest of honor. He, or should I say it, is joining us any second now."

Dancer felt his skin crawling with each utterance from the mage's lips. He could comprehend the sick pleasure he took in his own weird appearance and his perverted greeting. Morgan stiffened beside him and then let go of his hand to step forward.

She stopped shy of the blood Pentagram. "Lucien, you cannot control a major demon. I know you believe differently, but that is a fact. If you try to summon one, it will destroy you."

"You think so?" He was flippant, totally unaffected by her warning. "I think that is your fear talking. But then again, you were always easily frightened, weren't you, little sister!"

Morgan looked down at the arcane symbol. Her hands moved.

Almost too late, Lucien realized what she was trying to do. He flung a volley of fireballs at her, diverting her attention from her intent to disperse the Star.

She deflected them easily. "Why, Lucien? You are my mother's son. She was not of the Dark. Why must you choose that way?"

He gave no answer. Another shower of fireballs darted toward her, but again she spun them away. Dancer was awed by the magical sparring. Every time Morgan evaded a fireball, it flew about the room and then vanished in a puff, leaving behind a thick carbon stench. Naturally the air was getting warmer by the minute.

Lucien was clearly frustrated, but he managed to control his emotions. When he spoke, it was in a clear, modulated tone.

"I curse you, Morgan Rein, in the names of all the demons of Hell. I summon aid to remove you from this plane, from my path, and from my life. Forever!" His words boomed in eerie echoes about the rectangular room.

Morgan wouldn't retreat. "Lucien, remember Kalavela's warning! Save yourself, before it's too late!"

At the mention of his old nemesis, he glowered at her. His face was a relief of wickedness and unrecognized despair. "I will win, here and hereafter. Look into the Star, sweet sister! LOOK!"

Dancer saw her shudder. He knew, in some unexplained way, that Morgan was trying not to turn her gaze to the Pentagram. But Lucien forced her to look. As she stared, Lucien stepped out of the pattern.

Behind him, at its center, something was starting to form. The warlock was panting with triumphant effort as he continued to summon, at long last, a major demon.

The thing rose like a column of billowing smoke from the middle of the circle, looming larger and larger in the room. Scales rasped across the carpet and ugly, long claws gleamed in the faint candlelight, their glints reddish and their tips shiny-sharp.

Dancer rubbed his eyes. This couldn't be happening!

The thing, and it was there, seemed to be rising out of the floor… and perhaps the spaces beneath the floor and the building and even the earth beneath that. Something was climbing out from the depths of Darkness and it was taking shape right before them.

Refusing to be cowed by its appearance, Morgan struggled to confine the thing. Dancer could feel the energies pouring from her as she waved her hands at it, weaving one pattern after another. But Lucien was also busy, bombarding her with more fireballs, while the monstrous shape took on solidity. As its plated skin materialized, it gave off a rank smell of decay. Dancer felt himself gagging, gasping for breath.

More than anything, he wanted to turn and flee. No sane person had any business being there. But the sight of Morgan, battling on against two fronts, rooted him firmly. Fireball after fireball flew at her, only to be repelled while at the same time she continued weaving new spells against the emerging demon. She was purely magnificent.

Lucien bent forward, trying to focus his entire will upon her. It was disgustingly obvious now that she was proving stronger than he had ever imagined she could be. Strong enough to defeat him!

He had to break her concentration. An inspiration made him shout at her, "I killed our father!"

Morgan turned her head, all else forgotten.

He grimaced at her in glee. "Yes, yes. You stupid child. I did it. I made him fall asleep at the wheel of the car. He went off the road into a stone wall. It was so easy."

She looked right into the wizard's eyes. "Why?"

The monster behind her was groping outward, with half-a-dozen tentacles that were nearly substantial, now.

"Because I thought it would bring you back for the funeral. I would have had you then, witch or no witch. But you disappointed us, Morgan. Papa and me. You didn't come and it was all for nothing. What a pity."

Morgan sighed. "I was sick."

"How lucky for you."

"Lucien, you are mad, you know."

He laughed. Suddenly he thrust at her with all his strength of will. She fell back a half step.

The gigantic demon was virtually complete, now. Almost able to grab her with tangible tentacles and claws. Standing on hideous legs, the thing rose above her, its head and shoulders cramped by the ceiling. The monster pushed and plaster and wood rained down. It began to extend one of its many arms towards its foe.

Lucien started shrieking. "I am the summoner! The debt is to me! Take her, I command it!"

The demon bellowed in return. Dancer, as well as the two witches, felt it squirm under the warlock's mental command. The three of them were all tied together in some mystical fashion. Dancer watched as Morgan warded off the initial clutch of clawed tentacle, all the while pushing the demon back toward the center of the Star.

Frantically looking for a way to assist her, he grabbed a chair piled with other against the wall and yanked it up over his head. Then he charged past Morgan and smashed it down on the slimy, twisting limb.

"Dancer! NO!" Morgan's cry was too late as a second tentacle whipped out of nowhere and hit him across the back. Like a swatted fly, Dancer sailed across the room and slammed into far wall. He was hurt.

Seeing Morgan distracted, Lucien pressed his attack harder. Relentlessly he exerted every ounce of strength, of will, of power that he had gained over his long years of study. She gave… just a bit, but it showed that she was beginning to weaken.

Dancer lifted his head from the floor and groaned. Morgan was faltering as Lucien increased his barrage against her.

The warlock exulted.

Morgan fell to one knee, her arms heavy, her face covered with sweat. She didn't have anything left.

Except a word.

All three felt, rather than heard, the word that now pierced her heart, her memory.

"Surrender!" rang through Morgan and on through her brother, like a blade.

Lucien knew the bitter tang of Kalavela on the word, and even Dancer understood the power of it. Morgan's resistance ceased, with terrible suddenness.

Caught off balance, Lucien's control wavered. Like a rubber band that has suddenly been cut, Morgan's energy was now feeding into the demon rather than against it. She was force feeding it, making it too strong for any earthly craft to coerce.

Back on her feet, Morgan wore a grim smile as she sent wave after wave of energy into the unholy agent. Lucien found himself flooded with alien strengths that poured through him and in to the demon. He was drowning in powers uncontained, uncontrolled. He gasped, his arms rising like a swimmer in the smoke-laden air.

He was helpless to stop Morgan as she moved around the giant beast and, using her foot, broke the line of blood that had confined it. The demon was free.

It roared and surged forward, but its burning white eyes were not focused on Morgan. Rather it turned to Lucien, the disturber of its slumbers. The one who would coerce it against its ancient will.

It reached out a tentacle and curled it around Lucien.

"NOO!" he pleaded. "I am the one who called you forth! Take her! NOT ME!"

But the demon made no sound as it drew its struggling victim lazily into the Pentagram. The tentacles moved, folding the pattern of the Star!

Dancer shook his head in disbelief at what he was witnessing. The Pentagram had come free of the carpet like a lace formed of lines and blood. The demon looped that pattern about Lucien's twisting body.

It became a cage.

The warlock shrieked again as the monster folded the ethereal cage shut about him. Then it began to shrink, compressing him more and more tightly into himself.

The imprisoning web became solid as it shrank. Lucien Wicker was sealed into it permanently, shut away from everything knowable to humankind. Shut away into some claustrophobic dimension known only to demons.

Forever.

CHAPTER 31

The nightmare did not end with Wicker's disappearance. Dancer, still dazed by the horror he had seen, was doing his best to stay awake. Rising slowly to his feet, he realized that the demon itself was still there. A reddish glow was beginning to form around Morgan.

He struggled to move, but he seemed frozen in place, as the room filled with steam and a sulphurous stink. He remembered what Morgan had said. He stopped fighting and focused his attention inside himself.

The image of the house where he had been reared formed on the screen of his mind. The freshness of early spring mornings. The tender, loving care of his mother and father. The innocence of that time and place. The cleanliness of it.

And then he could move. He went after Morgan, toward the heat that was growing worse every second. He shielded his eyes and caught the girl around the waist. He moved away, pulling her with difficulty from the spot where the glow was growing. The massive demon itself was fading into a searing spot in the middle of the floor that seemed to go down into infinite depths.

But it didn't want to leave empty handed. Its tentacles flailed about, seeking a new prize.

"Morgan!" He couldn't seem to make her hear him. Her battle with Wicker had taken its toll on her. She was virtually defenseless against the demon's actions.

Now the glow was dimming and, with it, Morgan as well. She was starting to fade in his arms, her skin rapidly becoming transparent as if she were simply a mirage, a see-through woman like the anatomical charts he'd studied in college. Somehow the witch's energy discharges had formed a connection with the demon from beyond and that bond was taking her away with it.

Dancer bit his tongue. He tightened his hold on her, afraid that any second his arms would pass through nothingness and she'd be gone.

"Hold on, Morgan! I won't let you go!" he yelled above the din created by the gyrating beast.

He held on, as its seeking tentacles crashed into the walls, shaking the very frame of the building. More and more debris collapsed all around them. One of the slithering arms drove through the plate glass partition and smoke and dust were suddenly sucked out.

Dancer maintained his hold and began pushing them away from the pit that was widening like a whirlpool behind the demon. Every inch of his body was agony, as the demon roared again. The sound was like a million dentist drills, only they were going right through his skull.

Cool, wet air blew into the room. It had started to rain outdoors and the wind was picking up. The demon screeched at its first-ever contact with water. Its pain was unbelievable in its magnitude.

Morgan began to grow solid again as Dancer moved them further from the agonizing hellspawn. He was now able to move with less difficulty toward the door. Bit by bit they were leaving the demon and its portal to the eternal pit behind them. With every step, the torture lessened until Dancer started thinking they just might make it after all.

He caught his breath and reached for the doorknob. He was weak. Weaker than he had ever felt before.

But something was happening behind them. Back in the room there was a shrill wailing. It grew louder. The beast was shouting in mindless frustration. Its pitch reached a range that could shatter stone.

Frantically Dancer jerked the door open. At the same time the floor heaved beneath him. He fell to his knees, one arm around the comatose Morgan and the other still clutching the bronze knob. Everything was slanting downward towards the spinning vortex where the demon was slowly sinking.

A single, scaly gray tentacle slinked up and wrapped itself around McCoy's right leg, just below the knee. He tried to shake it off, but it was futile. The foul appendage wouldn't release its hold. Morgan was oblivious to it all.

Dancer looked at the hall beyond the door. He put both his hands on the witch's waist and shoved her away from him. Morgan fell backwards into the corridor and her body rolled out of sight. The thing holding his leg pulled at him. Dancer had only a half second to slap the door shut as he was yanked away.

The demon slid out of view into the opening maw and as the entire room imploded in on itself, Dancer was pulled into bottomless hole.

* * * *

In the hall, Morgan came to. She was lying on her back midway between what had been Lucien's apartment and the elevator. The apartment was gone! The entire section was simply sliced away like a piece of cake, exposing one half of the building to the elements. Which was now a cool, evening rain.

Morgan lifted up on her elbows. Blood spilled from her lips. She kept looking at the open vista before. Had the entire apartment been sucked or blown or translated into another dimension entirely? She was too tired to speculate.

Sirens sounded in the distance. Her temple throbbed unmercifully and she used the remaining wall to get to her feet. Rain hit her face and she welcomed it. Her breath was ragged and she brushed her black hair from her face.

"Dancer?"

Where was he? It was over and somehow, some way, they had won. But where was Dancer?

Then she knew. Standing at the ragged edge of the cut-out, electrical sparks flying in ruptured lines, Morgan Rein realized what the price of her victory was.

Dancer was gone.

EPILOGUE

Scratch had teased a ball of yellow yarn from the knitting bag and was batting it all over Morgan's living room. The scars of Lucien's vandalism had been healed as well as possible, and Morgan was now sitting on her blue couch, laughing at the cat.

"At least you've forgiven me," she said. It was good to laugh again, even over small things.

Scratch pounced on the ball and gave it a good trouncing. He had been more than upset at her abandonment. He hadn't liked the vet's accommodations at all. He had let her know his displeasure in no uncertain terms, when she came to pick him up.

Then, in his wordless fashion, he became aware of her sadness and gave up his pretense of being slighted. He quickly set about trying to both comfort and cheer her up, something no other had been able achieve since that awful day.

Morgan looked down at the latest Stephen King novel in her lap and realized she didn't remember a single word she had read in the last ten minutes. She dropped the book on the floor. It was pointless. Who was she kidding?

The past week had been the most strenuous she had ever known. Even for a witch, the events had seemed more than a touch incredible.

But now most of it was finished. Thanks in great part to Connie Hines, that human dynamo. The evidence they had uncovered, with what the DA's office had been given, had put the thieves at C.C.I. into legal jeopardy for a long time to come. Even with appeals, it didn't appear that they could escape the consequences of their dirty deeds. Justice was moving at long last.

The company, important as it was to international commerce, was now in the hands of a group of government appointed receivers. They would administer it under the careful scrutiny of the courts. Even so, its credit had been badly shaken. When people lose faith in such an institution, it takes a long time to recover its prestige. If ever.

But Lucien was gone. That was the single result of the entire affair that made it all worthwhile. The threat that had hung over her life, and to a large extent the world at large, for so long was ended, dissipated into whatever space now held her errant brother.

She would later learn that she and McCoy had not really been alone in their battle. Claire Maxwell had visited the day after everything hit the television and newspapers about the big explosion on the east-side.

"We knew what was happening, to some degree," Claire had told her. "Once I sensed that you were going to face Lucien, I linked with the group, scattered as we were. We concentrated on you with all our talents.

"I'd like to think our sending was of some help to you."

"I know it was," Morgan believed. She was enjoying the other woman's timely visit.

"No one in our order has ever faced a major demon and survived the encounter. You are the first. That was a stupendous achievement."

Morgan sighed. "I suppose so. I just… wish Dancer had …" She began to cry and Claire hugged her.

"There, there, let it out. All of us feel so sorry, Morgan. From what you've told me, he was a really brave young man."

She tilted Morgan's chin up and dabbed at her cheeks with a lace handkerchief. "Who loved you very, very much. Don't you ever forget that."

"But why did he have to die, Claire? Why?"

"You know none of us can answer that. But I'd like to think he gave his life for yours because it was his wish and you will only dishonor that act if you allow yourself to wallow in despair."

"I'm just so lost."

"I know, Morgan. But you do have friends. And we are all here for you. Whenever you need us."

That had been three long days ago. Morgan, although appreciative of the coven mother's offer, was simply in no mood for any company. She wanted to grieve in solitude in her own way.

The hardest part was not actually knowing how he had met his end. Having been unconscious, Morgan could only guess at those last moments after her brother had vanished. It was obvious that she had collapsed and should have been an easy morsel for the hellish creature. Yet, somehow, be it through his courage, intelligence, or a combination of both, McCoy had managed to save her. It was a sacrifice she would hold in her heart forever.

Eventually she would come out of her depression and get on with her life.

There were many things yet to do.

She looked down at her shirt with the MAGIC across the front and recalled she had been wearing it the first time he had come to see her.

Her world was totally opposed to all the things he had believed in. But that had not stopped him from committing himself to her cause, with all his heart and soul. She closed her eyes and she could see his quirky smile, the way he ran his fingers through his brown hair.

Why? Dammit, why?

Was she cursed to be alone?

The doorbell chimed and Morgan sat up. Now that was odd. No one was allowed access to the building without a formal announcement from Biff at the lobby station. So who was ringing her bell? Her senses were calm and she trusted them.

Unless it was somebody from building maintenance. Of course, that would explain them not having to go through Biff.

As she went to door, Scratch purred and followed at her heels. Another sign that there was nothing wrong.

She opened the door and looked at Dancer McCoy.

"Hi, Princess."

Morgan's mouth dropped and her eyes doubled in size. Then she leaped at him, arms flung wide.

"DANCER!!!"

He caught her and fell back a half step. Their lips met and she held on to him with such fierceness, he thought his ribs were going to crack. Around their ankles, the white cat circled happily.

"You're alive!" she squealed, still refusing to let go.

The lopsided smile. "Apparently so."

"But how? I don't understand."

Together, arm in arm they left the hall and Scratch pushed the door shut behind them.

"I don't either," he confessed, touching her cheek where new tears were streaming. "It was all so weird."

"Tell me, please."

"Well, that demon pulled me into the pit with him. Wasn't a thing I could do to stop. Then just like that I was falling in this well of pure emptiness. Everything was just black all around me and I couldn't see a thing. I just kept falling and falling. Part of me knew that once I reached bottom, there would be no going back.

"Suddenly there was this light, from out of nowhere. I can't describe it any better than that. It was just a hot flash and something grabbed me by the collar and pulled me out of the darkness."

"Into the light?"

"Right. Man, I was totally going goofy by then. I mean, there was nothing but light.. all around me. And Morgan, it felt so perfect. Like nothing wrong could ever exist there. Everything was just... good. Then this old lady pops up right in front me and starts bitching at me."

Morgan blinked. "Old lady?"

"Huh, huh. Crazy. Anyhow, she says I've no business going down to THAT place, it just isn't my time. At which I tried to reply, but she shut me right up. Waved this finger at me like my own grandmother used to do and says, 'Morgan needs ye, Dancer McCoy, so you get back there and love her.' I wasn't about to argue with her."

Morgan's tears were coming faster as he listened to Dancer's tale of salvation. "It was Kalavela."

"I think so, Green Eyes. Anyhow she blinked me out of that light and the next thing I know, I'm laying in a pile of rubbish in an alley behind some Chinese restaurant down on Conklin Avenue way across town and it's a week later.

"I managed to get a cab and got home, where I have been asleep for the last two days, I think. Anyway, when I woke up a little while ago, I almost called you but then decided it would be better to come on over instead. And I told Biff I wanted to surprise you."

"To the point of having a heart attack," she said, slapping him playfully.

She kissed him. "Oh, Dancer. I thought I'd lost you forever."

"Me too. Please, let's never do that again, okay?"

"Deal."

"Oh, and I almost forgot. Just before the old woman sent me back, she gave me a message for you."

Morgan's heart stopped. Somewhere beyond time, as Dancer mouthed her words, she heard Kalavela's familiar voice in her ears.

"…their feet began to float off the floor."

"She said..'Be happy.'"

Morgan's smile was a big as the universe. "I am, I am, I am."

And once again, she and Dancer were molded together, the rest of the world forgotten. Scratch meowed whimsically as their feet began to float off the floor. They stopped a good foot in the air.

Without breaking the embrace, Dancer arched an eyebrow and peeked down with one eye. Hmmm, interesting. Then he closed his practical eye and went back to kissing his beautiful witch.

After all, it was only magic.

THE END

Bio, Ardath Mayhar

Author of sixty novels, forty of them published by standard print publishers, the late Ardath Mayhar began her career in the early eighties with science fiction novels, fantasy, and westerns. Doubleday, Atheneum, Zebra, and TSR published many of these. She has used several pseudonyms, westerns written as Frank Cannon, mountain man novels written as John Killdeer, and a historical novel as Frances Hurst. Four prehistoric Indian books under her own name came out from Berkley, one of which has been reprinted by The Fiction Works. Presently all of her work except for material otherwise committed is being reissued as electronic books, then as trade paperbacks by Renaissance E Books at http://renebooks.com. Now in her seventies, she lives in the deep woods and does book doctor work, as well as instruction for a national writing course.

Bio, Ron Fortier

A Vietnam veteran, Ron Fortier is most known for his work as a comic book writer and has over three hundred titles to his credit. He has written the adventures of such notable characters as POPEYE, PETER PAN, RAMBO, THE TERMINATOR and THE GREEN HORNET.

With Ardath Mayhar he penned two sci-fantasy novels, TRAIL OF THE SEAHAWKS and MONKEY STATION. His most recent efforts include the revival of the classic pulp hero, Captain Hazzard, in a series of brand new novels. His first play, a romantic comedy, WHERE LOVE TAKES YOU was produced two years ago. At 58, he and his wife, Valerie, reside in New Hampshire. He currently working on new graphic novel retelling of an old horror film classic, THE DAUGHTER OF DRACULA with artist Rob Davis.

Visit his webside at http://www.Airship27.com

Bio, Rob Davis

Illustrator of a variety of comic books, role playing games and novels, Rob Davis has been a practicing artist since 1986. Such diverse projects as STAR TREK, STAR TREK: THE NEXT GENERATION, STAR TREK: DEEP SPACE NINE, QUANTUM LEAP, PIRATES OF DARK WATER, as well as comics covering the life of MERLIN of Camelot and ROBYN OF SHERWOOD with publishers like MARVEL, D.C., MALIBU, INNOVATION and others have crossed his drawing board. His latest projects include a slew of pulp novels and anthologies and collaborating with Ron Fortier on his gothic, adult retelling of THE DAUGHTER OF DRACULA as well as a "reboot" of ROBYN OF SHERWOOD with writer Paul Storrie. Rob lives with his wife and two children in the wilds of Mid-Missouri.

Visit his website at robmdavis.com

Situated in the rural back country of Edwardian England is an old, mysterious house whose unique owner earns his living as a Spirit-Breaker, a hunter of ghosts. A former military veteran, Sgt. Roman Janus has devoted his life to aid those haunted, both emotionally and physically by obsessive wraiths whose spirits are still anchored to our world.

Airship 27 Productions is thrilled to present *Sgt.Janus – Spirit Breaker* by Jim Beard. Part detective, part occultist, Janus is himself a man of mystery whose own past is shrouded and the motivations behind his calling kept hidden. Within this volume you will find eight tales as narrated by his clients, each with his or her own perspective on this uncanny hero and his amazing career. Filled with suspense, terror and agonizing pathos, each a solid mesmerizing journey into the unknown world beyond.

PULP FICTION FOR A NEW GENERATION!

AVAILABLE FROM AMAZON.COM AND AS A PDF EBOOK FROM AIRSHIP27HANGAR.COM

AN AIRSHIP 27 PRODUCTION

NEW **PULP**

The Return of Baron Gruner

In 1902 Sir James Damery enlisted the aid of Sherlock Holmes to prevent the daughter of an old friend from marrying a womanizing Austrian named Adelbert Gruner who was suspected of murdering his first wife. Dr. Watson chronicled the case as "The Adventure of the Illustrious Client." By its conclusion, Gruner's evil intent was exposed to the young lady when Holmes came into possession of an album listing his many amorous conquests. A former prostitute mistress of the Baron's then took her own revenge by throwing acid in his face – permanently disfiguring him.

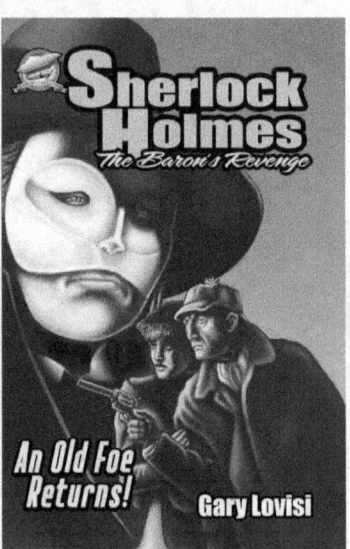

Holmes believed the matter concluded. He is proven wrong when a hideous murder occurs rife with evidence indicating the Baron has returned. Soon the Great Detective will learn he has been targeted for revenge in a cruel and sadistic fashion. Not only does the Baron wish his death but he is obsessed with causing Holmes emotional suffering. He desires nothing less that the complete and utter destruction of the Great Detective in body and soul.

Gary Lovisi spins a fast paced tale of horror and intrigue that is both suspenseful and poignant, all the while remaining true to Arthur Conan Doyle's original stories. "The Baron's Revenge" is a thrilling sequel to a classic Holmes adventure fans will soon be applauding.

AN AIRSHIP 27 PRODUCTION

NEW **PULP**

PULP FICTION FOR A NEW GENERATION

AVAILABLE AT AMAZON.COM AND AIRSHIP27HANGAR.COM